MURDER IN-LAW

Also by Paul Engleman

DEAD IN CENTER FIELD
CATCH A FALLEN ANGEL

A MARK RENZLER MYSTERY

MURDER IN-LAW

PAUL ENGLEMAN

THE MYSTERIOUS PRESS

New York • London

Any similarity between the characters depicted herein and actual living people is pure coincidence with one exception: The celebrities mentioned did exist and, for all I know, still do.

 The Mysterious Press, 129 West 56th Street, New York, N.Y. 10019

Printed in the United States of America

First Printing: November 1987

10 9 8 7 6 5 4 3 2 1

Library of Congress Cataloging-in-Publication Data

Engleman, Paul.
  Murder-in-law.

  I. Title.
PS3555.N426M8   1987   813'.54   87-42704
ISBN 0-89296-186-4

This is for three others who survived Wayne Valley High School: Selma and Tom Rayfiel, and John Sheehan, the world's second worst caddy.

Thanks to my father and Tom Young for research, my brother Mark and Barb Carney for editing, and Michael Seidman for taking a chance on me.

CHAPTER
1

It was one of those unspeakably beautiful spring days that make TV weathermen cluck smugly, as if nice weather is something they're somehow responsible for. The moment I stepped out of my apartment building on West Seventy-second Street, I could sense that the city was caught in a vise-like grip of unnerving good cheer.

One of the counter ladies at Chock Full O' Nuts winked at me. Men in business suits were sidestepping the winos. Even the cabbies seemed civic-minded, actually stopping for a red light or two.

It was the kind of weather I'm inclined to dislike even when I'm not suffering from a first-degree hangover.

The night before, I had watched the Boston Bruins trounce my New York Rangers and win the Stanley Cup. I take my hockey losses with a grain of salt and a fifth of tequila, so I was operating at less than my usual seventy-five percent when I crossed Eighth Avenue and headed to Jim Downey's steak house.

As I escaped from the criminally bright sunshine into the

1

comforting darkness of Downey's bar, it was damn near impossible to see anything. But it only took me a moment to spot the guy I was looking for.

Mike O'Leary was parked right where he said he'd be, second stool from the far end, same place he was sitting the last time I had seen him, four short years ago.

That was 1968. A lot of things had changed since then. I was no longer married to his daughter, for one. He was no longer my attorney, for two. We were no longer on speaking terms, for three.

Until yesterday.

His phone call had caught me off-guard, as phone calls often do these days. I haven't been getting very many of them. That's usually a bad sign for a private investigator. But lately I didn't have any complaints.

Six months back I had come into a sizable sum of money, at least by my standards, and I've never seen much point in working unless it's absolutely necessary. I've never been a proponent of saving for the future, either. But after turning forty last year, I decided it was probably time to start thinking like a grown-up. After a few excruciatingly dull evenings with the likes of an insurance man, an accountant and a stockbroker, I finally developed my own investment plan.

At absolutely no cost to you, here's how it works: There's a blue-chip pacer named Albatross that's probably the best horse in the history of harness racing. I bet five thousand dollars across the board every time he races. The return on my investment has been modest, but it's a no-risk proposition. If only his trainer, Stanley Dancer, wasn't planning on retiring him at the end of year, I'd probably be set for life.

Given the comfortable state of my finances, it's hard to say why I agreed to have lunch with my ex-father-in-law. It probably had something to do with being in the unusually good mood that comes over me when I'm anticipating a Rangers' victory. That or wanting to get off the phone with him as fast as possible.

Or—and this I hate to admit—maybe I was feeling a trifle

nostalgic for the days when Mike O'Leary and I used to drink the gloom out of a winter afternoon on the last two stools at the far end of Downey's bar.

O'Leary was grinning his familiar leprechaun grin as I ambled over and took the seat beside him. Mike's the sort of jerk who makes you want to hide under the covers on St. Patrick's Day. But he's a thoughtful jerk, so there was a tumbler of bourbon waiting for me on the bar.

He extended a paw that was just as small but a little flabbier than I remembered. "I assume you're still drinking Grand-Dad."

"Until last night. It's baseball season now."

"Oh yeah, that's right, gin and tonic." He began to flag the bartender, but I stopped him.

"That's OK. I'll break tradition and pretend it's still hockey season."

"Did you see the game last night?"

"I was there."

O'Leary chuckled, and I recalled another good reason for not talking to him. He was a Boston fan, probably the lowest form of animal life on the planet.

"I watched it on TV," he said. "Great game."

"It stunk."

"From where you were sitting, I suppose it did. Three-zip! Your boys were never in the game. What happened to the famous GAG line?"

The GAG line was a nickname some sportswriter had invented for Jean Ratelle, Vic Hadfield and Rod Gilbert, the Rangers' all-star forwards. GAG was an abbreviation for the Goal-A-Game they could be counted on to score every night. Well, almost every night. From now on, it would stand for joke or choke.

"I don't know," I said. "We had lousy seats."

O'Leary laughed again. "Yeah, and I'll bet you paid a bundle for them."

I nodded and finished off the bourbon.

"That's what you get for rooting for a bunch of pussies."

I cringed. One of the major disadvantages of following

hockey is having to listen to softies like Mike O'Leary raise questions about players' manhood from the safety of their barstools.

"I hope you didn't invite me here to talk about hockey," I said. "Because, as I recall, it's one of the many subjects you know absolutely nothing about."

"I love it. You're just as sarcastic as ever." O'Leary was still simpering. The permanent grin—that was an essential part of Mike's charm. And his obnoxiousness. The only way to get rid of it was to punch him in the nose.

I speak from firsthand experience. The only time I saw O'Leary not smile was the last time I had seen him, seconds before I had knocked him off the chair he was now sitting in. It felt good at the time, but not so good later. Mike O'Leary is twenty years older than I am and a foot shorter. He's built like the proverbial fire hydrant, and I can testify to one occasion, after an afternoon of drinking, when a stray mutt on Seventh Avenue mistook him for one.

I guess you could say I lost my temper. O'Leary can have that effect on you.

He slapped me on the back. "It's been a long time," he said.

"Maybe not long enough."

"Oh, come on. You're not still sore at me. All I was doing was looking out for my baby's interests. You can't blame a guy for that."

No, I couldn't. Except that O'Leary's baby was now pushing thirty-three years old. She was twenty-five when I married her. She had inherited her mother's good looks and her father's bad habits. Foremost among them was an affinity for booze and an inability to handle it.

We met at McCabe's bar on West Seventy-second Street. Kathy worked behind the bar, and I worked in front of it. We did the foolish thing in 1964. Her first, my second. It lasted until 1968.

It was supposed to be a clean split, quick and simple, spic and span. Or at least that's what I had thought.

Stupid me. O'Leary played a few surprise cards at the

divorce hearing that resulted in my having to ante up once a month for a couple of years. After a while, I just stopped paying. But I learned a couple of valuable, if expensive, lessons. One, never trust a lawyer. Two, never trust your father-in-law.

So what was I doing even talking to Mike O'Leary? It could have been because, as my mother used to say, I'm just a slow learner. Or maybe I derived some unconscious satisfaction from knowing that O'Leary had to be in dire straits to come asking for my help—and I had the option of turning him down.

But as I finished off the second bourbon and looked over the grinning little man that I had once seen a small dog piss on, I realized it was all very simple. Basically, I just liked the jerk.

"No, I'm not sore at you anymore, Mike. You're a prick, but you're not a bad prick."

He gave me a friendly jab on the shoulder. "That's the kind of talk I like to hear. Let's have another round."

CHAPTER
2

"How's the old schnozz look to you?" he asked, angling to give me the benefit of a profile. At my suggestion, we had retired to the dining room and ordered London broil. I thought it would be a good idea to have something sticking to my ribs if I was going to spend another day sticking it to my liver.

"Same as ever. Too red, too big, too ugly."

"You broke it in two places. Cost me two grand to get it fixed."

"You got off easy," I said. "That's only half of what you took me for in alimony."

"Oh hell," he said, "let's just call ourselves even. Besides, you would've lost it at the track or blown it on booze anyway."

"Not like Kathy. I'll bet she put it toward something worthwhile."

"Hey, watch that. She's been off the sauce for two years now."

"Yeah, I heard. Best thing she could have done."

"I guess you must've heard she got remarried, too."

6

I nodded. He sighed.

"Guy she married is a colossal bore. Nice guy, but he's about as exciting as a preseason hockey game. He doesn't drink, either. They bought a house out near me, in Verona. I go over there on Sundays sometimes, I go crazy. You remember how you and me used to sit around guzzling beer and watching the ball game? We sit around there *sipping* ginger ale. By three in the afternoon, I've got the goddamn shakes. I've got to slip out to the car and sneak a shot. I know it's better for her, but it's not like the old days anymore. You know what I mean?"

Of course I did. I get sentimental, too, but I didn't miss the old days as much as O'Leary. Unlike him, I was glad they were gone. You can only kiss the past's ass for so long.

"Why don't you tell me what's on your mind, Mike."

He looked at his watch. "What's the big hurry? You got an ambulance to chase or something? I thought maybe we could do a little catching up with each other."

After three drinks, you could spend hours catching up with O'Leary and still lose ground. We were starting on our fourth.

"We can stroll down memory lane later," I said. "I think it's a good idea for you to tell me what kind of trouble you're in now, while you're still capable of walking a straight line."

"Trouble? There you go jumping to conclusions, same as always. What makes you think I'm in trouble?"

"A couple of things. You probably wouldn't have come all the way into the city from Jersey if it wasn't important. And you certainly wouldn't have come all the way in here to talk to me unless you were desperate. What happened? Did *you* finally chase the wrong ambulance?"

"No, smartass, I didn't. This is totally legit. You need a detective out in Jersey, all they've got is rent-a-cops. I need somebody good, so I thought of you. I've got no problem separating business from personal. Just because you make a lousy husband doesn't mean you're not a good detective."

"Thanks for the compliment." I didn't bother telling him that *all* good dicks make lousy husbands. I pushed away the plate and finished off the bourbon. Tradition dictated it was time to order Irish coffee. "You're not exactly what I'd call a world-class father-in-law, either. In fact, you're not even what I'd call a mediocre lawyer."

I caught him in mid-swallow. He let out a guffaw that was accompanied by a spray of scotch. Mike was a class act all the way. A waiter and a busboy rushed to the table, no doubt hoping we were ready for the check.

I'm afraid he disappointed them. "Looks like we could use a couple of refills over here," he said. Then he turned back to me. "Well, I hope for your sake you never have to go up against a *good* lawyer, Renzler. Because this mediocrity sitting before you today had no trouble stealing the god-damn shirt right off your back."

With that he let out a genuine belly laugh, the first of many I'd have to listen to if we didn't get to business pretty soon.

I waited a moment for his laughter to subside. "Time to get serious, Mike."

"What? You want to start drinking doubles?"

He would have erupted again if I hadn't nailed him with a frown. It was a wonder to me that I had known this guy four years and only punched him out once. "Time to cut the shit, Mike."

"OK, OK." O'Leary leaned back and straightened his tie. There was nothing he could do about the gravy stain. "Dwight Robinson. Does that name mean anything to you?"

It most certainly did. Any casual follower of baseball had heard of Dwight Robinson. I tend toward fanaticism where the national pastime is concerned, although the players' strike at the start of the season had convinced me I could wait until July to begin paying attention and probably not miss very much.

A couple of years ago, Dwight Robinson was the New York Yankees' top prospect, the most highly touted player in their organization since Mickey Mantle. That's what they were calling him—the black Mickey Mantle. He was a sure thing, a can't miss, a natural. More than that, he was the classic American success story, living proof that the system works.

He grew up in a housing project in Paterson, which is possibly the grimmest city in New Jersey. If you've ever seen the likes of Newark, Trenton or Camden, you know that's quite a claim. By the time he graduated from John F. Kennedy High School, Robinson had broken nearly every baseball record in the book—including one of mine, but that's another story.

In 1971 Dwight Robinson's ride to the top came to a screeching halt outside the drive-up window at a Hardees' hamburger stand in Wayne Township. I knew about that lovely section of the Garden State, too, although I didn't follow its progress like I had Dwight Robinson's. My parents lived there for a while in the early fifties, long before anybody had thought of tearing up farmland and replanting it with neon-lit cheeseburgers.

Robinson was busted for possession of marijuana with intent to sell. That means he was holding more than the police thought he could smoke by himself in one sitting. You didn't see much pot smoking around Wayne when my parents lived there, either. But I gathered that it had become one of the most popular forms of recreation out in the suburbs these days.

Robinson got a good lawyer—not Mike O'Leary—and managed to get off with probation and stay out of jail. But the Yankees decided to kiss their bonus baby good-bye. There were rumors that a few other teams were thinking about signing him, but the commissioner of baseball put the hush on that talk fast. He banned Dwight Robinson from the game.

Some people thought the commissioner was being too harsh in trying to make an example out of him. I was one of them. But then I can be surprisingly hip for a guy who's forty. Besides that, I had a short-lived career in minor league baseball myself a couple of decades back. I had seen enough to know that Dwight Robinson's indiscretions were not without precedent.

The story gets worse. Being suspended from baseball was a mere swan song compared to the nosedive Dwight Robinson wound up taking a few days ago. According to the papers, Robinson came home on Tuesday night, May ninth, and found his twenty-one-year-old wife, Cynthia, dead on their living room floor. He called the cops, who came out to his house and promptly charged him with first-degree murder.

I'm inclined to give people the benefit of the doubt. I'm especially inclined to doubt cops. For good reason. I used to do some of that kind of work—for the New York police. But from everything I had seen and heard, this looked like one of those occasions when the cops had gotten the right guy.

"Of course I know about Dwight Robinson," I told O'Leary. "Aside from J. Edgar Hoover finally kicking the bucket, it's practically the only thing that's been in the papers all week. What does he have to do with you?"

"I've been hired to defend him."

"Jesus Christ." This time I took the lead in flagging the waiter. "I'd say you've got your work cut out for you."

"That's right." A big grin. "And now you've got your work cut out for you."

I raised my arm in defense. "Not so fast. Aren't you being a little quick on the draw?"

He shrugged. "A little. But you've always been a sucker for lost causes. And this one's got your name on it. Look at the similarities." He began counting off on his fingers. "Kid from North Jersey. Budding baseball star. Career ends before it even starts. With a couple of exceptions, this could be your life story."

"A couple of *big* exceptions, counsel. You're stretching things a bit. I didn't end my career. Someone ended it for me. And I didn't kill my wife."

O'Leary stopped grinning for a moment. "Neither did Dwight Robinson," he said. "You missed something, Renzler. But it's not your fault. It hasn't been in the papers. It's something nobody else knows about. The kid's innocent."

"How do you know? I heard he doesn't have an alibi."

"He has an alibi. He just hasn't used it."

"Why not?"

"I'm not at liberty to say."

I took the last drag off my cigarette and crushed it out. The busboy had been pretty dutiful about switching ashtrays, but we were still doing a good job of piling up the butts.

"How did you get involved in this?" I asked.

"I used to watch Robinson play. I thought he got a raw deal from the commissioner. Smoking pot's nothing these days. I felt sorry for the kid." That grin again. "And, like you, I'm a sucker for lost causes."

"*Pro bono*?"

He nodded. "Practically."

"Bullshit. You never did anything for free in your life."

O'Leary feigned bruised feelings. "Maybe I've changed since you knew me."

"For the worse, if at all. Who hired you?" He was baring stained teeth now, an ear-to-ear grin. "I know, I know," I said. "You're not at liberty to say."

"That's right."

O'Leary bent over and reached to the floor, nearly tipping over his chair in the process. He came up holding a briefcase. It was a black imitation leather model that set him back at least five bucks. You couldn't really say it had been battered beyond recognition, because I doubt anyone would have recognized it as a briefcase to begin with. Except perhaps me. I was with him when he bought it—at a department store in Jersey called Two Guys.

"I've got everything you'll need to see to get started right here," he said, pushing a bundle of folders across the table. "Police report, depositions, background stuff. There's a list of people you should talk to. I figured you could read it over the weekend." He paused. "You do know how to read, don't you?"

"Yeah, fatso. I even had two years of college. Maybe someday I'll write away and get a diploma. You wouldn't happen to remember the address of the place where you got yours, would you?"

He laughed and slapped me on the arm. "Just like old times again, isn't it?"

"Yeah, Mike. Just like old times."

"After you read it, if you've got any questions, we could discuss it over a drink."

Oh yeah, great idea. How about tomorrow morning at nine? "I don't think that'll be necessary. We can talk about it over the phone. But there is something we should discuss."

He nodded and pulled a wallet out of his jacket pocket. It was the match to his briefcase. "I'm a step ahead of you." He peeled two fifties off a short stack. "Fifty a day if my memory serves me correctly."

"Your memory's fine," I said. "But it's double for working in Jersey."

He shrugged. "OK, no big deal."

"And it's triple for working for you."

"You're kidding."

I smiled my charming smile. "Would I kid you, Mike?"

CHAPTER
3

I killed off most of Saturday sorting through the stack of files that Mike O'Leary had given me. Actually, the day was already half-dead by the time I managed to lift my aching bones out of the sack and make my way to the couch in the living room, which doubles as my office. On the way I swallowed down six aspirin and four cups of coffee. My lunch with O'Leary had lasted until midnight.

O'Leary is as compulsive about collecting information as he is about drinking, so there was no shortage of material to read. Even so, I had already seen quite a bit of it. Any time there's a murder in the suburbs, you usually see some news coverage—at least in the papers I like to read. When a woman is murdered and her husband is charged, you usually see quite a bit. When the woman is white and the husband is black, you just can't avoid it.

But the case of Dwight Robinson and his wife, Cynthia, was more than just a big news story. It was a full-fledged scandal, the American Dream turned into a nightmare, the stuff that motion pictures are made of. I wondered if O'Leary had made any inquiries about buying the rights to it.

Dwight Robinson married Cynthia Vreeland on June 13, 1970. He was twenty-one, she was nineteen. I suppose you could say they had a lot in common. He was the next Mickey Mantle, she was a high school homecoming queen. They both grew up in planned developments. His was a housing project in Paterson called the James Baldwin Homes, reserved exclusively for the dirt poor. Hers was a private community in Wayne Township called Mountain Lake, reserved exclusively for the filthy rich.

They met at the Mountain Lake Country Club, which her father had founded and where Dwight worked as a caddy. They were at least two rungs apart on the social ladder, but he was willing to take a step up in class if she'd go down one. They compromised into a split-level house in a middle-class section of Wayne. Less than two years after their wedding, he was out of baseball and she was out of this world.

You rarely see an airtight case, but the one against Robinson was about as close as you get. According to Dwight, Cynthia was already dead when he got home Tuesday just before midnight. His older brother, Dexter, was with him when he called the police. They said they had been out drinking together. Unfortunately for Dwight, Dexter had been out drinking—alone.

It didn't take the cops long to round up a few witnesses who had seen Dexter. And it didn't take long before Dexter admitted that Dwight had called him up and asked him to come over. After a little more interrogation, he said they had ransacked the house to make it look like a burglary.

It was strictly an amateur job.

The coroner said Cynthia died from a severe blow to the side of the head that had been delivered with a blunt instrument. In a garbage can at the end of the next-door neighbor's driveway, the cops found one of Dwight's Little League Baseball trophies. Strangely enough, there weren't any fingerprints or traces of blood on it. It didn't take a genius to figure out somebody had wiped it clean.

One of the first things cops look for when charging somebody for murder is a motive. As far as they were concerned, Dwight Robinson had a good one. A couple of weeks before, Cynthia had told her father she had decided to get a divorce. According to Thomas Vreeland, she was planning on breaking the news to Dwight the night of the murder.

Then there were the witnesses.

Robinson's next-door neighbor, an elderly lady name Anna Paslawski, heard Dwight and Cynthia arguing earlier in the evening. She saw him leaving around seven when she was on her way to church. She heard him come back around ten, but he went screeching away in his car a few minutes later.

Old ladies who spend their evenings going to church don't always make the best witnesses. But guys who pass the time looking out their picture windows often do. That's where a fellow named Warren Shepherd was stationed around ten o'clock.

Shepherd lived across the street. He saw Robinson throw something into Anna Paslawski's garbage can and speed off in his car, which was parked at the curb behind Shepherd's. In the process of pulling away, Dwight smashed the left taillight on Shepherd's Pontiac. When the cops checked, they found that the right headlight on Dwight's white Cadillac was broken.

It was good to know that Robinson had a secret alibi. For his sake, I hoped it was a good one. Despite what O'Leary had told me, I was hard-pressed to believe that his client wasn't guilty. Even with an alibi, there was still a good chance he'd get convicted. But things aren't always what they appear once you start digging below the surface of a police report. Come Monday morning, I was going to have a lot of shoveling to do.

When I was done reading and ready to face the world, I called up my friend Nate Moore. We had a tentative date to make an investment at Yonkers Raceway, where Albatross was running in the seventh race. I also wanted to see if I could interest him in taking a drive out to New Jersey. I expected this proposition to be something of a long shot.

For the last fifteen years, Nate has been my partner, more or less. Playing detective is merely a hobby for him. He finds it a refreshing alternative to his major vocation, painting. Canvases, not houses. Luckily, he isn't dependent on me to make a living. If he were, he'd probably have to go hungry a lot. And that simply wouldn't do.

Nate has a big appetite. He's a big guy. He's also just about the strongest son of a bitch I've ever met. I don't have to tell you what an asset he can be in my line of work.

Last summer Nate became my benefactor, as well as my strong-arm. In honor of my fortieth birthday, he presented me with an enormous painting acknowledging my New Jersey heritage. Titled "The Garden State," it depicts one of those ugly green trash dumpsters with a dandelion growing out of it. A mosquito the size of a pigeon is chomping on the dandelion.

In terms of artistic accomplishment, the painting is one of Nate's lesser efforts. But, like God and criminals, the art community works in mysterious ways.

By prior agreement, "The Garden State" was put on display alongside some Andy Warhols at a trendy gallery in the West Village. The day after the opening, I got a call from a guy who makes his living acquiring art for a guy who makes his living doing nothing in a mansion in Nantucket.

He offered me fifteen thousand dollars for the painting. I told him it wasn't for sale. He offered twenty.

When I told Nate about it, he almost went through the goddamn roof. "Jesus Christ! Are you crazy? Ask him for twenty-five, and I'll paint you another one just like it."

We split the cash, and the rest is history. Except that he's been besieged with offers ever since. After thirty years of painting, Nate Moore has finally hit the big time. After decades of groveling for dates, he's got dames calling him up at all hours, begging him to take them out. He's done the talk show circuit and college lecture tours, and there's even been some talk about a feature story in *Rolling Stone.*

I'm glad to report that my friend is taking it all in stride. "I'm this year's Peter Max," he likes to say. And despite his busy schedule, he still manages to find the time to spend an occasional Saturday night at the track with me.

"How did it go with your ex-father-in-law?" he asked. "Were you able to restrain yourself from slugging him?"

"Oh yeah. I was very civil. In fact, I agreed to do some work for him."

"That's advancing the notion of reconciliation beyond reasonable limits, don't you think?"

I conceded the point. Mike O'Leary was one of Nate's least favorite people. "It's an interesting case," I said. "O'Leary's client is Dwight Robinson."

"That *is* interesting. And exceedingly bad news for Mr. Robinson. With O'Leary representing him, he'll probably get the chair *and* the gas chamber."

"I could use a little help. Are you in the mood for some cruel and unusual punishment, or are you still going out with that woman named Hortense?"

He sighed. "Aren't we in a witty mood today. You'll be glad to know that Hortense has gone back to her sculptor friend in Queens. And for the record, I only went out with her twice. If you had been that lucky, you would have been lining up at the altar by now."

Nate is what you would call a confirmed bachelor. The mere idea of attending a wedding can make him physically ill.

"I take it you're talking about a trip to New Jersey," he said.

"Yeah, probably a few of them. The first one's Monday morning."

"Now why in the world would I want to go to New Jersey?" Nate likes playing hard to get.

"For one thing, it's the source of your newfound notoriety."

"For another?"

"I'll buy you lunch at a Howard Johnson's."

"Now you're talking. Let me check my calender."

Up to last year, Nate seldom knew what the date was. Now he never left the house without his pocket calendar. He kept another one on his desk for backup. I heard him open the pop-top on a can of beer, as he came back to pick up the phone. How did I know it was a beer? Call it an educated guess.

"I'm clear all week, except Wednesday," he said. "I'm taping *Joe Franklin.*"

The program was a local talk show that had been running for at least twenty-five years. The official name was *Down Memory Lane,* and it featured withering celebrities on their way down and unknowns who were destined only for small things. Nate was a faithful watcher.

"What's the matter? Has your star faded already?"

"Are you kidding? It's my dream in life. Joe Franklin's like a god to me." He paused, and I could hear him working on the beer. "By the way, wasn't Dwight Robinson's wife from a town called Mountain Lake?"

"That's right. Why?"

"I got an invitation to play in a celebrity golf tournament out there on Memorial Day weekend."

Small world. "Sounds like they're lining up all the big stars. Is Joe Franklin going to be there?"

"I don't know. I'll have to remember to ask him."

CHAPTER
4

There was a steady drizzle welcoming us to New Jersey as we crossed the George Washington Bridge against the flow of morning commuter traffic. Thanks to Nate, we were off to a late start.

He had brought along a cooler and insisted on stopping for ice and beer before we left the city. Running out of beer is probably his biggest fear in life.

"Just in case," he explained, as he crammed himself into the Corvair.

"It's only a forty-five-minute ride," I said. "And there are a million places to buy beer out there."

"Is that so? Well, you never know when this old heap is going to break down. It might be days before they find us."

He had a point there. Although the Corvair only had fifty-thousand miles on it, I had been driving it for eleven years. If something went wrong with it, I'd probably have to buy a new car. Someone who knows about those things had told me parts were scarce. I think that was back in '67.

Due to some changes in the highway system since I had last been out to Jersey, my estimated driving time was a little

19

on the short side. I've got my own traveling phobias, so by the time we pulled into Paterson at ten-fifteen, we had finished off the thermos of coffee I had brought along, just in case.

I suppose there are worse places to live than the Passaic County Jail, but offhand I couldn't think of one. From what O'Leary had said, it looked like Dwight Robinson would be calling it home for the next few months. His bail had been set at five hundred thousand dollars. Even if O'Leary managed to get it reduced, as he was trying to do, it would be tough to come up with the ten percent needed to spring him.

"I think this is the joint where they were holding Mike Bloomfield last summer," Nate said, as we walked up the drab brick steps.

"Who's that?"

"You've never heard of him? He had a band called the Electric Flag. He got busted out here somewhere." Nate prided himself on keeping abreast of what young people were up to. It made him forget he would be turning fifty in two years.

"Aren't you a little old for that stuff?"

"That's one way of looking at it. I prefer to think I was just born too early."

We had to submit to a search by a pair of burly guards who seemed to enjoy their work. Nate's a little touchy about being touched, so he was less than cooperative with his examiner.

"Are you planning to finish the job with a proctology exam?" he asked.

The guy paused and hit him with an empty stare. "Is that a wisecrack, pal?"

Nate shrugged. "Have a look, and you tell me."

"Huh?" The guy turned to his partner for clarification, but the remark had apparently gone over his head, too.

"Let 'em go, they're clean," my man said. Then he waved to another stiff, who led us down a long grim corridor to a small grim room where Mike O'Leary and Dwight Robinson were waiting.

I had seen pictures of Robinson in the papers, but they didn't do justice to his imposing physical presence. He was only an inch taller and maybe ten pounds heavier than my six-two, one-ninety-five, but he gave the impression of being much bigger. Maybe it was the extra layers of muscles rippling under the sleeves of his T-shirt. Or it might have been the hard angles on his face and the large probing eyes, which combined for a cold, serious, distrustful gaze.

O'Leary introduced us, and Robinson crossed me up with the alternative handshake that blacks and hippies have taken to using. Nate handled it like a pro. I'd have to get him to teach it to me one of these days.

We took seats across from Robinson at a battered aluminum table with a dirty plastic ashtray on it. Next to it was a paperback book called *Soledad Brother*, by George Jackson. Apparently, Dwight had decided to do some reading. From the marker, I could see that he was about ten pages into it.

O'Leary remained standing, with his arms folded, in the corner of the room. He was wearing his involuntary grin, but I knew he was in a less garrulous mood than when we had talked on Friday. That would change—after lunch.

"Renzler and Nate are going to be a big help to you, Dwight," he said. There was the trace of a fatherly tone in his voice. "Things will go a lot better and move a lot faster if they can find out who killed Cynthia. I thought it would be a good idea for them to get a chance to meet you before they begin investigating."

O'Leary had warned me that his client tended to be uncommunicative. That turned out to be something of an understatement.

Dwight shrugged and fixed me with a hollow glare. I wondered if it was the same expression he used when he was standing at home plate, staring down a pitcher. I returned the look until his eyes wandered to the cinder block walls. I used to stare down pitchers, too.

I didn't really expect to learn much by talking to him. One of the ground rules I had agreed to with O'Leary was not to ask any questions about Dwight's secret alibi. That obviously was going to hamper the investigation. But sometimes you can learn a lot just by looking at a person. Dwight Robinson, for instance, was an easy read. He looked like someone who just might bash in his wife's skull with a baseball trophy if he was in a bad mood.

"I'd like to ask you a few questions," I said.

"Go ahead. I got all day."

"I've read the police report. Is there anything you can think of, anything you've remembered since they questioned you, that might be of help to us?"

Dwight's eyes continued to wander the walls. He answered with a barely perceptible shrug. Time to get specific.

"I'd like to know why you ransacked the house. Why didn't you just call the cops as soon as you got home?"

Dwight turned to O'Leary, who was leaning on the corner of the table. "What's this jive, Mike? I thought they were supposed to be helping me."

O'Leary gave me an I-told-you-so look. "Just tell them what you told me," he said patiently.

Dwight let out a heavy sigh, then began staring at me again. "Where you been, man? You ever been picked up by the pigs? You think they're going to believe some nigger?" He pointed his finger at me. "You got a lot to learn."

I grimaced. So this was how it was going to be. But at least he was talking.

"You figured they'd charge you anyway, so you decided to make it look like a burglary," I said.

"*Figured!* Man, I *knew.* They don't like niggers living in honky town. They were out to bust my black ass from the minute I moved in. I didn't have a chance."

From what I knew of Wayne Township, I figured he very well might be right. But I wasn't the one who was dumb enough to move there, and that didn't excuse the stupidity of trying to cover up a crime he said he didn't commit.

"There was no sign of a forced entry," I said. "Who else besides you had a key to the house?"

"We never locked the doors, man. It was a nice, safe, *white* neighborhood."

"Until you moved in," Nate reminded him, grinning. Dwight managed the faintest trace of a smile in response. "Yeah, that's right," he said.

"What about the trophy?" I asked. "Did you see it when you came home?"

"I told the pigs, man. I don't know shit about no trophy."

"They found it in your neighbor's garbage can," I said. "How do you think it got there?"

Robinson threw up his hands, then pulled them down and covered his face. After a moment, he got up from his chair and began pacing the room.

"He thinks the police might have put it there," O'Leary said.

"You think the cops framed you for it?" I asked. It was an interesting angle, one that I hadn't considered. Of course, it didn't explain who killed Cynthia.

"White justice," Robinson muttered. He came back to the table and took his seat. He picked up his book and held it in the air. "White justice. You know what that is? You ever hear of Hurricane Carter?"

We both nodded. That didn't stop Dwight from telling us who he was.

"White justice convicted Rubin Carter. He could have been the middleweight champion of the world. They said he killed some honkies in a bar. He wasn't even *near* the bar, man. The pigs in Paterson didn't like the idea of a nigger boy driving around town in a fancy-ass car showing them up. So they set him up. Just like me. It's the same thing exactly."

Nate let out a sigh. He tends to get impatient when he's hungry. We had skipped breakfast.

"You better hope it's not exactly the same, bro," he said. "Because Rubin Carter's rotting his life away in jail as we speak."

That was something to think about. I had a feeling Dwight Robinson hadn't been thinking about it enough. I didn't know what his secret alibi was, but if he thought things through about white justice a little further, he just might realize there was no guarantee a jury would buy what he had to sell. Especially if, like Hurricane Carter, he ended up facing a jury with twelve white faces on it.

"Who do you think killed your wife?" I asked.

Robinson rubbed his chin and gazed into space. After a moment, he looked at me and said, "Shake Johnson."

"Who's he?"

"He's the caddy master at Mountain Lake."

"Is he a brother?" Nate asked.

Dwight almost cracked a smile again. I think maybe he liked Nate. "Yeah. A real badass. And he's got a big black dog that goes by that name, too."

"What makes you think he killed Cynthia?" I asked. It had occurred to me that if Robinson's wife was planning to file for divorce, there was probably another man in the picture. If Dwight knew about him, that might explain why he didn't seem to care much that she was dead. But in all the news coverage so far, nobody had emerged to fill the role.

There was a possibility that her family would have kept it quiet. There was also the possibility that the person she was seeing might have been the one who killed her.

"I got my reasons."

"You want to tell us what they are?" I figured he didn't. He surprised me.

"I owed him money."

That hardly seemed sufficient reason to kill a man's wife. If it was, then Shake Johnson must have been a *real* badass.

"How much did you owe him?"

"About a thousand."

"What for?"

He let out an impatient sigh. "Bet money. I hit a bad streak."

"Did you tell the cops about Johnson?" I asked.

Dwight rolled his eyes and began watching the walls again. "Come on, cut with the cop jive, man. I already told you where they're at."

O'Leary looked at his watch. "Time's just about up," he said. I wasn't sure if he meant that Dwight had to go back to his cell or if he was feeling the need for some lunch.

A guard entered the room and clarified the point.

"One more question," I said, as Dwight was getting up to leave. "How did you smash the headlight on your car?"

"Are you planning on talking to Shake?"

I nodded.

"Why don't you ask him."

"Do you want us to give him your regards?" Nate asked.

"Yeah, I'd like that a whole lot. You tell him I'll see him and you tell him where."

The guard led Dwight out the door without giving me a chance to practice shaking hands. After an hour of sitting in that room, I felt like I had been sent to jail. I wondered what it felt like for him.

O'Leary was somewhat more animated as we trudged down the corridor to the freedom of the outside world. The arrival of lunchtime can have that effect on some people. I was content just to be getting out of prison.

"The kid's a tough nut to crack," he said.

"No shit," I answered. "I think you better work on his court manner before you put him in front of a jury."

"I don't expect to have to go that far. That's why I've got you guys on the case."

"Wish us luck," Nate said. "We'd have a little more cause for optimism if you'd let us in on what his alibi is."

O'Leary shook his head. "That I can't do." He motioned toward the row of dingy but official-looking buildings along Hamilton Street. "But I can buy you lunch. I know a place that has five-dollar steaks and fifty-cent drinks a couple blocks over."

Nate shot me a look of protest. It wasn't necessary. I knew better than he did that Mike O'Leary was a low-dosage proposition. We had already gotten our day's fill.

"I'm overwhelmed by your generosity," I said, "but our workday doesn't end at noon."

"It's your loss, smartass."

We watched him lumber away, then walked back to the Corvair, which was parked at a broken meter on Marshall Street. The windshield had acquired a parking ticket and a leaflet for a topless bar since we had left. Nate pulled them off and looked for a trash can. I told him he was standing in it.

He shrugged and dropped them on the sidewalk. "Yeah, I guess a little paper won't alter the esthetic balance."

No it wouldn't. And we were in one of the nicer sections of town.

CHAPTER
5

Getting lost in Paterson is easier than getting drunk at a hockey game. It's the oldest city in New Jersey, and it looks it. Alexander Hamilton and a group of his followers founded the place in 1790, ten years or so before he got himself killed in a duel with Aaron Burr over in Weehawken.

It always sounded like a ridiculous tale to me, but an argument could be made for modern-day politicians to settle their squabbles in a similar fashion. The world wouldn't be any worse off if Richard Nixon and Mayor Daley had fought to the death after Daley stole the 1960 election for Kennedy. If Daley had come out on top, it might even be a little better. At least it would make a lot of jerks think twice before running for office.

After our third random interrogation of gas station attendants, we managed to locate Preakness Avenue, the long-winding hill that connects the city of Paterson with the township of Wayne. It's only a two-mile ride over the hill, five minutes when there aren't too many trucks. But distance and time aren't the appropriate standards of measure for the gulf that separates the two communities.

In terms of age, Wayne is no spring chicken, either. But it's one of those areas that went right from farmland to shopping centers, better late than never for developers looking to make a fast buck after World War II. Ten years ago, it had thirty thousand residents. By 1970, there were fifty thousand. Paterson has three times that many, but they're crowded into a space the size of a postage stamp. Wayne, by contrast, is spread over twenty-five square miles. And, as with many adjacent towns in North Jersey, there are significant differences along lines that I think sociologists like to refer to as cultural.

Dwight Robinson probably wasn't the first black person to move into Wayne. But it wouldn't have surprised me if he was the second. The town where I grew up, Clifton, has a population of about eighty thousand, but you pretty much had to cross over into Passaic if you wanted to see a black face. For some reason, a lot of people from Clifton stayed out of Passaic. And the folks from Passaic knew better than to wander into Clifton. It made for great rivalries at high school football games.

In Wayne, being black was not the only ethnic affront you could commit. A few years back, a member of the township school board had mentioned it might be a good idea to keep Jews out of administering the school budget because they're inclined to spend too much money on education. The comment sparked a media controversy that spread to the front page of *The New York Times*, a paper you don't see much in Jersey. Many of the town's citizens were outraged. But not that many.

The man who made the remark soon left the school board and went on to be elected mayor.

Lucky for us, orange roofs were a more common sight than black faces, so we didn't have any trouble finding a place to get Nate filled up with fried clams. We thought about paying a visit to Shake Johnson after we left Howard's, but we decided that could wait a while. It seemed like a good idea to collect some more information before confronting him. Knowledge is power, after all, and I wasn't exactly feeling like Superman after our meeting with Dwight Robinson.

With the help of a local map that I picked up at a store that sold everything from adult novelties to diapers, it only took us a few minutes to find Willow Way, the street that Dwight lived on. It was in the older section of town, relatively speaking, and reminded me of the neighborhood where my parents used to live. Maybe it was. But that was twenty years ago and I had only been out there a few times, so I couldn't be sure.

The houses were modest and built close to the street on small yards. Most of them still had trees, which seemed like something of an oddity based on my suburban wanderings. These days, bulldozing away anything that takes in carbon dioxide seems to be the first order of business when starting a development. If you want a tree on your property, you just go down to Two Guys and buy one.

The streets were narrow. Although they had been recently paved, they weren't bordered with sidewalks and three-foot-high curbs. Only a few of the houses had driveways, and there was no evidence that the neighborhood had ever been assigned a cutesy name, like Cherry Valley or Tall Oaks.

As I looked over the brown-and-white split-level that Dwight Robinson lived in, it occurred to me that moving there might have been as big an adjustment for Cynthia as it was for Dwight. Her father being a wealthy real estate magnate, I would have expected something a little more impressive. But Dwight Robinson being black, there was always the possibility they didn't have a whole lot of options. And then I recalled seeing a grief-stricken Thomas Vreeland on the TV news the week before. He said he had known his daughter was making a big mistake when she married Dwight Robinson. Maybe Daddy had been less than forthcoming with a contribution toward the down payment.

After a few minutes of pressing the doorbell at the house next door to Dwight's, we were just about ready to give up on Anna Paslawski. But as we descended the cracking concrete front steps, which nobody had ever taken the initiative to paint, Nate detected some movement behind the curtain at her living room window. Dwight and Cynthia may not have locked their doors, but this old dame was holed up like Ma Barker dodging the Feds. I wondered how she felt about a black guy moving in next door.

Once she realized we had spotted her, she gave herself up by moving to the front door. She peered out at us through a large, diamond-shaped window with a United Way sticker on it. But she didn't open the door—no sir.

"Go away or I'll call the police," she shouted. For an old gal, she had a pretty good set of pipes.

"We are the police," I called back. Just to prove it, I held up my ID. It works on kids all the time. Why not a senior citizen? "We just want to ask you a couple of questions."

Ever so slowly, the door opened a crack. The outer glass door was locked, so she still had a layer of protection in case we turned out to be lust-crazed dope fiends. To put her mind further at ease, we backed down off the top step of the porch.

Anna Paslawski was wearing a tattered blue bathrobe over pink pajamas. My guess was that she had seen seventy a few years back, but once they pass sixty most ladies look about the same age to me. Her hair was pulled back under what appeared to be a shower cap. The few strands I could see hanging out belonged to the same color family as the bathrobe. She was wearing bifocals, the frames of which matched the pajamas. She opened the door just wide enough to stand in the crack. She leaned against the molding for support.

"Are you the police? You don't look like police." She was squinting hard, as if she needed a new prescription. I figured the one she had was probably as old as the bathrobe.

I explained that we were private investigators.

"Oh," she said, clasping her hands together. "You mean like *Mannix*."

"Exactly." I smiled my charming smile. I can be a killer

when it comes to old ladies. It's the young ones I seem to have problems with.

I held my ID up to the window and told her our names. "We'd like to ask you a few questions, if you're not too busy."

She studied the badge a moment, then eyed me above her lenses, which had slipped down the brim of her nose. "Go ahead, shoot," she said.

"It's about—"

"I'll bet it's about the murder of that poor girl!"

"That's right. I know that you spoke to the police—"

"Terrible, terrible." She was shaking her head. "It's not our place to question the work of God, but sometimes you have to wonder why he lets things like that happen."

Uh-oh. I had a feeling Anna Paslawski was one of those people who don't stop talking once you get them started. I suspect the combination of too much TV and church can do that to you. Especially if you live alone.

"Why do you suppose God does that?"

"Maybe he was asleep when it happened," Nate suggested. I don't think she heard him. I don't think she heard me kick him. She seemed to be caught up in her own world of wonder.

"That husband of hers! I knew he was a no-good loafer the minute I laid eyes on him. It was a terrible thing, terrible. I'll never understand why she married him. Personally, I think there ought to be a law against it. She was such a nice, pretty girl. And she came from such a good family. Her father is a living saint!"

"Oh, so you know Thomas Vreeland," I said.

"Know him! Why he's the one Ed and I bought the house from in the first place!" She sounded surprised that we weren't privy to this information. You can be sure I didn't make the mistake of asking who Ed was.

"And did you know Cynthia well?"

"Why of course! We were next-door neighbors! We used to exchange magazines. Of course I used to bring more of them to her than she ever brung to me. She was such a pretty girl.

I guess God must have thought she deserved it. He was probably trying to teach her a lesson."

"What about her husband?" I asked. "Did you talk to him?"

The incredulous look that began spreading over her face was sufficient answer, but she supplemented it with a verbal assault. "Are you *kid*ding? That loafer? I'll never understand why she married him in the first place. Not in a million years. And not only him, but all those other ones that were always coming and going at all hours. I don't know how in the world she could stand it!"

"By other ones, you mean blacks," Nate said.

"That's right." She adjusted the glasses and they promptly slid back down her nose. "Who else would I mean? Coming and going at *all* hours."

"His friends probably," Nate said.

"Oh no, hers too!" she said. "That's the funny thing about it."

"How do you know that?" I asked.

"Well, he used to go away and play baseball somewheres. I don't know where, but somewhere far from here, because she told me he did, and when he was gone they still came over, so I guess they must have been her friends too. Isn't that funny?"

I nodded. It was a laugh riot. "Did you ever ask her about it?"

"Are you *kid*ding? Never in a million years!" She began to chuckle. It was closer to a series of soft shrieks than a laugh. I felt a little sorry for Ed, wherever he might be.

She stopped laughing abruptly. "Young man, I'm not a nosy woman. I've always believed that people's business is their own business."

"I agree with you completely," I answered, matching her lie for lie. I make my living being a snoop, but I was willing to bet my nose was a whole lot cleaner than Anna Paslawski's.

She unlatched the outside door and pushed it open slightly. Apparently, our charm was working. "You want to know what I think?" She edged out closer to us and spoke in a lowered voice. "Personally, I think they were drug addicts. I think they were selling drugs. Isn't that terrible?"

I ignored the question and asked one of my own. "How many of them were there that used to come over?"

She leaned her head back and thought it over for a moment. "Sometimes one, sometimes two or three."

"Were they the same people all the time?"

She laughed again. The shrieks were louder this time. "Are you *kid*ding? How on earth would you be able to tell?"

While waiting for her laughter to subside, I was tempted to ask her if she knew how to get a one-armed Polock out of a tree. I restrained myself. It wouldn't have served any purpose, and she probably wouldn't have gotten it anyway.

"You told the police you saw Dwight Robinson leaving his house on the evening of the murder."

"That's right. I was on my way to seven o'clock mass. He was in an awful big hurry. They were having one of their fights again. They were always fighting, you know."

"What were they fighting about?" Nate asked. "Were you able to hear?"

"No! Of course not! I never listened. But they were having a doozy. Who should I run into on my way out to church but him. Of course he didn't look at me. They never do, you know. She was still yelling at him when he got into the car."

"So she was definitely alive when he left," I said.

"Oh yes, of course! He didn't kill her until he came back." She explained it with the surety of a truth we hold to be self-evident.

"And when was that?"

"Ten o'clock. Right on the dot." She wasn't wearing a watch, but she pointed to her wrist.

"Did you see him come back?" I asked.

"No, it was dark. But I heard him come up my driveway— you know he was always walking in my driveway. And then I heard him go into the side door of their house."

Either we had won her trust completely or Anna Paslawski

was getting carried away with the momentum of her story. She stepped outside the door and began walking past us down the stoop. It was still damp, even though it had stopped raining. She gripped the railing for balance, but she looked agile enough to skip down all four steps without assistance.

We followed her a few paces along the walk until she stopped and pointed. "He was right there. He always went in that door."

"Did you hear them fighting again?" I asked.

"No. He just killed her and left." She pointed to a run-down house across the street. "Mr. Shepherd saw him leave. And he threw the murder weapon into *my* garbage can! The nerve!"

"It seems strange that they weren't fighting, don't you think?" We were walking back up the steps now.

Anna Paslawski came to a sudden halt, peered at me and raised a finger in the air. "Not when it's premeditated. That was just his *modus operandi*. Now you or I might have gone about the whole thing different, but not him. I don't think he was too smart. He just barged right in there and clobbered her upside the head before she even knew what hit her!" She swung her arm to demonstrate. "It was one, two, I kill you. Three, four, out the door."

Either she had watched an awful lot of *Mannix* or Mrs. Paslawski was a *McCloud* fan, too.

"Just one more question," I said, as we reached the steps. "What time did you get back from church that night?"

"Nine o'clock. Like I always do. Mass starts at seven and ends at eight. I always stay and do a rosary and the stations of the cross. It takes me forty-five minutes."

"I see." I'll say one thing for the old lady. She must have been in pretty good shape. If you've ever done the stations of the cross, you know what I mean. "Well, thank you, you've been a lot of help."

"You mean you're going so soon? Don't you want to come inside? I just made a pot of sauerkraut soup. It was Ed's favorite."

Sure, I'll bet it was. Maybe it even had something to do with the reason Ed was no longer with us.

"No," I said, "we have to—"

"Actually, I wouldn't mind using the little boy's room," Nate said.

She chuckled as we entered behind her. Nate has a way with the old gals, too. I just hoped it was the beer and not the fried clams that had given him the urge to try out her can.

The house had that closed-up, musty odor that old people's homes always have. Somebody once told me it was the smell of death, but I always thought of it as the lingering stench of TV dinners and chicken pot pies.

She led Nate by the arm a few steps to a hallway. "It's around the corner to your right," she told him. "There's a sign on it that says 'Ed's Room.'" She turned back and smiled at me. "He was always sitting in there reading the newspaper, so I had them make up a sign down at that store on Route 23. You know the one I mean?"

"Pinky's?"

"Pinky's! That's right. They've got everything at Pinky's."

Indeed they did. From street maps to signs for your bathroom door.

I turned down another offer of sauerkraut soup and surveyed the living room. It was cramped, the typical size of a forties starter-house. I had a feeling Ed Paslawski hadn't made a whole lot of money. Either that or his wife was sitting on a pile of it.

The TV set was right where you'd expect—in the center of the room. An easy chair like they used to make was five feet away from it. On a coffee table beside the chair was a pack of Chesterfields, an unfinished bowl of soup and a magazine called *Inside Detective*. The cover featured a staged photo of a cute young thing being throttled by a knife-wielding assailant. The headline promised "The Case of the Bullet-Riddled Blonde in the Ballpark Grave."

Interesting reading for a Monday afternoon. My guess was

that she bought it at Pinky's. I wondered if Cynthia Robinson had gotten a chance to read it.

Nate returned from his bathroom mission in record time. His eyes were bulging like a pair of Slinky toys, and I could tell he was trying to restrain himself from laughing. He was already out the door by the time I thanked Anna Paslawski for her hospitality.

As we walked down her driveway and across the street to Warren Shepherd's house, he said, "Someday, when you've got a few hours, remind me to tell you about 'Ed's Room.'"

"That good, huh?"

"Better than you could possibly imagine."

CHAPTER
6

I didn't expect Warren Shepherd to be home in the middle of the afternoon, but I thought it might be a good idea to knock on his door while we were in the neighborhood just in case.

It was. He even answered the bell more promptly than Anna Paslawski. But he wasn't any less suspicious.

"Yeah, what do you want?" Saying that his tone was gruff doesn't quite do it justice. I felt like we had awakened a slumbering bear.

Maybe we had. Through the screen door, I could see sleep lines on Warren Shepherd's face. It was a chubby face, with a few days of growth around the edges. He was a chubby man. Judging by the age lines, I'd say he was about fifty-five. But it was a little tough to tell. He had chosen to fight the battle against baldness with a black hairpiece that made him look months younger.

Shepherd was wearing a pair of madras shorts and one of those sleeveless T-shirts that we used to call Italian dinner jackets when I was in high school. Judging from the stains, his looked like it had been worn to quite a few dinners over the years, and maybe a recent breakfast. It was stretched to the limit, but not far enough to conceal a rather unsightly bulge of flesh that hung out over the elastic waistband of his underwear. Warren Shepherd and I had something in common. He was a jockey guy, too.

"We're private investigators," I said, holding my ID up to the door. He opened it a crack and I passed it in to him. "We want to ask you a few questions about the murder of Cynthia Robinson."

He opened the door farther and leaned against it, stepping out onto the porch. "I already talked to the police," he said, handing the ID back to me.

"I know. I read the report. But I just wanted to double-check a couple of things."

He sighed and shook his head. "Damn shame. She was a great-lookin' broad. I'll never figure out what she was doing married to a nigger." A look of recognition started to spread slowly over his face. "Who are you working for—the Vreeland family?"

I shook my head.

He snorted. "You're working for him," he muttered.

"For his attorney," I answered.

"Same difference."

"Can we come in for a minute?"

He shrugged. "Just for a minute. I don't got all day to waste."

"No, I'm sure you're a busy man," Nate said.

We followed him into the living room, where he proceeded to flop down on an easy chair that you couldn't have paid the Salvation Army to carry away. The layout of the house appeared to be identical to Anna Paslawski's, only reversed. A quick glance around the living room suggested that they used the same decorator.

Shepherd wasn't as good a housekeeper as his neighbor, but he had a color TV parked in the same approximate spot. Like Mrs. Paslawski, he had an ugly coffee table next to the chair. There was a pack of Chesterfields on the table, along with an unfinished bowl of soup. I thought I recognized the aroma of Campbell's Scotch Broth, but he might have been the victim of Anna Paslawski's Christian charity.

The set was tuned to the *Flintstones*, and the volume was cranked up to a level that could test the limits of human endurance. I'm a heavy sleeper myself, but one Yabba-Dabba-Doo would have sent me reeling right back to the Stone Age. Apparently, Warren Shepherd was the kind of guy who could sleep through a nuclear war.

He leaned forward and turned down the volume. "They got nothin' but crap on TV in the daytime," he said. He picked up a can of Bud that was sitting on the arm rest and took a swallow. I didn't expect him to offer us one. He didn't.

"Home from work," I said abruptly, more a statement than a question.

"Yeah, vacation day," he answered, giving me a look that said none of your business.

There were no chairs for us to sit in without having to rearrange his wardrobe, so we remained standing.

"What do you do?" Nate asked. His tone was casual, but it had an official ring to it.

"I'm a forklift operator." He pointed with the beer can over his shoulder. "At the Felsway Corporation, over on River-view Drive."

"I hear that's interesting work," Nate said.

Shepherd glanced at him suspiciously, while I ambled over to the picture window. I spoke without looking at him.

"According to the police report, you were standing here when you saw Robinson come out of his house on the night of the murder."

"Yeah, that's right. He came running down Mrs. Paslaw-ski's driveway, then he dumped the baseball trophy in her garbage can. Then he hopped into his car and pulled away. The bastard smashed the taillight on my car."

"Where was your car parked?" I asked.

"On the street."

I turned and stared at him. "Maybe you'd be willing to show us," Nate said.

Shepherd let out a low groan, then got up and moved

slowly to the window. I figured the guy was a real pleasure to work with.

"Mine was parked across the street, right out in front of their house, just like it is now." He pointed to a rusted gold Pontiac that was about ten feet from the edge of Anna Paslawski's driveway. "His was parked behind mine. There was another car parked behind his."

"Whose car was that?" I asked.

He shrugged and moved back to his chair. "I didn't notice."

"What kind of car does Robinson drive?"

He smirked. "What is this, a trick question? He drives a fuckin' pimpmobile, like they all do. And I'll bet it ain't paid for, either."

"Did you see him pull up to the house?"

"Hey, I'm not the neighborhood watchdog, Jack."

I didn't bother to correct him on the name. "So you don't know how long he was inside."

"No. But Mrs. Paslawski saw him come home. He wasn't in there but five minutes."

"Did you call the police about the accident?"

"Do I look like a fuckin' idiot to you?" I assumed it was a rhetorical question. "Of course I called the police. They came out here and wrote up a report."

"You must have been pretty pissed off," Nate said.

Shepherd rolled his eyes and glanced back at the TV set. "No. I was jumping for joy."

Nate smiled. "Effective use of sarcasm. I guess you must have been waiting up for Robinson when he came home."

"Huh?"

"Didn't you think about confronting him when he got back?"

"A buck nigger? The asshole's thirty years younger than me and used to be a star athlete. Plus he probably carries a razor. What would you have done? I went to sleep. The next thing I know the cops are poundin' on my door wantin' to ask me a bunch of questions." He paused. "*You* got any more questions?"

"Yeah," I said. "Did you ever talk to Robinson or his wife?"

"As little as I had to. I mind my own business."

"What about your wife?"

Shepherd was standing up now, our signal that it was time to leave. "I don't got a wife."

I figured as much, but I just wanted to make sure. Details like that are sometimes good to know. "Mrs. Paslawski said there were a couple of other black guys who used to go in and out of Robinson's house," I said. "Did you ever notice them?"

"I don't run the neighborhood boogie watch. If she said so, it's probably true."

"Does that mean that she does?" Nate asked.

Shepherd answered the question by opening the screen door. Once we were outside, the idea that we were leaving seemed to imbue him with a sudden burst of friendliness.

"I hope you guys are getting paid well," he said. "Because you're working on a lost cause." He closed the door. "Sorry I couldn't be of any help."

"Actually, you were quite a bit of help," I answered. That wasn't true, but it never hurts to leave the witnesses a little room for second thoughts. With Warren Shepherd, you'd have to leave quite a bit of room.

I turned back when we reached the bottom of the steps. "By the way, was it dark the night of the murder?" I asked.

I caught him by surprise. He had to think about that one for a minute. Even through the screen, you could see his mind laboring over whether or not there was a correct answer.

"No darker than any other night," he said at last. Not a bad response. In a courtroom, of course, he'd have to be more specific.

"We were wondering about that because, without street lights, Mrs. Paslawski says it's hard to see them in the dark."

Shepherd frowned, then pursed his lips into the first stage of a smile. He had to think about that one a minute, too.

"Yeah," Nate said. "I hear some people even have trouble telling them apart during the day."

We left Warren Shepherd chuckling nervously behind his screen door. He didn't bother to close the inside one, so I could hear Fred Flintstone screaming "Wilma-a-a" as we pulled away. No doubt the *Jetsons* would be coming on next.

"What do you think?" I asked Nate. "We've still got time for another house call."

He cracked open two beers and handed one to me. "I think I've seen just about all the white trash I can stand for one day."

CHAPTER
7

I picked up Nate and his cooler at nine the next morning. Even if I made all the same wrong turns as the day before, that left plenty of time to make our eleven A.M. with Hal Pucinsky, the Wayne Township chief of police.

When I spoke to him on the phone, Pucinsky had reluctantly agreed to "find fifteen minutes" for us. I'm sure the guy stayed a lot busier than Warren Shepherd, but I didn't think being the top cop in Wayne could be all that demanding. They had a murder out there once every five years, and the latest one was already solved, as far as Pucinsky was concerned. Other than that, police work in Wayne probably consisted of little more than busting kids for pot and setting up speed traps. Not what you'd call high-pressure work.

"I'm beginning to feel like we're in a goddamn car pool," Nate said as he crammed himself in behind the dashboard. "Maybe you ought to consider buying something with room for an adult."

No man in his right mind would argue in favor of bucket seats. "At least it beats taking the bus," I said.

"Jumping off the goddamn Brooklyn Bridge beats taking the bus."

"Sleep well last night, sugar plum?"

"As a matter of fact, I didn't."

"What's the problem? Up all night worrying about George Wallace?" Wallace was the cracker governor of Alabama, and he was running in the Democratic presidential primary. He had been shot the day before by a man named Arthur Bremer at a shopping center in Laurel, Maryland.

"Hell no. That was the best news I heard since J. Edgar Hoover kicked. Hortense called me up at three A.M. She's thinking about taking up suicide again."

"Is *she* worried about George Wallace?"

"Are you kidding? She's probably never heard of him. I don't think she even knows who's president. She's apolitical. Not by principle. It's just a by-product of her egocentrism. Her sculptor from Queens has decided to carve out a niche for himself that doesn't include her. Whenever that happens, she decides to kill herself."

"What did you tell her?"

"I told her it has its pluses and its minuses, but it's not something you want to jump into lightly."

"You ought to be a psychotherapist."

"I ought to get a new phone number."

The drive went so smoothly that we had time to stop at the Dunkin' Donuts in downtown Clifton. Had I remembered that Nate actually likes to dunk his donuts, I wouldn't have made the suggestion.

When we got to the Wayne police station on Valley Road, my suspicions about the police chief's grueling schedule were confirmed. Hal Pucinsky had just finished slipping a putter into a golf bag when the desk sergeant led us into his office.

Pucinsky was a stocky guy with a ruddy complexion and reddish brown hair. He had a fairly large nose that looked bigger than it really was because his eyebrows had grown together, giving the illusion that the beak started in the center of his forehead.

When we shook hands and did the introductions, he seemed friendlier than he had been on the phone. "I've been doing a little work on my putting," he explained sheepishly. "There's a big tournament coming up over Memorial Day."

"That wouldn't be over at the Mountain Lake Country Club, by any chance?" Nate asked.

Pucinsky leaned back in his chair and lit a cigarette. I think he thought he might like us. "Matter of fact it is. You ever shot over there?"

"No, but they sent me an invitation."

"Well, you must be some kind of celebrity then."

Nate got an "aw shucks" expression on his face. "They seem to think so."

"I hear we got quite a lineup this year," Pucinsky said. "There's even talk that Frank Sinatra and Dean Martin are coming. I guess Mr. Vreeland is a friend of theirs."

"Thomas Vreeland?" I asked.

"That's right. He's the one that started the tournament to begin with. Him and Congressman Winchester. It's dedicated to the memory of Mr. Vreeland's wife, the congressman's sister. Of course there's a big cloud hanging over the whole thing this year, thanks to your client going and murdering his daughter."

All of a sudden, Pucinsky began giving it to me with both eyeballs. I sensed something of a chill in the room. I resisted the temptation to remind him that a man was innocent until proven guilty. I couldn't see any gain in antagonizing him.

"Listen, Renzler," he said. "I spoke to George Grimaldi about you, and he says you're good people."

"So's George," I said.

Grimaldi used to be the assistant police chief in Wayne. I met him in 1961 while protecting a baseball player from some low-rent mobsters. The reason George liked me was because I set him up to make a collar that got his mug splashed all over the North Jersey papers. Every year since, his wife has sent me a Christmas card. Grimaldi retired a few years back, but I figured it wouldn't hurt to drop his name when I spoke to Pucinsky on the phone. Apparently, it hadn't.

"George and me are golfing buddies, so I try to believe what he says. But I've kind of got my doubts this time. I don't know how you got mixed up with Robinson and this O'Leary jerk. For all I know he's your brother-in-law—"

"Father-in-law," Nate corrected.

"*Ex*-father-in-law," I clarified.

"Oh, so that's it." The police chief nodded, revealing years of apparent experience with in-laws. "Anyway, if it wasn't for what George says, I wouldn't even be giving you the time of day." He glanced at his wristwatch. "Starting now, you got exactly five minutes."

Thanks a lot. It sure helps to have connections.

"You seem awfully certain that Dwight Robinson killed his wife," I said.

"There's not a doubt in my mind. That's why this is a waste of both our time. It's an open-'n'-shut case."

"Robinson seems to think a guy named Shake Johnson might have been involved. Did you talk to him?"

"Bullshit. I talked to him." Pucinsky snorted, and the beak wrinkled up like a week-old pierogi. He got up from his chair and began pacing the room. "Let me tell you something about Dwight Robinson," he said, stopping and pointing his finger at us.

I leaned back in my chair and got ready for a lecture.

"The kid's a born troublemaker. Back maybe five years ago, I had him and his brother caddying for a foursome over there. One of the guys loses a fifty-dollar bill he had in his bag. So I asked Dwight about it. You know, casually. He gets all hot and bothered and starts saying the guy probably never had the money there in the first place, he's just making it up. That's Dwight Robinson for you. A born liar."

"There's a big difference between stealing fifty bucks and murder," Nate pointed out.

Pucinsky had resumed pacing but came to a sudden halt. "Fine, you want to hear some other stuff? Since he moved into Wayne, he's been picked up for speeding *three* times. We got him on disorderly conduct twice. We could have got him for assault, but we gave him the benefit of the doubt. That was our mistake. You give his kind an inch, they'll take a mile."

The chief walked over to his golf bag and pulled out his putter again. "Then last year we picked him up with enough grass to get the whole town high. We gave him a break again. If it wasn't for Mr. Vreeland intervening all the time, we would have put his ass in the slammer a long time ago. But he wouldn't listen to me. Now he's sorry he didn't."

There was something a little disturbing about the tone of reverence Pucinsky used when referring to Dwight Robinson's father-in-law. I wondered if Dwight was the only person Vreeland practiced legal intervention for.

"Me and Mr. Vreeland had a heart to heart last week," Pucinsky said. "He told me Robinson was gambling a lot. Cynthia had to get money from her father to pay off his debts. Then it turns out Tommy, that's Mr. Vreeland's son, says Cynthia told him Dwight used to smack her around sometimes after he had a snootful."

Pucinsky put the putter away, then came back to the desk, where he sat down and lit another cigarette. He had snuffed out the last one almost as soon as he started smoking it. He was what you'd call the nervous type.

"Big fucking baseball star! Beating up on his own wife." He started giving us the eyeballs again. "What do you think of that?"

Neither one of us answered the question. It wasn't easy to speak up on Robinson's behalf. Speeding tickets and disorderly conduct don't mean much, but wife beating's a little tough to defend—assuming it was true.

"What about Shake Johnson?" I asked.

"Oh, he's another one. But there's no way he would've killed Cynthia. He's practically Tommy's best friend. Mr. Vreeland likes him, too. He's the caddy master up at Mountain Lake."

"You checked him out?" It was more of a statement than a question, but Pucinsky seemed to get indignant nonetheless.

"Of course we checked him out! We check everything. Shake had an alibi." He smiled. "Unlike Robinson, his was a good one."

"Do you mind telling us what it was?"

"Be glad to. He was drinking. With Cynthia's brother. At a bar down in Mountain View called Pete's. It's owned by Pete Becker. He's the golf pro up at Mountain Lake."

"You mentioned that Vreeland told you Dwight had gambling debts," Nate said. "Do you know who was putting the heat on him?"

He shook his head. "Beats me. I don't know and I don't particularly care."

That seemed like a strange comment for the police chief to make. After all, gambling is illegal. "No chance it would have been Shake?" I asked.

"Doubt it. Probably some of his friends from Paterson. We don't have that kind of crap here in Wayne."

Oh no, not here.

"Where can we find Shake Johnson?" I asked.

"He lives in Mountain View, but you can probably catch him up at the golf course."

"And the Vreelands?"

"Now listen." Pucinsky stood up again. "I'm telling you this once and I don't want to have to tell you again: I don't mind you guys talking to people, but don't go stirring up any trouble. We've had enough of that already."

"Scout's honor," I said, raising my right hand. I didn't see any gain in telling him we could talk to anybody we damn well pleased.

"Did anyone ever mention you got kind of a bad attitude?" he asked me.

I gave him my charming smile. "Plenty of times."

Pucinsky ground out his cigarette. "The Vreelands live in Mountain Lake, up on Hogan Drive. But I doubt you'll be able to get past the guard."

"They've got a guard at the house?" Nate asked.

"They've got a guard at the gate into town. You want to

see somebody in Mountain Lake, you got to have an appointment."

"Is that where you live?" I asked.

"You kidding? On my salary? Where would I get that kind of dough?"

I didn't bother offering to put him in touch with some New York cops I knew who could have given him a few ideas. Maybe if he had been a little nicer.

He shifted his eyeballs from us to his wristwatch. "Time's up. In fact, you got a lot more than you should have."

Nate stood up. "Got to get to work on that putting, right?"

Pucinsky grinned. I don't know how Nate did it, but he had a knack for sending his sarcastic jabs just over the heads of his intended victims. If I could perfect that tone, maybe I wouldn't have so many people complaining about my attitude.

"I've won the men's side of the tournament two years straight," the police chief said. He padded to a bookcase that was starved for books and motioned to a pair of trophies. "Of course not the overalls. Terry Vreeland—that's Mr. Vreeland's other daughter—she's got that all sewed up. They might as well just give her a permanent trophy."

"Did Cynthia play golf?"

"Not really. Cynthia Vreeland didn't do much of anything except sit around and look pretty."

"Do you have to live in Mountain Lake to play on the course?"

"You're supposed to. But I got kind of a special deal."

Nate shook the chief's hand. "Maybe I'll see you at the tournament."

"Great." He looked at me. "Are you playing, too?"

I shook my head. "I don't have any special deals. But you'll be seeing me again. I'll give you a call when we figure out who killed Cynthia Robinson."

CHAPTER
8

Variety being the spice of life, I decided to surprise Nate by taking him to lunch at another Howard Johnson's I knew, on Route 23. On the way there, we heard a radio report that George Wallace had been taken off the critical list but doctors expected he would be confined to a wheelchair for life.

"If this doesn't get his campaign rolling, nothing will," Nate said. "I bet it'll improve his sex life, too."

"You want to make a little bet on the outcome of today's primaries?" I asked.

"What did you have in mind?"

"I'll take Wallace and you can have the field."

"Oh, sure, great deal for me. Who do I get—Ed Muskie, Scoop Jackson, McGovern? Any dark horses in the race?"

"I don't know. I'd have to check the Racing Form."

"I think we should check out somebody who might have something good to say about Dwight Robinson."

Not a bad idea. O'Leary had suggested we talk to Ed Gallo, Dwight's high school baseball coach, but he was probably busy teaching school. We settled on Dwight's mother. She lived with his older brother, Dexter, in the delightful little town of Singac, just over the border of Wayne and a mile down the road. Actually, I was more interested in speaking with Dexter. He had been at Dwight's house the night of the murder, and there was a chance he wouldn't be as reluctant to talk about it.

I'm sure Singac was a step up from the housing projects of Paterson, but Dahlia Robinson was not basking in luxury's lap. She lived in a tiny, wood-frame house on a narrow street behind Willowbrook, an enormous enclosed shopping center that was being billed as the world's largest indoor mall. The house was a winterized summer bungalow, situated within spitting distance of the Passaic River, about two miles south of where the Pompton River empties into it. It was no doubt built back in the days when the area was a vacation spot for wealthy New Yorkers. Those days had ended long ago, around the advent of highways.

Nobody with any sense went swimming in the Pompton or Passaic anymore, but residents of towns like Singac and Mountain View didn't have much choice. Every couple of years during the springtime, the rivers came to them, spilling into their living rooms and ruining their bean bag chairs and shag carpeting. They were compensated for their inconvenience by having their pictures splashed across the Jersey section of *The New York Times*. In years when the flooding was severe, they made the front page.

Dexter, we learned, had a part-time job scooping ice cream at a shop in the mall. We spent a few minutes with his mother just to be polite.

Dwight had always been a good boy, she told us, and she was sure he couldn't have murdered his wife. She was glad that nice chubby lawyer was going to prove his innocence, and she was happy to know that nice men like us were helping him out. It was Dwight, she said, who paid for her house, immediately after receiving his bonus for signing with the Yankees. She thought there must be a way to put up the house to pay his bail, but he wouldn't allow it. So the only way she could help was to keep saying her prayers.

Dwight had bought the house from Thomas Vreeland through some kind of deal that was too complicated for her to understand. "Now I'm not so sure," she said. "I don't understand," I said. "What aren't you sure about?"

"Mr. Vreeland, he was wanting to buy the house back from me and then give it to some other lady. He said I would get a thousand extra dollars and wouldn't have to move. But then he called back one day, saying he didn't want to buy it after all on account of the other lady might not be so trustworthy. He was saying I could make some extra money if I'd be willing to be the owner of other houses. I didn't understand it all, but of course I said I would, on account of you can never have too much money these days."

Nate and I exchanged puzzled looks, while Dahlia Robinson paused to catch her breath. "Now, after what happened, I don't suppose he'll be thinking about giving us any deals," she said. "Not after the way he's been talking about my boy on the TV."

"How long ago did he call you?" I asked.

"Oh, a couple of months ago, I guess. I never did get all the details because he only mentioned it that once."

As we made our exit, she stopped to show us her proudest possession, an old maple hutch with window shelves. The shelves were lined with trophies. "It got so I didn't have enough space to keep them all after a while. They're Dwight's mostly, but Dexter, he got a couple, too."

We admired the trophy case for a few seconds, then Nate moved out to the front stoop. I had a feeling Dahlia Robinson didn't want us to leave so soon. I could see tears forming at the corners of her eyes. They were nice eyes. Big, brown and round. She was a pretty woman.

"Please help my boy," she said. "I know he's got problems and troubles, but he never would have done anything as awful as they're saying."

"We'll do everything we can," I assured her. "In the meantime, you just keep on praying."

"When did you become such a staunch advocate of the

power of prayer?" Nate said, as we rumbled over the ruts in the road.

"And people think *I've* got a bad attitude," I replied.

We spent what seemed like an hour trying to find a way into the mall and half of another wandering through it before we found the Barricini candy shop, where Dexter Robinson worked. Behind a counter on the left side of the store, we spotted a tall black guy in a white cap scooping ice cream for a sweet young eyeful in an Indian print dress. Dexter was a lot thinner than his younger brother, but you couldn't miss the resemblance in the long, sharp lines on his face.

We reached the counter just as he was leaning across it and handing a giant cone to the girl.

"For you, beautiful, no charge," he said.

"Hey, thanks," the girl answered.

"Think nothing of it." An easy-going smile spread over his face as he leaned closer to her and whispered. "Meet me after work tonight and I'll put some cream between your buns that'll satisfy like nothing you've ever experienced before."

"Fuck you, jerk off."

Dexter's grin turned instantly to a frown, but he tried to force it nonchalantly back into place when he noticed us off to his right.

"Chicks!" He shrugged and put his hands up. "They just don't know what they're missing."

"You keep giving it away for free, you're going to lose your job," I said.

"Shit. I don't need this dumb job. What do you fellas feel like today? Boss is out to lunch, so I can give you a good price on rum raisin. Of course, I got to make sure you're old enough, so you got to show your ID."

I surprised him when I did. "You're Dexter, right?"

"Who's asking?"

I guess the badge scared him so badly, he didn't get a chance to read the name. I showed it again. "Your mother said we could find you here. We're trying to help your brother."

"Oh yeah? How is the dude?"

"He's in fucking jail," Nate said.

"Whoa!" Dexter backed away a step and put out his arm. He spoke to me. "This dude here got a temper."

"So do I. We're trying to figure out who killed Cynthia."

"Don't look at me. I sure didn't do it."

"Neither did your brother."

"Yeah, that's what he says."

"You mean you don't believe him?"

"No, man, sure, I believe him. He's my brother. I stood up for him. I gave him an alibi. I told the pigs we were out drinking together."

"We heard. We also heard that you were seen drinking alone that night."

"This is true. But that was only for a little while, early on. I could've been drinking there and then been with him someplace else later."

"But you weren't," Nate said.

He nodded. "Yeah, this is true."

A short, beefy guy padded up and ordered a scoop of rum raisin and a scoop of blueberry cheesecake. Dexter didn't bother asking to see his ID. As I watched him scoop, I noticed a tiny object in the rum raisin that didn't look like a raisin. Then I noticed that there were strips of fly paper hanging from the ceiling over the ice cream containers. The strips were covered with flies.

"This guy's a big help," Nate whispered. "I'm glad we found the time to see him."

Dexter gave the beefy man a cone that was considerably smaller than the last one he had scooped. The guy gave him exact change. Dexter began to slip the money into his pocket, but he glanced our way and had second thoughts. I'll bet the boss didn't know how expensive his lunches really were.

"OK, so where were we?" Dexter said, clasping his hands together.

"You were out drinking," Nate reminded him.

"That's right. At Pete's."

"That's the place in Mountain View?" I asked. "The one that's owned by the golf pro?"

Dexter nodded. "This is true."

"Your brother said he thought a guy named Shake Johnson might have killed Cynthia," I said.

"Could be," he answered. "I saw him down at Pete's that night, but I was out of there by nine. Shake's a bad dude. Dwight owed him some cash, you know, and Shake didn't like to be kept waiting. Last week, you know, he bashed in the headlight on Dwight's car."

"Did you see him do it?"

"No, man, but I heard about it."

"Who from?"

He shrugged. "From the bro. And Shake was bragging about it. He told Dwight he might have to take his pay off of Cynthia."

"What did he mean by that?"

Dexter leaned forward and put his hands close together. He made a circle with the index finger and thumb of his left hand and poked his right index finger through the circle. "You know what I'm talking about, man."

"We heard Shake's a friend of Tommy Vreeland's," Nate said.

That's exactly what I was thinking. What kind of person would even joke about raping his friend's sister?

"They hang out and stuff." He shrugged. "Tommy might think they're friends, but Shake ain't a friend of nobody's."

A man's voice called Dexter's name from a room in the back.

"I got to go," he said. "See what dumb shit he wants me to do now."

"Just one more question," I said. "Did you go to Dwight's house a lot?"

"Sure, lots of times."

"Did you ever go there alone, when he wasn't there?"

"You mean to see Cynthia?" Dexter looked from me to Nate, then over his shoulder, as the boss called his name again. "Not too often. Only when she invited me. She and me used to rap once in a while." He turned and began heading for the back. "Catch you later."

Nate called to him, stopping him in his tracks. "You didn't go over there to rap with her the night she was killed, did you?"

Dexter spun around to face us. Without the smile on his face, the resemblance to his brother was very close. "*No* way, man. That's crazy jive."

"I wonder," Nate murmured, as we turned to search for an exit.

My sentiments exactly.

CHAPTER
9

We headed north on Route 23 and got stuck in a logjam of cars. The problem could have been caused by commuters returning home from New York, locals being released from their industrial-park cages or housewives hunting for bargains at the shopping mall. I figured it was probably a combination of the three. I also figured that if you took the trouble of moving twenty-five miles from the city, you shouldn't have to deal with that sort of shit.

"Aren't you glad I thought to bring the beer?" Nate asked.

"We're only going a couple of miles," I assured him, taking a frosty one nonetheless.

"I should have packed a goddamn case. Where are all these people coming from?"

"They live here," I said.

"There's got to be a better word for it than that."

I crossed over two lanes of traffic and pulled off at the Mountain View exit, pissing off some of our fellow travelers in the process. Nate answered their honking horns with his middle finger.

"Time for a little chat with Shake?" he asked.

"I think we ought to wait on that. I thought we'd pay a call on Thomas Vreeland and his son."

"Do you have an appointment?"

"No, but you've got to register to play some golf."

"Think again, pal. That's not in my job description."

"What's the matter? Don't you want to meet Frank Sinatra?"

"Only if he brings along Sammy Davis Jr."

"Isn't he Frank's caddy?"

"You're thinking of Jack Carter. Sammy Davis is *Nixon's* caddy."

"That's right." How could I have forgotten? I was no match for Nate in the celebrity ID game. "Well, it might do you good to get out in the sun and get some exercise for a change."

"Then again, it might not. I've never golfed in my life. I don't have a set of clubs. I don't even know anybody with a set of clubs. If I did, I wouldn't be on speaking terms with them."

Despite his opposition, I could hear equivocation creeping into his voice. "We'll get you some," I said.

He frowned, then broke into a smile. "OK, I'll do it. But you've got to carry my bag."

"Naturally." I figured that was coming.

"And, under no circumstance am I going to dress up like a goddamn fruit salad."

Just before we crossed the railroad tracks in Mountain View, we passed a drab, two-story cinder block building with a Rheingold logo on it. A handpainted sign on the front window said: "Pete's—Where Friends Meet."

"Looks like a charming little place," Nate said.

"It's a charming little town," I replied.

Mountain View was one of those dirty old burgs with about eight narrow streets and eighty seedy bars. The town square had a run-down shopping center with a bakery, a hardware store and fifteen laundromats. Two side streets running off the main drag were lined with car-repair garages and stores for rent. Only one storefront was freshly painted—Vreeland & Son Realty.

Two blocks and four bars past the tracks, we turned right and began ascending the short, winding hill that led up to Mountain Lake. Whoever named the two towns had taken some liberties with the language. As far as I could see, the highest point in the area was the Route 23 overpass. It would have been more accurate to call the mountain Big Lump of Asphalt. But I guess that doesn't have much of a ring to it.

Half a mile up we came to a green booth with an electric gate across the road. A radio was blaring acid rock music at earsplitting volume. I could detect the smell of smoke, but it wasn't from a cigarette or cigar. As I stopped the car, a pimply-faced kid leaned out of the booth. He looked all of sixteen, but I figured he was older, because school was still in session.

"Who you here to visit?" he shouted. On second thought, I figured he was probably a high school dropout.

"This is Nate Moore," I yelled. "He has to register for the golf tournament."

The kid squinted through the car window and started giving Nate the once-over. He turned down the radio, but it was still loud enough to cause temporary hearing loss. "You're supposed to send it in the mail."

"Yeah, I know," Nate said. "I meant to do that, but my cat puked all over it. It happens every goddamn time I buy one of those discount brands."

The kid got a puzzled expression on his face, then began to laugh.

"I didn't think Tom Vreeland would appreciate having his mailbox smell like a bedpan, so I decided to come out in person. Besides, I thought it might be a good idea to scope out the course."

"Well, I better check the list anyway. It could take me a few minutes."

It did. He began sorting through a stack of papers, pausing over each one as if he were deciphering hieroglyphics. "They must have taken it back. I guess I got to call up to the pro shop."

"Don't bother going to all that trouble." I pulled a ten out of my wallet and held it out the window. English may have been his second language, but I figured money talks.

"Well, I don't know." His voice was hesitant, but he didn't hesitate to snatch the bill from my hand.

"It's OK," I assured him. "Buy yourself a little Panama Red."

The kid grinned vacantly. He did something with his hand behind the window, and the gate lifted. I thought about adding that he might spring for some Clearasil but I restrained myself. That kind of comment can traumatize a kid for life.

"By the way," he said, as we started to pull away. "It usually takes a double sawbuck, but I'm giving you guys a break."

For all its pretensions of grandeur, Mountain Lake was less magnificent than the Land of Oz. But it was the result of somebody's bad dream, nonetheless.

The streets were as wide as a hockey rink, but they weren't paved with gold or yellow brick. They were painted bright green. All the houses looked big enough to sleep ten, but there was nothing distinctive about their design.

"Hey, take at look at that," Nate said, pointing at a street sign. "Sam Snead Drive."

Mounted on the same pole were crude drawings of a sailboat and a golf ball with an arrow indicating the way. Maybe it was no accident that the kid at the booth didn't know how to read.

We followed the arrows to the golf course, taking a right on Arnold Palmer Way and a left on Gene Sarazen Street. Along the way, we passed the lake, which constituted another liberty with the language. It couldn't have been any bigger than the saltwater pool at Palisades Park. The country club was on the east shore, at the end of Dwight D. Eisenhower Court.

"I sense a little inconsistency here," Nate said.

"Ike was an avid golfer," I explained.

"Mamie, too?"

"No. She just liked to sit around the clubhouse bar getting cockeyed."

"Isn't a golf course supposed to have sixteen holes?" he asked, as I parked the Corvair between two Lincolns.

"Eighteen."

"The sign says this one only has nine. That's kind of a half-assed job, wouldn't you say?"

"Take it up with Mr. Vreeland."

There was a kid working in the pro shop who could have been the brother of the guard at the gate. Maybe he was. For all I knew, the kids in Mountain Lake all had six fingers. This kid worked like he only had one hand. It took almost half an hour before Nate was an official entrant in the Tenth Annual Sarah Winchester Vreeland Memorial Golf Tournament. He got a packet of promotional materials to prove it.

"Is Mr. Vreeland here today?" I asked.

"He was earlier. Him and Tommy and Mr. Winchester played together. They might be in the bar or they might've went home."

"Want to check?" Nate asked, nodding toward the entrance.

"You got to be a member," the kid said.

Nate waved a free drink coupon that he had found in his registration packet.

"That's only good for the day of the tournament."

"I figured there had to be a catch."

For a moment, I thought about slipping the kid a ten. A pair of lizard-skinned ladies staggering out of the bar changed my mind. If they were typical of the clientele, I didn't want to take any risks with the glasses.

"So much for being a celebrity," Nate muttered. "I bet they wouldn't have turned away Dean Martin."

I reminded him that we had beer in the car, but that didn't seem to satisfy his thirst for respect. "Someday, young man, I'm going to own this place," he said.

We didn't have any trouble finding Ben Hogan Drive, the

street where the man who owned Mountain Lake lived. We didn't have any trouble finding his house, either—it was the only one on the street. If the residents of Mountain Lake ever decided to expand the golf course to eighteen holes, all they'd have to do is put a few pins and sand traps on Thomas Vreeland's front lawn. You could have finished off a six-pack in the time it took to drive from the street to the garage. The front of the house was framed with rose bushes, and the massive marble walk leading up to it was lined with life-size statues of golfing legends.

"Something tells me golf plays an important role in this man's life," Nate said.

A heavyset black woman in a maid's outfit answered the bell. She let us into the foyer, which was about the size of Dahlia Robinson's living room. She returned a few moments later, trailed by a tall, silver-haired man with a permanent tan. I figured Thomas Vreeland for about sixty, but it was a healthy sixty. He was followed by another man, who looked identical in almost every regard, except that his hair was blond and he was probably thirty-five years younger. If you wanted a reference point for defining chip-off-the-old-block, you wouldn't have to go any further than Tommy Vreeland. As I began to speak, I noticed a young woman come around the corner and stand behind father and son.

Introducing ourselves went smoothly enough. That was as far as we got. I hadn't thought it was going to be easy. Before I got through explaining that we were working for Dwight Robinson's attorney, Thomas Vreeland's tan turned a curious shade of red. His son's face changed too, a sympathetic protective coloration.

"How dare you come into my house!" Vreeland squawked, "Working for that filthy murderer!"

"We have good reason to believe that Dwight Robinson didn't murder your daughter," I said. "I know it's a very difficult time for you—"

"Get the fuck out of here!" This time it was Tommy Vreeland doing the talking. He took a step forward, and I could sense Nate bracing for combat beside me. I hoped that wouldn't be necessary.

Thomas Vreeland stuck his arm out as a barrier in front of his son's chest. "Get the hell out of my house or I'll have you arrested for trespassing," he yelled.

I understood their being upset, but I hadn't expected quite so much hostility. Vreeland had lost his daughter, but if it turned out Dwight hadn't killed her, the person who did was still on the loose. And he wasn't so broken up that he couldn't go out and play a little golf.

I opened the door with one hand and pulled a business card out of my pocket with the other. "We don't want to cause any trouble," I said, holding out the card. Nobody came forward to take it. "Perhaps when you're feeling—"

"Get the fuck out of here, asshole," Tommy shouted.

Nate gave him a patronizing smile. "We're on our way, junior."

I let go of the card and watched it flutter to the floor. It landed about a foot from Tommy Vreeland's feet. The maid hurried over to pick it up.

"Friendly folks," Nate said when we hit the walk. "I think the youngster might have a gland problem."

I looked back over my shoulder and saw Thomas Vreeland and his son standing at the top of the steps and glaring at us. "It could be genes."

Nate gave Jack Nicklaus a friendly pat on the ass. "Watch out for those frog ponds, buddy," he said.

CHAPTER
10

$\mathbf{I}$ was at Bowie Racetrack in Maryland, waiting to put fifty grand down on a horse called Bremer's Boy. Just as I got to the betting window, someone pulled down a shade over it. The shade was a color poster of George Wallace. I walked outside to the grandstand and pushed my way through a throng of people. I asked a fat guy wearing a straw hat with Wallace's picture on it if I had missed the third race. He answered in a southern drawl.

"Y'all come for a *horse* race? This ain't no horse race, sonny. This here's the presidential race. You must be at the wrong track."

Indeed I was. As I looked around, I saw that everyone except me was wearing one of those dumb hats. I saw George Wallace standing atop the tote board, shouting into a megaphone. He was wearing one of those dumb hats.

Wallace was saying that folks shouldn't feel inferior to all them slick-talking, fancy-pants fellas in the three-piece suits carrying attaché cases to their jobs on Wall Street.

"Them guys might look important, but you know what they're carryin' in them fancy briefcases of theirs?" he yelled.

The crowd fell silent. Evidently, I was the only person who knew the answer to the question. I had heard the speech before.

"There ain't nothin' in them briefcases but a *peanut butter sandwich!*"

The crowd erupted with laughter until the sound of machine-gun fire exploded off to my left. I ducked for cover and found it—back in my apartment, under the sheets on my bed.

On my night table, the machine-gun kept firing. Of course, it wasn't a machine-gun. Just the telephone. As far as I'm concerned, that can be just as lethal a weapon. Especially when it goes off at seven in the morning.

I crawled out from behind my J.P. Stevens bunker and picked it up. Mike O'Leary's voice exploded like a grenade in my ear.

"Wake up, Sleeping Beauty. You're supposed to be working."

"Do you know what fucking time it is?" I had been making a concerted effort to cut back on my cussing following a particularly vulgar exchange with a fat lady on the Broadway bus a few weeks before that had embarrassed the shit out of two young nuns. But instinct tends to override resolution when you're teetering on the brink of consciousness. I'm not what you'd call a morning person, by any stretch of the imagination.

"What the fuck do you want?" I asked.

"I thought I'd check in with you, let you in on a little good news."

"What is it?" Except for the occasional -ing ending on an expletive, I'm strictly a monosyllable guy before coffee. I told him to hold on while I went to the stove to make some.

"I managed to get Dwight's bail cut in half yesterday—we're only looking at a quarter million now."

"That's still a lot."

"It's an improvement. If we could figure out a way to come up with twenty-five grand, we'd be able to post bond."

"Put up his house."

"He doesn't own the house. Didn't I tell you that?"

"No."

"Technically, the house belongs to Cynthia. Her father arranged all the financing. If it hadn't been for him, they never would have been permitted to move into that neighborhood."

"Why not?"

"Think about it a second, Einstein."

"Oh yeah."

"There are laws to protect minorities from discrimination, but that doesn't eliminate the problem. You can't stop realtors from winking at each other with legislation."

Thanks for the civics lesson, counselor. I'm not stupid, just asleep. And that would be changing any minute. I was sipping coffee and smoking a cigarette now. Watch out, world, here I come.

"Have you made any progress on your end?" O'Leary asked.

"I've managed to get it out of bed, if that's what you mean."

"That's not what I mean, and you know it. You shouldn't waste the little energy you've got in the morning trying to be funny. Tell me what you've come up with so far. Have you got any suspects?"

"A couple of possibles, but basically we're still at square one. And that's probably where we're going to stay unless you let me in on your little secret."

"That I can't do."

"OK, have a nice day." I could hear O'Leary hollering as I started to hang up the phone. I waited until he finished before I put it back to my ear.

"I need more to go on, Mike. We haven't talked to Shake Johnson yet, but the police chief says he's got an alibi. I'm willing to believe Dwight's comments about white justice, but so far he's still the number-one guy. You want to know who the number-two guy is?"

"Yeah."

"His brother, Dexter."

"Aw come on, that's ridiculous."

"Tell me about Dwight's alibi, Mike."

O'Leary let out a sigh. "I can give you some of it, but not all of it."

"Give me what you can."

"The person who hired me was in bed with Dwight the night of the murder. She's a wealthy woman with a reputation to protect. Naturally, she doesn't want her name mixed up in any of this."

"Naturally. This woman's married, I presume."

"I didn't say that. Don't start putting words in my mouth."

"So she's not married."

"I didn't say that, either."

"Is she white?"

"Yeah, she's white. Through me, she's offered to pay Dwight fifty grand not to say anything. That's why he's being so tight lipped about the whole thing."

"Is that why you're being so tight lipped? How much is she paying you?"

"None of your goddamn business."

"I've got an idea. Why don't you put up his bail."

"Hey, I'm an attorney—not Santa Claus."

"Don't worry. Nobody's liable to mistake you for him. Is this wealthy lady the reason Cynthia filed for divorce?"

"No, I don't think so. Dwight says Cynthia didn't have any idea he was fooling around."

Maybe, maybe not. Wives usually know more about what their husbands are doing than their husbands like to think.

"Is she willing to come forward and testify at the trial?"

"That all depends."

"On what?"

"I'm not at liberty to say." He paused and I heard him slurping coffee. At least I figured it was coffee. O'Leary usually doesn't get started on the booze until lunchtime.

"If you'd find the murderer, we wouldn't have to worry about a trial." He said it like a statement of fact, not a directive to try harder.

"Why doesn't she put up Dwight's bail?" I asked.

"She doesn't want to. She seems to think he might not be safe. That, and I guess she's afraid he might be more tempted to talk if he's out and about."

"I want to talk to her."

"Tough rocks. I've already told you more than I was supposed to."

"It could save you both a lot of money. Working in an information vacuum, my expenses are really starting to pile up."

"Oh Christ, I'll see what I can do. Now how about a report from your end."

Fair enough. I gave him the blow-by-blow, from Anna Paslawski to Warren Shepherd, from Hal Pucinsky to Dexter Robinson. He laughed when I told him about our encounter with Thomas Vreeland and son.

"I wish you punched him out," he said. "Vreeland's a first-class jerk. But you've got to be careful around him. He's a powerful guy. He owns half of North Jersey. His brother-in-law's a jerk, too. Bob Winchester."

"That's the congressman, right?"

"Yeah, but he's running for Senate. You want to guess where he gets his financial backing."

I didn't have to. "Do you have a researcher on your staff?" I asked. "Somebody who knows something about real estate?"

"My secretary can handle it, if it's not too complicated."

I told him about Thomas Vreeland's offer to set Dahlia Robinson up in the real estate business. "I'd like to get a list of everything he owns," I said.

"That won't work. He's probably got most of his holdings hidden. You'd never be able to figure out what was his."

Of course. Dahlia Robinson had even told me as much. "How about checking the names of home owners on the flood plain?"

"I'll do better than that," he said. "We'll do a check on all the houses along two-eighty-seven."

"What's that?"

"Just an interstate highway they're planning on building."

"That wouldn't happen to be one of Congressman Bob's pet projects."

"Is the Pope Catholic?"

I heard a female voice in the background say "yes." At first I thought she was answering the question, then I realized it was O'Leary's secretary telling him he had another call.

"Ask her to hold for a minute," O'Leary told her. Then, to me, he said, "Along with fighting busing and keeping the death penalty, I'll bet that highway's at the top of Bob Winchester's agenda."

"Well, you've got to go," I said, sensing an opportunity to get off the line and refill my coffee cup. "Thanks, Mike. You're not as dumb as you look."

He ignored my comment. "Speaking of agendas, you wouldn't want to come out to Kathy's house for dinner on Sunday, would you? She said she'd like to see you."

"I take back what I said. Not only are you as dumb as you look, you're probably the dumbest person I ever met."

"Aw, come on. It'll be just like old times."

I told O'Leary what I thought about old times by hanging up. Two minutes later, the phone rang.

"No, absolutely not," I said, expecting him to file another plea.

"But you haven't even heard my offer yet," the voice on the other end of the line said.

It was a female voice. The voice chuckled. There was a pleasant, throaty lilt to it. "That's the fastest I've ever been turned down."

I mumbled an apology, something about the previous caller trying to sell me land in New Jersey.

"You don't know me," the voice said. "My name's Terry Vreeland. We almost met last evening. My brother tore your business card into a thousand little pieces. It took me nearly all night to tape it back together."

"I'm glad you made the effort."

"Do you still want to talk about Dwight Robinson?"

I assured her that I most certainly did.

"Meet me on the first tee at Mountain Lake tomorrow morning at nine."

"Are we going to play golf?" I tried to suppress the horror in my voice, but I'm sure some of it came through.

"Yes, you know how to play, don't you?"

"I understand the basic concept."

"That's half the battle. See you then."

"Wait a second." I caught her just before she hung up. "How do I get through the gate?"

"You managed all right yesterday."

"Yesterday was a special circumstance." I didn't see any point in telling her that all it took was a ten-dollar bill. I'd probably get the kid fired. Plus I wasn't that eager to throw around any more money, even if it was Mike O'Leary's.

"I'll give them your name. You shouldn't have any problem. If you do, ask to call the pro shop. They'll be able to find me."

I thought about asking her if you could rent clubs at the pro shop, too, but I was afraid she might reconsider. Based on the way I had answered my phone, she probably had enough doubts about me already.

I put down the phone and mulled over some doubts of my own. Somehow I didn't think it was just a coincidence that Terry Vreeland had called me so quickly after I had spoken to O'Leary. I wondered if she was the person he had put on hold. I wondered if she was the person who had hired him.

I poured another cup of coffee and started to make a list of the people I knew who owned golf clubs. I came up with two, then I remembered that one of them had died three years back. That kind of narrowed it down.

It wasn't a phone call I wanted to make, but I figured it would be worth the price, no matter how high. I had a feeling my outing with Terry Vreeland was going to be just the break we needed. It was about time.

I picked up the phone and started to dial, half hoping I wouldn't get any answer. I wondered how much it would cost to buy a set of clubs. I wondered if my brother-in-law still hated my guts.

Probably. After all, I still hated his.

The line was busy. Maybe he had died, and my sister was making funeral arrangements. Fat chance, but you can't blame a guy for hoping.

I sat back and tried to imagine myself playing golf. It wasn't a pretty picture. I thought about all the time I had put in as a caddy. That wasn't such a nice thought, either. Just thinking about all that walking made me feel tired and hungry.

I got up and looked around the kitchen. Then I did something else I hadn't done in quite a while. I made myself a goddamn peanut butter sandwich.

CHAPTER
——11——

The trip to Jersey seemed a little longer without somebody to ride shotgun. Nate was off fulfilling his Joe Franklin fantasy. But he had given me the cooler, so I wasn't exactly going solo.

O'Leary told me I would like Ed Gallo, the baseball coach at Kennedy High School in Paterson and apparently the closest person to a father figure in Dwight Robinson's life. Dwight's real father had died in Korea when Dwight was a baby, a casualty of our efforts to stop the spread of Communism.

Gallo had invited me to visit him at practice, but I opted out of another venture into Paterson and we settled on a saloon off Van Houten Avenue in Clifton, where Gallo lived. In addition to being my old hometown, Clifton is close to the highway and blessed with a wide selection of taverns that you wouldn't mind being caught dead in. When you go to a bar in Paterson, you take your chances.

It wasn't hard to pick Gallo out of the lineup of overweight guys at the bar. He was wearing a Kennedy High School windbreaker and had a whistle dangling from his neck. He looked to be about my age and weight, but he was a few inches shorter and nature hadn't been as kind to him about distributing it. We ordered beers and shuffled over to a table in the corner.

"You probably don't remember me, but I remember you." He grinned, revealing a set of crooked front teeth, and showed me the ring on his right hand. "Montclair High, Class of Fifty-one."

"You played baseball?" I asked.

"Yeah," he said. "I was a pitcher. You went four-for-four against me."

I've got a good memory, but the details of my high school days are pretty much a blur. "No offense, Ed, but if you gave up four hits to me, you probably made a wise decision to go into coaching."

He shrugged. "I was only a sophomore then. I got better, but not that much. If my salary was as high as my earned run average, I'd be a rich man today. But you didn't do so bad for yourself—until the accident, I mean."

I nodded. Apparently, Ed Gallo had kept up with my career beyond high school.

"It was a tough break," he said. "You hate to see anybody's career end on account of an injury. I was thinking of writing to you when I read about it, but I don't know, for some reason I never got around to it. I figured you probably had enough mail to answer anyway, and maybe the last thing you needed was to be reminded of it."

"You figured exactly right," I said. I had gotten mail by the truckload. At first I tried to answer it, but I gave up pretty soon. I always wondered if the people I hadn't written to thought I was unappreciative. I wasn't. I just couldn't think of anything to say. It's nice to find out people care, but when you're busy feeling sorry for yourself, sympathy cards only make you feel worse.

I had a feeling Gallo was curious about how it happened, so I gave him the *Reader's Digest* condensed version. It didn't upset me to talk about it. But after twenty-three years, I had told the story so many times that I couldn't put much energy into the narrative.

"It was a fastball. Caught me full force on the left eye," I said. "When I woke up in the hospital, I couldn't see anything out of that eye. Still can't. It seemed like the end of the world then, but it turned out it wasn't. It kept me out of the army, at least."

Gallo chuckled. "I got out, too. Bum knee from football. You were in triple-A, right?"

"Yeah, the Richmond Sailors. We had a good team that year." I named off five guys who had gone on to play in the majors. "And what about you?"

"I had a tryout," he said. "It didn't take a genius to figure out I wasn't up to snuff. I've been teaching at Kennedy for ten years now."

"Do you like it?"

"I can't complain. It's a challenge, you know, working with city kids. Not many people want to do it, but I enjoy it. Plus I like having my summers off."

"What do you teach?"

He took a long mouthful of his beer. Two more swallows like that, and he'd need a refill. "I'm kind of a utility infielder. A little history, driver's ed. Coaching's the thing I like to do most."

"You have any good prospects?" I realized now why he had wanted me to come to practice. I felt a bit guilty for turning him down.

"Not since Dwight Robinson." He shook his head. "What a goddamn shame. He was the best baseball player I've ever seen. There was no way he could've missed."

"You were close to him," I said.

He sighed. "As close as anybody could get. Dwight's not exactly the easiest kid to reach."

"I know. I met him."

"I went down there to see him last week. He's buttoned up tighter than I've ever seen him. I couldn't get through to him. It was kind of frustrating."

I had a feeling nobody was more disappointed in Dwight Robinson than Ed Gallo. I ordered another round of beers.

"Did you ever meet his wife?" I asked.

"Oh yeah. They had us over to their house a couple times. She swept him right off his feet."

"He was having an affair with another woman," I told him.

"Oh yeah? Well, that's good for him. Because she sure wasn't."

"You didn't especially care for her."

"She was a little flirt. Spoiled rotten. Hooked herself a big baseball star. As soon as Dwight got busted, she wasn't so impressed with him anymore."

"Did Dwight tell you that?"

"Well, more or less. You could see it in the way she acted around him. The tragedy is, he never should have been busted in the first place."

"Why not? You don't think Dwight smoked pot?"

"Oh yeah, I'm sure he smoked it. Take it from me—just about all the kids have tried it. It's like booze was to us when we were in school. But he wouldn't have been selling it. He didn't have any reason to. If you ask me, I think it was his brother. I don't trust him any farther than I could throw him. The story I heard is Dwight was holding it for Dexter."

"That's not too smart."

"Yeah, well, nobody ever accused Dwight of being a Rhodes Scholar."

"Who told you about it? Dwight?"

"No, he clammed up on me when I asked him. Got real defensive. I heard it from some of the kids at school. The word gets around. They kind of talk to me about things."

"Why do you think Dwight would have protected Dexter?"

Gallo drained his beer. "Beats me. Maybe he figured he'd be able to get off, and Dexter wouldn't. I certainly figured he would. If you ask me, I think he got screwed. Dexter's his older brother. He didn't have a father. Down in the projects, families have to stick together to survive."

That made sense. But I thought it was ironic that Dwight Robinson didn't start having trouble surviving until after he moved out of the projects.

"Do you think Dwight could have killed Cynthia?"

"Absolutely not." Gallo began wagging a finger at me, as if I had made an accusation. "Take my word for it: Dwight may not have been any angel, he may have hated her, but he never would have murdered her."

"According to the Wayne police chief, Cynthia's brother said Dwight used to beat her up."

"Bullshit! Total bullshit!" Gallo took a glance around the tavern to make sure he hadn't offended anyone. "Pardon my French," he said.

"No fucking damage done," I assured him.

"He's another one, that Tommy Vreeland. Rich brat, thought he was going to be a major leaguer. He couldn't have carried Dwight Robinson's jockstrap. Once that became clear, he started getting jealous."

Gallo finished off his beer, then held up the empty glass. "Sorry to get so mad," he said. "Once I start drinking, I sort of let it all hang out. I can be kind of a hothead."

I suggested another one to cool him off.

"No, better not. If I come home drunk, the wife will make me sleep out in the garage. You want to come back to the house for supper?"

I liked Gallo, but I didn't have much interest in seeing his garage. "Thanks. I've got other plans."

"Did that lawyer O'Leary tell you about the rally we're having on Sunday?"

"He mentioned something about it."

"We're trying to raise Dwight's bail. Even if we don't, it should be a boost for morale. We'll get some good publicity out of it, at least. Show those bastards like Thomas Vreeland that not everybody thinks Dwight Robinson killed his wife, like they've all been saying in the papers. You know, it's like he's already been convicted! It's goddamn frustrating! You try to teach these kids about how our system works. You tell them a man's innocent until proven guilty, then somebody comes along and throws them a big curve."

I watched Gallo squeeze his fist around the beer glass. I had a feeling he just might throw it.

"Ah, hell, I don't know. The whole thing stinks." He stared at the empty glass, then looked toward the bar. I got up from the table before he could change his mind about having another round.

"Don't worry, Ed," I told him. "Dwight won't have to take the rap for this one. I intend to find the killer."

"Call me Coach," he said, putting out his hand. "Everyone else does. And be sure to come to the rally. We need all the support we can get."

I promised I would. It was going to be a long weekend. I watched Gallo go out the door, then ordered another beer and moved to the telephone booth in the back.

My sister, Karen, answered on the first ring.

"How would you like an overnight guest?" I asked.

"Are you kidding? We'd love it. When?"

"How about tonight?"

"Oh, damn," she said. "You'll miss Dick."

"Why's that?" I tried not to let on how crushed I was by the good news that my brother-in-law wouldn't be home. Now I could glom his golf clubs without even having to speak to him.

"He's out of town on business. He would have enjoyed seeing you again."

"After last time, I wouldn't be so sure."

"What happened last time?"

Three years ago I spent Christmas at their house. It was against my better judgment, but Karen can be very persuasive. I was so bored I went on a bourbon jag that resulted in my punching the lights out of one of their asshole neighbors. I think he was spouting off about Jews and niggers, but he might have said something about liking the Boston Bruins. It wouldn't have been so bad if his kids hadn't been watching.

Karen chuckled. "Oh, I completely forgot about that."

Nonsense, of course. Karen can be very forgiving, but not forgetful.

"Well, Herbie will be glad to see you."

Ah yes, Herbie. When you don't have kids of your own, you're inclined to take a special interest in your nieces and nephews. It was a good thing Herbie was my only one. There was an awful lot of Herbie to take an interest in. As a young boy, his only hobbies had been eating and watching TV. But he did both of them very well, I had to hand him that.

"How old is the little guy now?" I asked.

"Thirteen. And he's not so little anymore."

I stifled the urge to remind her that he never was. "He spend a lot of time whacking off?"

"Not as much as you used to. He joined the baseball league this year."

"Great." I had a hard time imagining Herbie playing ball. "What position does he play?"

She laughed. Karen's always had a sweet laugh. She's always been a sweet girl. "Bench mostly. But sometimes they put him in right field. You'll never guess who his coaches are."

I didn't even try.

"The Jensen brothers!"

"Oh, Jesus." The Jensen twins were contemporaries of mine. The joke in grade school had been that if you looked up the word ugly in the dictionary, you'd find a picture of Jeff Jensen. If you looked up stupid, you'd find a picture of his brother Joe. Their idea of a good time was having fart contests in the lunch room.

"You should see their kids."

"No thank you."

"Where are you calling from anyway?"

"The Black Forest Inn."

"You're kidding! What are we doing talking on the phone? Get your ass over here."

Five minutes later, I pulled up to the front of their house on May Street. I didn't recognize the large figure huddled on the porch until he bounded across the front lawn and loomed up next to the passenger window. My nephew, Herbie, had grown a foot taller and put on another fifty pounds since I had last seen him. His face was ravaged with acne, and his mouth was outfitted with about ten grand worth of orthodontics' gear. Oh, those terrible teens.

Herbie had one fist wrapped around a baseball and the other stuffed into a glove. He tossed the ball about ten feet into the air. On its downward flight, it hit the heel of his glove and dropped to the ground.

"Hey, Uncle Mark," he yelled. "You want to have a catch before dinner?"

It didn't look like I had any choice.

CHAPTER
12

The idea behind staying at my sister's house was to avoid having to get up before dawn to keep my appointment with Terry Vreeland. Instead, Karen and I stayed up drinking until then, so I wasn't exactly operating on a good night's sleep when I set out for Mountain Lake.

Seeing her was worth it, just the same. Plus I got a set of clubs out of the deal, although I was a bit embarrassed carrying a bag that said Dick Derkovich on it. Try saying that one three times fast on a hangover without throwing up.

It turned out I'd soon have the pleasure of seeing old Dick after all. As head of the Clifton Jaycees, Karen told me, he was a regular at the Sarah Winchester Vreeland tournament. I thought inviting him was stretching the concept of celebrity mighty thin. But then I've never understood the appeal of Dean Martin.

The pimple-faced sentry already had his radio blaring and his hand out as I rolled up to the admittance gate. He looked crushed when I told him I was Terry Vreeland's guest.

"Tough break, kid," I said. "From now on, it's a free concert."

I saw Terry Vreeland waving to me, as I limped over to the first tee. In addition to a small brain, my brother-in-law has small feet. I'd be walking on a pair of blisters by the end of the day.

Terry was prettier than I remembered. Of course, I hadn't gotten a very good look at her the first time we almost met. She had shoulder-length brown hair that was tied back in a ponytail. Her eyes were big and round and green. They stood out sharply against her smooth, lightly freckled complexion. It was a nice contrast. She wasn't wearing makeup, she didn't need any.

She had on a man's button-down white shirt with the sleeves rolled up past her elbows and a pair of loose-fitting gray shorts. The outfit revealed that she had inherited her father's tan. I thought it looked far more becoming on her arms and legs. These were quite shapely, no doubt the result of regular exercise. Terry Vreeland was a living argument that there was something good to be said about golf.

"It's a beautiful day, isn't it?" she said, smiling as she held out her hand.

I took it and agreed without qualification. To be truthful, it was still last night as far as I was concerned, but why complain?

"This is the kind of day when you don't want to stop at eighteen; you just go right through and play thirty-six."

"Uh-huh." I tried not to let on what a terrifying thought it was, but my speechlessness was probably a tip-off.

"I thought we'd take a cart, if that's OK with you. That way we can talk privately."

"Great." Not to mention all the wear and tear it would save my body.

"Do you want to shoot first?" she asked.

"Oh no, please. Ladies before gentlemen." I figured I might learn something from watching her.

I did. I learned that I liked the way she looked when she bent over to tee up the ball.

"I haven't played with anyone for a couple of weeks," she said, as she surveyed the fairway. "I lost my regular partner."

"What happened?"

"He got sent to jail."

"Anyone I might know?"

Her muscles were taut as she leaned over the ball. She stared down at it for a moment, then swung the club back in a smooth, easy arc, twisting her hips backward. She stopped for a split second at the top of her swing, then twisted her hips forward as she brought the club down in another perfect arc. She drove the ball so goddamn far down the center of the fairway that I lost sight of it long before it landed.

I had logged quite a few slave hours as a caddy in my youth, so I should have been able to follow it. Of course I did most of my caddying for fat old farts, so I never had any trouble keeping an eye trained on the ball. Terry Vreeland presented something of a hindrance to the process. Her statuesque follow-through was a thing of beauty to behold, but she seemed totally unaware of my watching her as she stepped down from the tee.

"That's right—Dwight," she said. "He and I used to play every day, rain or shine. He was good, damn good. He was hoping to get on the PGA tour. That's why he quit his job at the real estate office. My father thought he was lazy."

Terry nodded her head toward the tee, a signal for me to shoot. I thought of suggesting that she do the golfing and I'd just drive the cart.

"Doesn't your father spend a good deal of his time playing golf?" I asked, going through the motions of lining up my ball.

"Absolutely. But he's not lazy—just rich. There's a big difference, as far as he's concerned."

"There is," I said, taking a few pointless practice swings for effect. "He can afford to be lazy." I was trying to delay the inevitable. Finally I put my head down and took a round-house swing at the ball.

Apparently, I didn't put my head down. I looked out over the center of the fairway, straining to pick up the flight of the ball, thinking I had gotten a pretty good piece of it, all things considered. When I failed to see it land, it occurred to me that I might be acting a bit optimistic in expecting accuracy, as well as distance. I scanned the fairway from left to right, adjusting my sights a little closer to the tee each time I panned.

I concluded that I was being far too optimistic. I found the ball just where it had been before I swung—perched on the tee, still waiting to be walloped.

I looked up sheepishly and saw Terry trying to suppress a laugh. "How many years since you've played?" she asked.

"What makes you think this isn't my first time?"

"You've got too good a swing."

"Thanks. Is that the positive mental attitude school of coaching?"

"No, I mean it. This time, keep your head down and your eyes on the ball. And don't try to kill it. Let the club do the work. That's what it's there for."

"Oh, now I get it."

It worked. I hit the little son of a bitch pretty solidly, probably 200 yards down the fairway. Unfortunately, it sliced about half that far over to the right and landed in a clump of trees.

"Not bad," she said. "Now all we've got to do is get you to straighten it out."

"Give me a few years."

She hopped into the passenger seat of the cart. "You ever drive one of these things before?"

I slid in beside her and took the wheel. "Yeah, but that was before I got my driver's license."

"You were a caddy once?"

"More than once. Those were the best years of my life."

She let out a laugh. The throaty lilt sounded more pleasant in person than it did over the phone. "Dwight caddied here all through high school. He hated it. He told me he used to step on people's balls when they weren't looking."

"The police chief told me Dwight once stole fifty bucks out of a guy's bag."

"Oh, bullshit," she said. "That was Dexter, and it was only a twenty. Dexter's a creep."

"Yeah, I know. I've had the pleasure."

It took me three more shots to get to the green. Terry was on in two. She one-putted for a birdie three. I two-putted for a six.

"Do you do this professionally?" I asked. "Or is it just a hobby?"

"I've been in a few tournaments as an amateur. I'm hoping to get on the LPGA tour. This is the last year. If I don't make it by next spring, I'm going to hang it up. I've decided if I can't make it by thirty, I better figure out something else to do with my life."

"You have any ideas?"

She sighed. "There's a career in real estate waiting for me."

"Are you living at home?"

"You mean at my father's house? You've got to be kidding."

"Yeah, I guess I was."

"Tommy still lives there. He'll probably die there, too. I'm renting a house from my father—over in Packanack Lake. I've been there for three months. For the last couple of years before that, I was living in Florida. You can golf there all year long. It's paradise."

Different strokes for different folks. Personally, I've always thought of Florida as an extension of South Jersey.

"You gave up paradise for Jersey?"

She shrugged. "Pretty dumb, huh? It seemed like a good idea—under the circumstances."

I didn't ask what the circumstances were. After she hit another perfect shot off the second tee, she told me.

"I was living with a guy. We had marital difficulties."

"That's too bad. I'd say it's his loss."

She smiled. "Thanks. But you don't know what a holy terror I can be to live with."

I didn't bother to tell her she couldn't be any worse than

my first two wives. "Who watches over your father's empire while he's golfing?"

"My little brother. Only he's not so little anymore—just dumb. That was the other problem Dwight had. He couldn't stand having my brother as his boss."

I hit another rocket down the fairway, but this one hooked to the left. Terry walked over and stood behind me. She put her arms around my waist and showed me how to keep my balance on the follow-through. I wasn't particularly interested in improving my game, but I didn't mind taking her instruction. I wondered if it was as good for her as it was for me.

"I don't mean to pry, but I get the distinct feeling you aren't on the best of terms with your brother or your father."

She tugged at a strand of hair that had fallen loose. "That's an understatement."

"Does that have something to do with Dwight Robinson?"

"Lately, yes. We're barely on speaking terms. But that's not the only reason we don't get along. There've been plenty of others." She pulled her hair back into place and refastened her ponytail. "I've got a very weird family," she said.

I didn't ask her to elaborate. "Am I right in assuming that you don't think Dwight killed your sister?"

"Absolutely. I know Dwight. He may have hated Cynthia, but he didn't kill her."

"Not even by accident?" I knew it was a dumb question. You don't hit somebody with a heavy object by accident. But there was always the chance she had tried to hit him first and he took it away from her and lost his temper. That's almost accidental.

Terry shook her head. "Absolutely not. Dwight isn't capable of doing something that awful."

"You seem awfully fond of him."

"I am. We're golfing buddies."

I had a feeling they were more than that, but I didn't press her on it. Terry was being rather forthright. If she was the woman Dwight was with the night of the murder, she'd probably tell me eventually.

I held the flag while she putted for her second birdie in a row. She sank it from twelve feet. "You're bringing me good luck," she said.

"I usually bring trouble. Did Dwight hate your sister?"

"I don't know. You'd have to ask him."

"Dwight isn't exactly a forthcoming guy."

"I know. He's very reserved and distrustful. He's got reason to be. It takes a while to get to know him. At least he's talking to Mike O'Leary. That's a good sign."

"You know O'Leary?" What a coincidence.

"Well, no, but Dwight told me about him. I went to see him yesterday. He told me about meeting you, too. I think he likes your friend."

I took that to mean he didn't much care for me. I didn't let it bruise my feelings. I wasn't sure I liked Dwight.

"Did he tell you anything about the night of the murder?"

"No. We kept it light. We just talked about golf. To be honest with you, I don't want to know any of the details."

It took me two putts to finish the hole. Four over par isn't bad. Of course we had only played two holes.

"I heard that Dwight was having an affair."

"Really." Her drive off the third tee sliced a bit, but she was still on the fairway. I hit mine pretty good, but the ball wandered off in its customary search for shade.

"You wouldn't know anything about that, would you?" I asked.

She shook her head. If I was being too forward with her, she wasn't showing it. "I've only been back here for three months. I make a point of minding my own business. But if Dwight was carrying on with someone, it would have made Cynthia crazy. She used to get jealous about us playing golf together."

I didn't bother to tell her that I could understand why. "Did Dwight tell you that?"

"No, my father did. He suggested in a not-so-subtle way that I should stop playing with Dwight. He was worried about people talking. Most of the members of this club prefer drinking and gossiping to golf."

"I understand Cynthia was planning to file for divorce. At least that's what the police report says she told your father. You wouldn't know if she was carrying on with anyone."

"No, I wouldn't. I'm the wrong person to be asking about that. I really do mind my own business. I knew about the divorce thing, but only because my father told me. That was after Cynthia was killed. She never spoke to me about it. But she was always talking to my father. There were no secrets between those two."

"Your brother told the police that Dwight used to beat Cynthia up."

"That little fucking liar!" Terry slammed her five-iron into the ground. Good thing we were on the green. She had already hit her second shot there, but we were still searching for my ball.

She was shaking, and I put out my hand to steady her. That's when I noticed that her eyes were moist.

"I'm sorry. I don't usually get so angry. It's just that things have gotten so screwed up around here lately. My brother and father are sure Dwight killed Cynthia. They'd say anything to get him convicted. But regardless of what they say, I just don't believe he could have done it. I don't believe he would have hit her."

She paused for a moment. The tears had stopped. "But if he did hit her, she would have deserved it."

I looked at her quizzically. "That seems a little harsh."

"Mr. Renzler, you didn't know my sister."

I suggested we put things on a first-name basis. "I take it you and Cynthia didn't get along very well, either."

"Not since we were kids." We were standing face to face on the edge of the green. "One thing you've got to understand: I've got a weird family."

"Yeah, you said that."

She touched my arm and leaned in closer. The combination of tears and sunshine gave her big green eyes a dimension of translucence. She was probing me with them. I felt a little shiver run down my back.

"I mean *very* weird," she said.

CHAPTER
13

Terry Vreeland smiled and took a long, graceful bow. She had just sunk a thirty-foot putt for a birdie on the seventh hole. That made it five out of seven. If she shot that well all the time, she wouldn't have just made the tour—she would have been the national champion.

I gave her a standing ovation, and she shrugged it off. "I know every lump and bump and nick and trick on this golf course," she said. "I ought to—I grew up on it."

I pulled the limo around to take her to the eighth tee. "How long ago was it built?" I asked.

"You want to hear the whole family history?"

"You bet." It sounded like she wanted to tell it.

"I'll give you the twenty-five cent version. I don't want to go back to my grandfather. That makes us sound like royalty. All you've got to know is he made a fortune in real estate, selling summer bungalows along the river. My father took over the business when he died."

"What year was that?"

She looked down the eighth fairway to where a couple of

old duffers were searching for a lost ball. It was the first traffic jam we had run into. She was right about the golf course not getting much use.

"Let's see. I was five, so that would have made it 1948. My grandfather's dream was to put a lake up here on the mountain and build a private community—you know, a place where only the right kind of people lived. But he croaked and my father had to finish the job. That was 1950."

"I'm surprised the town isn't named after him."

"Oh, no. My grandfather didn't want that. He just liked being rich. He didn't care about being famous. My father— he wants both."

Terry shook her head and let out a soft chuckle. "It's funny. My father's dream in life has always been for one of his kids to be a professional golfer. I'm sure you've noticed that there's kind of a golf theme running through this place. He donated the land and they built the course in 1953. I'm the oldest, so I guess he must have drilled it into me the most. The irony is that of the three kids, the one he liked least is the one who has the best chance of making it."

I had the distinct impression that Terry Vreeland was still struggling to resolve her family conflicts. That seems to be a pretty common problem among rich kids. The real problem was, she wasn't a kid any more. As far as I'm concerned, if you can't get that crap sorted out by the time you're twenty-five you might as well forget about trying.

"Another irony is that I'm not doing it for him. I'm doing it for myself. And he knows it."

"Is that a source of some dispute?"

She sighed. "My father and I have lots of things to dispute. Basically, we try to coexist. That worked a lot easier when I was living in Florida. I'm sure he's proud of me and respects me. At least he did until I came back."

"What about your brother? Is he any good?"

"He's OK. It's hard not to be when you grow up on a golf course. Unless you're like Cynthia. She took after my mother."

I asked her what that meant.

"My mother was an alcoholic. She spent all her time in the

clubhouse bar. She died fourteen years ago. Basically, she drank herself to death."

Terry was speaking in a matter-of-fact voice. I didn't have any sense that I was dredging up painful memories.

"I was fifteen, Tommy was eleven, and Cynthia was seven. We had a maid who came in every day, but I had to take on a couple of extra roles. I had to be mother to them and wife to my father." Terry was standing at the tee now. She gazed down the fairway, then looked at me. "It wasn't a whole lot of fun."

I'm sure it wasn't. Especially the second part. I didn't understand exactly what she meant. But my instinct told me we were getting into sensitive terrain. I didn't want to dig too deep.

"I'm sorry. I must sound ridiculous. I'm making it sound like I've had a terrible life. I've actually had it pretty easy, I know that. My father just happens to be at the top of my shit list."

I told her it was OK. You get to hear about all sorts of family problems in my line of work. After a while, they all start to sound the same. And they all come down to money and love. There's always too much or too little of one or the other—never the right amount. The most bothersome thing is that most of the people you have to hear it from think their problems are more important than anyone else's. Either that, or they think they're the only ones who have problems.

Terry Vreeland was something of an exception. At least she was aware of what she was saying.

Her tee shot came to rest on the edge of the green. It was a par-three hole. Despite her warnings, I sent mine right into the pond that she said must have had ten thousand balls in it.

"That makes ten thousand and one," I said. I had a feeling this would be the last time I went golfing for the next fifty years or so.

"Have you ever heard of Bob Winchester?" Terry asked.

"Yeah, the congressman." I didn't mention that I had seen him on the TV news the night before, sounding off about how we should make the death penalty mandatory for airplane hijackers. This seemed like a patently stupid idea to me. If the crazies were sure to get fried when they landed, what was there to stop them from blowing up a plane while it was in the air?

"He's my uncle," she said. "My mother's brother. In 1963, he and my father started a charity golf tournament in her memory. The proceeds go to fight alcoholism and provide flood relief for the residents of Mountain View. It floods down there practically every spring."

"I heard about it," I said. "I also heard that you walk away with the trophy every year."

Her face turned a lovely shade of red. It looked even lovelier when she smiled and rolled her eyes. I was tempted to ask her to do it again.

"Who told you that?"

"Hal Pucinsky."

She looked understandably puzzled when I told her I was planning to participate.

"As a caddy," I clarified. "My friend Nate is one of the celebrity entrants. He's a painter."

"My brother will be glad to hear that. Maybe you'll get assigned to his foursome."

"I'd prefer to be assigned to yours."

"I'll see what I can do."

We shook hands after she sank her putt to par the ninth hole. "That was fun," I said. "We'll have to do it again sometime."

Her eyes got bigger as she gave me an incredulous look. "That's only nine holes. We've still got the back nine to play."

I had a few more questions to ask her, and if she insisted on continuing, I gladly would have suffered through a few more holes to get them answered. But I hoped with a little charm, I'd be able to convince her to call it quits and continue our conversation in a more suitable setting.

First I told her about my brother-in-law's shoes. She didn't seem terribly sympathetic. Nor did she fall for the line about a heart condition.

"The holes are all the same," I said. "Why don't we just double our scores."

She laughed. "Why don't we get you an early lunch."

CHAPTER
14

We took one of two vacant tables on the patio outside the clubhouse. There were about sixteen tables in all. Apparently, we weren't the only people who had opted for an early lunch.

"There's something that baffles me," I told her, after soothing my parched throat with half a bottle of beer. Terry was drinking orange juice. I wondered if she was a teetotaler. "Your father and brother hate Dwight Robinson, right?"

She nodded. "If Dwight got the death penalty, they'd be fighting with each other to see who got to throw the switch—along with my Uncle Bob."

"I'm surprised your father allowed Cynthia to marry him."

"Dwight and my father didn't always hate each other. The real bad feelings only go back about a year or so, I think. And it wasn't like my father gave Cynthia his wholehearted approval. But she had her mind made up. So Dad didn't have any choice. He was afraid they would have run away together."

Terry caught the attention of the waiter, an elderly black man she called Pop, and we ordered lunch.

"You've also got to take into consideration that Dwight was a baseball star. He was phenomenal. If he hadn't gotten busted last year, he would have been playing for the Yankees right now. My father had his reservations, but he wouldn't have minded having a son-in-law who was known as the black Mickey Mantle. That was his nickname. My father's the one who made it up."

"I didn't know that." I figured it was probably the work of Ed Gallo.

"Dwight was one of our caddies," she said. She made a sweeping gesture with her arm. "Take a look around you. This place is my father's *plantation*."

That was an interesting way of looking at it. All the more reason to wonder how he felt about his children associating with the slaves.

"Tommy used to be the caddy master," she said. "He and Dwight were friends. They were both baseball stars, except Dwight was a lot better. And Cynthia . . . well, Cynthia was into black guys."

I told her I wasn't exactly sure what she meant.

"Did you notice that old building down along the ninth fairway? That used to be the caddy shack. Now they just use it for storing equipment. Cynthia used to call it 'The Stable.'"

Terry's eyes narrowed. I think mine were beginning to bulge. The implication was clear from her tone, but that didn't stop her from clarifying.

"Cynthia lost her virginity at an early age. Early and often. She once told me that life would be perfect if she could give a blow job every day." Terry smiled, but she wasn't amused. "She was fourteen years old at the time."

I didn't bother to tell her that when I was fourteen I thought life would be perfect if I got a blow job every day. Or once, for that matter. "Was your father aware of any of this?" I asked.

"My father has one of the world's most efficient denial systems. And I certainly didn't tell him about it."

I was about to ask her if Cynthia was friendly with Shake Johnson when a pair of well-heeled blondes tottered over toward our table.

"This is the problem with trying to talk here," Terry whispered, as she got up to greet them.

I mumbled an apology, but I wasn't sorry we had stopped golfing. It hurt just to stand up.

Terry's friends could have passed for sisters, but I later learned they weren't. Both of them were holding drinks, and you didn't need a breathalyzer test to figure out they were well past the first round. One of the women was a natural blonde, the other had gotten an assist from her hairdresser. My guess was they were in their mid-thirties. They made a good case for lounging on the patio and taking in the scenery—as long as you didn't have to talk to them. Evidently, Terry didn't want to. She remained standing and didn't invite them to sit down.

"Sorry to interrupt, darling," the natural blonde said. "But we just had to come over and meet the man you're lunching with."

I extended my hand, but the bleach job came over and leaned on my arm. "Yes," she said, giggling. "Tell us where you've been hiding him." She was wearing enough perfume to kill all the mosquitoes in Jersey. "Is there another one like you at home?" she asked.

I tried to smile my charming smile, but it probably came off like a blush. I'm basically a shy guy. "Yeah, but he's kind of wild and has lousy table manners," I said. "My mother still has to tie him up and feed him with a slingshot."

"Sounds like a perfect beast. I'd love to meet him." This time the natural blonde joined in on her giggle.

Terry did the introductions quickly. Miss Natural was named Melody Winchester, the unnatural one went by Monica Heatherton.

"I didn't think you were here today," Melody said to Terry. "I didn't see your car in the lot."

"It's in the shop," Terry answered. "I let Tommy borrow it last week, and he ran it into a fire hydrant."

"I'd be glad to give him a good spanking, if you'd like," Monica said.

Terry shot me a disapproving look, which I took to mean I-told-you-so. I thought chatting with the dames was slightly better than hitting out of a sand trap, but I could see why she preferred golf to lunch.

"Well, I'm sure you two want to be left alone," Melody said.

Monica ran her fingers through my hair, stopping at my bald spot. "Next time, I'll remember to bring my slingshot if you remember to bring your brother."

"It's a deal," I said.

As soon as they were out of earshot, Terry offered a little background. "Monica was once second runner-up in the Miss New Jersey pageant. She was last year's scandal at the club. She won a huge divorce settlement after finding out that her husband had taken up with an eighteen-year-old. I think she's feeling a little sex-starved."

"Yeah, I sort of got that impression. Who's Melody—your cousin?"

She shook her head and did the eye-rolling number that I liked so much. "She's my aunt."

Indeed. "She looks like she's only a few years older than you."

Terry nodded. "That's how Uncle Bob likes them—young and pretty. Melody's OK. She just drinks too much."

Pop returned with our lunch order, and we chatted with him for a few minutes. He told me Terry was his favorite girl and any friend of hers was a friend of his. Terry told him she had seen Dwight and he sent along his regards.

After he walked away, Terry said, "Pop's heartbroken about Dwight. Everyone else around here ignores him. Dwight used to sit around here talking with Pop for hours."

I thought maybe Pop and I should have a chat, but I was more interested in finding out about Shake Johnson. I asked Terry if he and Cynthia were friendly.

"Oh, God, do you know Shake?"

"I haven't had the pleasure yet, but I'm hoping to make his acquaintance before I leave. Maybe you'd introduce us."

"He's not here today, just on weekends. Why do you want to talk to him?"

"Tell me about him first. I'd be curious to hear your impressions before I say anything."

"Shake Johnson's a real prize." There was a sense of awe in her voice but no hint of admiration. "He's been caddying here for as long as I can remember. He's the unofficial court jester of Mountain Lake. He amuses the white folks with black jive talk. His nickname is Shakespeare, because he's always spouting off poetry."

"You make him sound kind of harmless. From what I've heard—"

"Oh no, I'm sure he's not. Shake's into all sorts of shady activities. I think he deals drugs, and I know for a fact he's a bookie. He's also one of my brother's best friends. Tommy's not the best judge of character."

"What about Cynthia? Was she friendly with Shake?"

"Oh yeah, I think so. But he was more friendly with Tommy."

I told her about Dwight's suspicions that Shake might have killed her sister. I also mentioned Dexter's story about Shake putting the pressure on Dwight.

"Well, I know Dwight thinks that, but I heard Shake was drinking with Tommy that night." She picked the toothpick out of her club sandwich and wagged it at me. "But the last person in the world you should trust is Dexter. I think even Dwight knows that now. As far as I'm concerned, he and Shake are cut from the same cloth. Plus he and Cynthia were an item before she started going out with Dwight."

I leaned across the table and lowered my voice. The people around us were keeping up a fairly steady stream of conversation, but I wanted to make sure no one overheard me. "Do you think Cynthia and Dexter were still involved with each other?"

She answered with a shrug. "I haven't been around here enough to know that kind of thing. But knowing Cynthia, I have to wonder how she was keeping herself entertained when Dwight was on the road. Take my word for it— Cynthia always needed a lot of attention."

I didn't hesitate to take Terry's word for anything. But I found it a bit disquieting that she was still harboring so much bitterness for her sister. Cynthia was, after all, dead. But I hadn't sensed even the slightest indication of loss or remorse on Terry's part. She seemed far less concerned with finding Cynthia's killer than she was with getting Dwight out of jail.

Terry had said that Cynthia was jealous of her playing golf with Dwight. I had a feeling that sentiment went in two directions. I also had a feeling there was much more to Terry's relationship with Dwight Robinson than she was letting on. But the thing that really bothered me, the thing I didn't even want to think about, was just how deep Terry's hatred for her sister really was.

That question was troubling because of another one that it led to: Were Dwight and Terry both in on Cynthia's murder?

I didn't have time to ponder the subject. Terry muttered "Uh-oh," and I looked over my shoulder. Brother Tommy was on his way to our table. Something told me he wasn't going to be as cordial as his aunt and her friend. I think it was the scowl that gave him away.

Tommy strode right up to the table and stopped to my left. He glared at me for a moment, then turned his attention to Terry. I took the opportunity to size him up.

He was about my height, maybe half an inch shorter, and probably five or ten pounds lighter. He looked to be in pretty good shape, but it's hard not to be when you're only twenty-five.

"What are you doing talking to this asshole?" he demanded. His voice was loud, and it put a sudden end to the chatter at the surrounding tables.

I thought about decking him just on principle alone, but I didn't want to make a bigger scene then he was already starting.

"Go away, mind your own business," Terry answered. She hit exactly the right tone without raising her voice.

"After you talk to him, are you going to fuck him?"

Terry stood up and emptied her orange juice glass on her brother's face. It left him looking like the victim of a golden shower, but I didn't think even that would have constituted a sufficient response to his remark.

He apparently thought she had overreacted. I stood up from my chair but not quickly enough to prevent him from swinging at her with his open right hand. It landed flush on the side of Terry's head, knocking her off balance and into her chair.

"You little prick!" she cried.

My sentiments exactly.

I like to avoid getting into family squabbles, and I've become less violent as I've gotten older. I've even tried to adapt to women's lib, but basically I'm an old-fashioned guy.

I grabbed Tommy's right arm and pulled him back toward me. The idea was to set him up for a sucker punch that he would remember until his dying day.

Tommy had another idea. He spun around and swung with a roundhouse left the instant I touched his sleeve. I had no problem ducking underneath it. Good thing I'd only had three beers. While I was down at gut level, I took the opportunity to crush the bottom of his rib cage with a solid right. He doubled over, and I stepped back to get a better angle for finishing him off. If you go to the trouble of beating somebody up, you might as well leave a facial reminder.

Of course, there's another school of thought on the subject. Namely, that the degree of humiliation in losing a fight is inversely proportional to the number of blows sustained. This was my thinking as I decided to refrain from hitting Tommy Vreeland again. It's a more refined approach. After all, we were at a country club. Besides, at just that moment, Kid Vreeland staggered toward the crowd that had gathered around us and humiliated himself more than I ever could have.

Tommy Vreeland puked his guts all over the front of Monica Heatherton's blouse. I figured it would be a while before she felt like giving him a spanking.

"What's going on here?" a voice rumbled behind me. I turned to see a blond, muscle-bound man in tennis shorts and a knit shirt pushing his way toward us. I figured he was either Mr. Universe or the golf pro, Pete Becker.

"It's all right, Pete," Terry said. "Tommy was just speaking out of school again."

Becker stood with his hands on his hips and began giving me the once-over. He had a large, square head. I had a feeling there wasn't a whole lot going on inside of it.

Terry took my arm and began to usher me out through the pro shop. "I think maybe you better get going," she said.

"Are you OK?" I ran my hand over the red streak that had formed on the side of her face.

"It's nothing. We used to fight all the time when we were kids." She smiled. "Thanks. I had a good time talking to you. I feel a lot better about things."

I assured her the feeling was mutual. "Maybe we could get together again, if you're not too busy."

"I'm not," she said. "I'd like that."

You and me both.

As I reached the gate to the parking lot, Pop, the old waiter, called after me. From the way he walked, I could see that he had at least one bad leg. I moved forward to save him the steps, maybe adding minutes to his life.

"I just wanted to shake your hand, sir," he said. He was grinning so hard, I could see wrinkles on his wrinkles.

I put out my hand and he clasped it with both of his. "Master Tommy's been asking for it for an awful long time. Only nobody around here ever had the nerve to give it to him. Except Dwight."

"Dwight and Tommy had a fight?"

"Yes, sir, last year. Down at Pete's. I didn't see it, but I heard he whupped his ass but good."

"Do you know what they were fighting about?"

"I think it was about Miss Cynthia, sir."

"Do you like Dwight?"

"Yes, sir, he's a good boy."

I was going to ask him about a couple of others, but Pete Becker stepped outside the pro shop and began yelling his name.

"I best be going," he said. "Master Tommy made quite a mess back there."

"Sorry about that."

"No worry, sir. Far as I'm concerned, you can come back around here any time you please."

I told him I didn't have any intention of doing so, but I had a feeling it was a promise I might not be able to keep.

CHAPTER
15

A week had gone by since my fateful reunion lunch with Mike O'Leary. Nate and I had accumulated quite a bit of background information, some of it rather interesting. But we hadn't uncovered any answers— only more questions. Slowly but surely, we seemed to be getting absolutely nowhere. So it was only fitting that we were stuck in bumper-to-bumper traffic in the Lincoln Tunnel, heading for New Jersey yet another time.

It was midday, not rush hour, which made the delay all the more inexplicable, all the more infuriating. A few impatient motorists started venting their frustrations by leaning on their car horns. I've never understood the benefits of this sort of behavior, but a psychologist I dated once assured me that it serves a viable therapeutic function, similar to punching a wall to release anger. I told her I couldn't see much value in that, either, and she proceeded to lecture me on catharsis, explaining that whatever makes people feel better is an appropriate and beneficial response.

What started out as a minor difference of opinion soon turned into a major knock-down-drag-out. She was startled and offended by my blockheaded insensitivity. I said any bartender could provide the same advice she did, only bartenders didn't have the gall to charge fifty bucks an hour. By the end of the evening, we were no longer dating. I went home in a stew and promptly punched a goddamn hole in the wall next to my refrigerator. It didn't make me feel any better. I spent the night in the emergency room getting a cast put on my hand. I still don't understand that kind of behavior.

Within seconds, every car around us had joined in the honkers chorus. I hoped it was making them feel better. It was giving me a goddamn headache. Pretty soon, it sounded as if every car horn in the universe was in use.

Except ours. We had a cooler full of beer and some catching up to do.

As with most dreams fulfilled, Nate's trip *Down Memory Lane* with Joe Franklin had turned out to be less satisfying than he had hoped. Nate was the last guest on a lineup card that included a poodle trainer from Great Neck, a toupee designer from Queens and a husband-wife team that was putting on *A Streetcar Named Desire* in Westchester. Joe introduced Nate as "a dear, dear friend of mine," just like he does with his other guests. For some reason, he kept calling him Nat.

"I don't think Joe is going to ask me back," Nate lamented, swilling down a beer.

"Why not?"

"While the hairpiece guy was running off at the mouth, I took the liberty of complimenting Joe on *his* rug. It turns out Joe doesn't wear a rug."

"You mean he combs it across that way by choice?"

"Evidently. You know, that's the first time in all the years I've watched the show that Joe wasn't smiling."

"Well, that alone makes it worth watching."

He shook his head. "I have a feeling they're going to edit out the entire segment. That was right after I insulted the dog trainer."

"You didn't."

He nodded sadly. "Yeah, I did. The little prick was sniffing my crotch, so I told her to get it away from me or I'd teach it to roll over and die."

"How did Joe react to that one?"

"Oh, Joe's the consummate professional. Cut right to a special message for denture wearers. As soon as it ended, he said we were out of time. The whole thing was a misadventure."

I filled him in on my misadventures of the last two days. He shared my suspicion that Terry Vreeland was Dwight Robinson's secret benefactor. But he was skeptical that she was involved in Cynthia's murder.

"You don't really believe that she hated her sister enough to kill her?"

"No, probably not. I certainly hope not. But I think she likes Dwight enough to invent an alibi for him."

We went down my list of likely suspects. After eliminating Dwight, it was a short one. There were only two people on it—his brother and Shake Johnson.

My suspicion of Dexter was based on the comments Ed Gallo had made about him and Terry Vreeland's revelation that he had once dated Cynthia. That wasn't much of a motive, unless he had still been involved with her shortly before the murder. Terry implied that he might have been, but if she was protecting Dwight, it was hard to accept her remarks at face value. The other consideration was that Dexter had provided Dwight with an alibi that was full of holes. He apparently had been willing to sit back and let his brother take the rap on a drug charge, so it was certainly conceivable he would do so again, especially if the charge was murder.

Shake was obviously the preferable choice. But he appeared to have an alibi. Of course, we didn't know for sure how late he had stayed at Pete's bar the night of the murder. And it was likely that Hal Pucinsky hadn't checked it out too closely. After all, he was convinced that Dwight had killed Cynthia. Given the feeble alibi Dwight had offered, I really couldn't blame him.

"You're forgetting some other possibilities," Nate said. His tone was only half serious.

"You mean Warren Shepherd."

He nodded. "And the little old lady next door."

"Not dear Anna Paslawski."

"You didn't see her bathroom."

No, but I had noticed her reading materials and her affection for police dramas. "Yeah, when are you going to tell me about that?"

"One of these days—if you're a good boy. I'm saving it for when we get stuck in a really big traffic jam."

We were flying along Route 3 now, nearing the junction of Route 46 near Montclair. The traffic tie-up had been caused by a broken-down bus, so it wasn't a major delay. Unless you happened to be riding on that bus.

"Shepherd saw Dwight throw something into her garbage can," I said. "Maybe it wasn't Dwight, but you've got to at least figure it was a black guy."

"Unless—"

I finished his sentence for him. "Unless Warren Shepherd was lying. In which case he probably killed her himself."

"Yeah, what do you think of that possibility?"

"Not too much." But it couldn't be eliminated. Solving a crime is a lot like handicapping a horse race. You have to concentrate on the likely contenders, but you can't ignore the longshots. And, because some people are inclined to lie, you can't assume that the information in the program is accurate.

"I think Shake is still the favorite," I said.

Nate finished another beer and smiled. "I'm looking forward to our chat."

So was I. I had hoped to have stronger grounds for suspicion when we went to see him, but you can only work with what you've got. As we crossed the railroad tracks in Mountain View and turned left onto Fayette Avenue, we didn't have much going for us except a willingness to intimidate. Sometimes, that can work wonders.

Shake Johnson lived on Cree Lane, a narrow strip of mud

and gravel running about fifty yards from Fayette Avenue to the Pompton River. It was a wonder that anyone had taken the time to think up a name for the street. The four rotting shacks along it didn't have house numbers, but we could hear the song "Papa Was A Rolling Stone" blaring out of a shanty with close to a full set of shingles and almost a complete coat of yellow paint. A bright red Mustang was parked next to it.

"I think we found the place," Nate said. "Cute little neighborhood they've got here."

Indeed it was. Down near the edge of the river, three white kids were playing baseball. They were using a crushed milk carton for a ball and a rusted tail pipe for a bat. A dirty-faced girl in pigtails was sitting in a truck tire hanging from a dead oak tree and watching them.

The kids stopped playing and stared at us as we approached the house. I pounded my hand on a wooden door that had been painted at least five different colors over the years. The last time must have been ten years back. There was no screen door or bell. Lucky for us, the song ended just as I started knocking. Or maybe Shake had been watching us through the little screen window to our right.

We heard his muffled voice from behind the door. "What's the jive, Clive?"

"Are you Shake Johnson?" I had to shout now, because the music was up again.

"Who wants to know, Joe?"

I told him our names. "We're friends of Tommy Vreeland," I added, thinking that might help. It didn't.

"So what?" he replied.

I looked at Nate. Together, we looked over the door.

"One shot is all it would take," he said.

I decided to take another stab at diplomacy—I lied again.

"Tommy says we might be able to do some business. He says you're the guy we should be talking to."

After a moment, the door opened a crack and I could see a black face peering out at us. Make that two black faces. I had forgotten about the dog.

"You buyin' or sellin'?" Shake's question sounded closer to a growl than it did to human speech, but I might have been picking up interference from the dog. He didn't sound terribly friendly, either.

"We'd like to get a look at who we're doing business with first."

"Who says we're doin' business?"

"Forget it," Nate said. "This guy's a small-timer. What we've got is too big for him."

The challenge piqued his interest. As we began to turn, he opened the door about halfway—just wide enough for us to get our look at him.

Shake was a burly guy. He was carrying about 225 pounds on a frame designed to hold 175. He was probably four inches shorter than I am, but the dog made him appear a foot taller. If you wanted to factor in their menacing expressions, I suppose you could add another foot. I'm not up on the different breeds, but the dog was a big, black, ugly one. A rottweiler, Nate later told me. Shake was holding it on a short leash. Not short enough, as far as I was concerned.

"Hey, what's the rush, bro? You wanna talk, or you wanna walk?" Shake motioned for us to come inside. As we stepped through the doorway, Nate lowered his hand cautiously to pat the dog's head.

Bad idea. It backed onto its hind legs and began snarling.

Shake laughed. "He don't like honkies."

"That's OK," Nate said. "I don't like dogs." He wasn't laughing.

Shake switched off the stereo, tugging the dog beside him. The goddamn thing didn't take its eyes off us.

"What's the pooch's name?" I asked.

"Badass." He pronounced it as if it had at least a dozen letters in it. I didn't bother to ask how he had come to settle on such a cute moniker.

"Maybe you'd want to put Badass outside," I suggested.

Shake gave me a look that made it clear what he thought of the idea. He snapped his fingers and pointed to the corner. Badass sauntered over and sat down. Still staring at us, he began chewing on a hunk of wood that had started out as a two-by-four. The section he was working on was a one-by-two.

Shake invited us to sit down by making a perfunctory wave at the available seating options—three metal milk crates and a pair of beanbag chairs. He took up residence on a folding chair next to a card table that was littered with wrappers from Burger Chef. We remained standing near the door—as far away from Badass as we could get.

"So what's the rap?" Shake said, putting his feet up on the table and making it wobble.

"Nice place you've got here," Nate said.

Shake gave him an uncomprehending look. I think he was starting to catch on that we were there for different business than we might have led him to believe.

"We heard you were hassling Dwight Robinson," I said. "We want to know why."

Shake tilted back in the chair and grinned. "You got five seconds to get your ass outa here, motherfucker, or Badass gonna think you're a *bone*." He looked at the dog and it began to growl.

In two seconds, I had my gun out. "You've got five seconds to start answering our questions or Badass is going to be a Deadass." I had no intention of shooting, but I thought I'd let Shake know the odds in case he decided to gamble. If it did come down to a choice between Badass and me, I'd probably change my mind.

I didn't have time to. I guess Shake liked to gamble. He snapped his fingers and the dog charged before I could get set to aim. In addition to being big and ugly, Badass was one quick son of a bitch.

Instinctively, I put my arms up to protect my face and throat, kicking with my right foot. That alone wouldn't have been enough to hold him off for long, but Nate's a pretty quick son of a bitch himself. He cut in behind Badass and stunned him with a karate chop behind the head.

The dog flopped to the floor on its side and began to yelp. His master let out a yelp of his own. He sprang out of the chair toward Nate, who was bending over to grab the leash. I stepped between them and let him have it upside the head with the butt of the gun before he could spit out the last two syllables of "mother fucker." At least that's what I think he was starting to say.

Nate gave the snarling dog another kick, then dragged him to the kitchen and shut the door. I stayed in the living room and held the gun on Shake, who was stretched out on the floor, rubbing his head.

"Motherfucker," he mumbled, beginning to rise.

I put the gun away, then pressed his head back down to the floor with my foot. "Why were you hassling Dwight Robinson?" I asked.

"Fuck you."

"Which arm would you like me to break first?" Nate asked. "You can choose the left or the right, but you've only got ten seconds to decide."

Shake thought it over and came up with an answer well before the allotted time had expired. "He owed me money."

"Did you smash the headlight on his car?"

"Who told you that, Dexter? That motherfucker."

Nate told him we were asking the questions and reminded him of his arm-breaking options.

"Yeah, I busted the light."

I removed my foot from his head and he pulled himself up to a sitting position.

"We heard you threatened his wife, too. You're a pretty mean guy, aren't you?"

He looked toward the kitchen, where Badass was barking and clawing at the door. If we didn't conclude our business soon, he'd probably eat his way through it.

"You threatened her life, and then she turns up dead. A guy could get in trouble pulling shit like that."

Shake gave me the grin again. It was just about time to give him another shot. "I got an alibi, motherfucker," he said.

"Is that your Mustang parked outside?"

"Yeah."

Nate wandered over to the coffee table where Shake kept his stereo and began sorting through a pile of papers. "You keeping track of some bets here, bro?" he asked.

"Get the fuck outa there."

"This guy's too dumb to be working on his own," Nate said. He handed me a sheet with a column of numbers on it. "He can't even add."

I nodded. "Atrocious penmanship, too." I looked at Shake. "Who do you work for?"

"Fuck you."

Nate walked back to the stereo and pulled a record off the turntable. He dropped it to the floor and stomped on it with the heel of his boot.

"Hey, motherfucker, what're you doin'? That's my new Temps album!" He began to get up, but I pushed him back to the floor.

"Diamond needle," Nate said, taking the stylus off the tone-arm. "These babies are guaranteed to last forever." He dropped it to the floor and stepped on it. "Unless, of course, they're subjected to something other than normal wear and tear."

"We've got all fucking day," I said, smiling. "Who are you working for?"

"Ray Salvino."

"Is he the one who told you to put the heat on Dwight?"

"Yeah."

"Where can we find him?"

Shake answered with brooding silence.

"All right, *Four Tops' Greatest Hits!*" Nate said, pulling an album out of its sleeve.

"Hey, man, don't—" Shake watched in horror as Nate broke another record. "He tends bar at Pete's. Talk to him. I didn't do nothin'."

"What a coincidence," I said. "That's the bar where you and Tommy Vreeland were drinking the night Cynthia was killed. What time did you leave?"

"I was there all night. Me and Tommy. Ask Ray. He'll tell you."

"Why should we believe Ray?"

Shake didn't have an answer for that. He looked toward Nate, who was still in the corner next to the stereo. "Hey, man, what the fuck are you doin'?"

I turned to see Nate pulling two small plastic bags out of a shoe box. He grinned at me. "Two lids of grass." Then, to Shake, he said, "Thanks a lot. These make great stocking stuffers at Christmas."

"Hey, motherfucker, that's my weed!" Shake was up off the floor this time. I gave him a two-hander and he took his seat again. For a guy with a big reputation, he wasn't putting up much resistance.

"Call the cops and report it stolen," I said. We began walking toward the door. "I've got a message from Dwight, by the way. He says he'll be coming back to see you."

"I'll be ready," he snarled.

"You better be," Nate said. "We'll be with him." He winked. "No need to get up, bro. We'll find our way out."

CHAPTER
16

The bar was called Pete's—Where Friends Meet, but it wasn't the sort of place where I'd want to meet anyone. As we entered, I had the distinct feeling we weren't going to make any friends there, either.

It was empty, except for the bartender, who was coming toward the door with a set of keys as we stepped inside. I figured Shake Johnson would call Salvino as soon as we left his house, but the place was only a two-minute drive.

"We're closed," he said. "You'll have to drink somewhere else."

"We didn't come to drink," I said. "We're looking for Ray Salvino."

"Too bad. You just missed him."

Nate and I exchanged looks. I was positive Salvino didn't have enough time to get out of there, even if Shake had called right away. I was even more certain that the place didn't have enough business to warrant two bartenders. If it did, Pete was making his money off something else. That, of course, was not out of the question.

"In that case, we'll stay and have a drink," Nate said. "I'm sure Ray will be coming back."

"I said we're closed," the bartender repeated.

He was a wiry guy with a dark, pockmarked complexion. I'd say he was about forty. I'd also guess he was Italian. I didn't need to guess about his rug. It was a bad fit. I figured he had gotten it at the same place Warren Shepherd had bought his. Probably a store called Pinky's.

"You keep funny hours," Nate said, looking at his watch. "According to the sign, Happy Hour begins in fifteen minutes."

"It's a funny bar," the guy replied. I couldn't say the same about him.

"Did Ray say where he was going?" I asked. "He told us to meet him here."

"No, he didn't say. He left in kind of a hurry."

"You know Ray," Nate said to me. "He's always been just about the most undependable asshole on earth. Plus he doesn't have a brain in that fat head of his." We shared a chuckle, but the bartender didn't join in.

"Well," I said, "we don't want to keep you if you're trying to close."

"That's right," Nate added. "We've got beer out in the car. I guess we'll just have to wait right outside until Ray gets back."

A worried look began to spread over the bartender's face. "I don't think he's coming back today," he stammered.

"Good thing we've got a lot of beer," Nate replied.

As the bartender followed us to the door, I noticed Pete Becker getting out of a white Cadillac in front. He looked like he was in a hurry. Apparently, the bartender had relayed Shake's S.O.S. Or maybe Shake had called himself.

The bartender tried to send Becker some silent signals when he stepped inside, but Pete didn't pick up on them. I think I commented previously on the apparent intellectual similarities between Becker and a box of rocks.

"Are these the two guys giving you trouble, Ray?" It took Becker a moment to remember me from the day before. Maybe it was hard to recognize me without my brother-in-law's golf shoes. "Oh no, not you again," he said. "This is the same guy that sucker-punched Tommy yesterday," he told Salvino.

I didn't bother to correct his details on my slugfest with young Vreeland. We had our own recognition scene to go through.

"So you're Ray!" Nate said, offering his hand for a shake that was refused. "What a sense of humor, putting us on like that."

"You're pretty funny yourself," Salvino answered.

"What do you want?" Becker asked.

"We wanted to talk to Salvino," I said. "But I guess Ray isn't exactly feeling like himself today."

"What exactly do you want to know?" The golf pro was sizing up Nate. Becker was built like the proverbial brick shithouse, and I figured he didn't get intimidated too often. But based on my little tango with Tommy and depending on how much he had heard about our encounter with Shake Johnson, he probably had cause to wonder.

"Shake Johnson says you ordered him to do some strong-arm work on Dwight Robinson," I said.

"He's full of shit," Salvino answered.

"Notwithstanding that, he also threatened to hurt Robinson's wife, evidently at your request," Nate said. "What do you have to say to that?"

"He's still full of shit." Salvino seemed a lot more confident with Becker on hand.

"So why did you give him an alibi for the night of the murder?" I asked.

We didn't get an answer. And we weren't going to. Pete Becker pulled out a .38. I guess he must have figured we had the basic manpower advantage. The gun made it his power play now.

"You've got one minute to get the fuck out of here."

I used it to leave them with a parting thought. "You provided Shake with an alibi," I said to Salvino. "But Dwight Robinson's next-door neighbor saw him go into the house the night Cynthia was killed. You might want to double-check your story."

It was a lie, or course, but sometimes you can learn a lot

from the way people react to false information. This proved to be one of those times.

Salvino glanced nervously at Becker before issuing a denial. It was a short look, but long enough for me to figure out that Shake Johnson hadn't been in the bar drinking all night. I wondered about Tommy Vreeland, but I didn't ask.

As we began to walk out, Becker lowered the gun. Nate was behind me, so I don't know exactly how he did it. But I turned the instant I sensed the commotion, and just in time to see the gun drop to the floor.

Salvino looked at it, then at me, then thought the better of it. Nate had Mr. Universe in a hammerlock, and I had my foot on his gun. Becker let out a grunt of pain. There was probably an element of embarrassment in it, too. Nate let go after a few seconds, shoving him forward as he released his grip. Becker landed headlong on one of the Formica-topped tables along the wall.

"It's all a matter of leverage," Nate said.

That and being incredibly strong. I knew he still worked out at the gym once a week, but I had never seen him lift anything heavier than a quart of beer on a regular basis. Of course, he did a lot of that. He had thrown the discus and shot-put in high school, and he had been the all-state wrestling champion in Massachusetts one year. But he also smoked a pack of cigarettes a day, and he was pushing fifty years old. The man was a marvel of human engineering.

Nate put out his hand and I gave him the gun. He emptied the chamber and put the slugs in his pocket. Then he tossed the gun onto the bar.

"That's not a toy," he said to Becker. "You shouldn't point it at anyone. It's impolite and somebody could get hurt." He pointed his finger. "If you ever try that on us again, that somebody could be you. You get the big picture, Pete?"

I think he did, but we didn't wait around for his answer. We stopped at another dingy bar a few blocks away, where they actually served drinks during Happy Hour. We stayed until the country-western band started playing.

CHAPTER
——17——

After five straight days of Jersey, I was in bad need of a vacation. Naturally, that was out of the question, but I decided to spend Saturday seeking temporary relief from the week's confusion by working on my investments. This might sound demanding, but it isn't. All it involves is reclining on the couch, drinking beer and reading the racing program.

I found a few interesting prospects, but my friend Albatross had also decided to take the day off, so there weren't any big-money propositions. My friend Nate had a date with the fabled Hortense, and I didn't have the energy for a solo pilgrimage to the track. It looked like a day to do my banking at home. I called my bookie, Angelo Albani. Now that they've got off-track betting in New York, you can play the horses legally. But Angelo has lower service charges and I like to stick to tradition. Plus he usually has good jokes.

"Joke del giorno," he said. "How do you tell the difference between a dead rat on the highway and a dead lawyer?" I never attempt to guess, so he went right to the punch line. "You can see the skid marks in front of the rat."

The joke made me think about checking in with Mike O'Leary, but I decided that could wait a day. He was scheduled to attend the rally for Dwight, so I'd have the opportunity of talking to him then. Besides, sometimes your thinking about a case will become clearer if you shut down your mind for a day. The therapist I used to date had a technical term for this process. In the parlance of my profession, it's called Sleeping On It.

I got plenty of sleep, but I can't say my perspective was any clearer when I set out for Kennedy High School on Sunday afternoon. I still had that lingering feeling that we were getting nowhere. But I had a dinner date that night with Terry Vreeland, and I was hopeful I might learn more from her.

My memory of Jersey roads was getting sharper each time I drove out there, so I didn't have any trouble finding the school. Of course, my route selection was considerably less scenic than you'd get from the American Automobile Association. I got off Route 80 in Clifton and came into Paterson on Main Street. It was a warm, sunny day, and the people were lined up outside their two-family row houses watching the garbage pile up along the sidewalks. Ordinarily, this is a summertime activity, but I guess they wanted to take advantage of the nice weather.

Kennedy High School is a massive gray brick building that looks only slightly more inviting than the county jail. It's located on Preakness Avenue at the Passaic River, a few blocks over from the so-called historic district.

In the early 1900's, Paterson was one of the biggest textile manufacturing centers in the country. In 1913, it was also the scene of the one of the nation's ugliest strikes. Close to twenty-five thousand workers struck the mills, with help from Big Bill Haywood and the IWW, who were coming off a big win up in Lawrence, Massachusetts, the year before. The strike lasted six months and culminated when a thousand workers, organized by a guy named John Reed, marched from Paterson all the way to New York to reenact picket line scenes in a fund-raising pageant at Madison Square Garden. Despite a massive turnout, the event netted all of one hundred and fifty dollars. With the Paterson cops smashing skulls with reckless abandon and the town fathers inviting in the rival AFL to offset the Wobblies, the great Paterson silk strike wobbled to a close.

One look at the cars and bicycles crammed into the Kennedy High School parking lot told me that Big Bill Haywood would have been proud of the organizing job that Ed Gallo had done. I just hoped the people who turned out at the rally for Dwight would have more change to spare than the ones who had attended the Wobbly affair at Madison Square Garden.

With the lot full, I had to park over on Spruce Street near the Great Passaic Falls, a city landmark that William Carlos Williams had waxed poetic about in his famous Paterson poems. Williams thought the history of the town lived on in the disembodied roar of the falls. But as I hoofed it back to the school, the only neighborhood institutions that seemed to have any life left in them were a pair of hot dog stands called the Falls Diner and Libby's Lunch.

There were probably a thousand people, mostly kids, gathered in a riverside park behind the school. The park didn't appear to have a name, but I was familiar with it. I had been there several times in my childhood to see the world's first submarine. I never understood why it was there, and my scout leader had been hard-pressed to come up with an explanation. It was one of the great mysteries of my childhood. As with the Blessed Trinity, I had long since lost interest in trying to figure it out.

As I made my way through the crowded park, I spotted Coach Gallo on a makeshift stage near the edge of the river. A short, overweight woman whom I took to be his wife was standing beside him. My ex-father-in-law was standing next to her. Except for me, the cops, a TV crew and a few newspaper reporters, they were about the only white faces in the park.

Dahlia Robinson and her son Dexter were also standing on the platform, alongside a few other people whom I didn't recognize. Ed Gallo was just stepping up to a microphone to address the crowd when I reached the side of the stage.

It wasn't exactly the Gettysburg Address, but you could tell the coach was no stranger to public speaking. You could also tell that the kids respected him, because they began listening attentively almost as soon as he started talking. I doubt many of his fellow teachers would have commanded that much attention.

Gallo's speech was short and sweet, a brief lesson on civil rights mixed with sports metaphors and a pitch for money in any denomination. He said Dwight was facing the biggest at-bat in his entire life, fourth and ten with his back to the wall. This time it didn't matter how he played the game, the only thing that counted was whether he won or lost. And the only way he could win was if all his fans gave him their complete support. Gallo finished by starting up a chant that the crowd joined in on for five minutes or so: "Things ain't right till we free Dwight."

It probably would have outraged the head of the English department, but it was a direct hit with the audience.

The crowd cheered when Gallo introduced Dexter and Dwight's mother. Dexter didn't say anything, but Mrs. Robinson spoke briefly about the importance of prayer and believing in God. The crowd listened politely and started up the chant again when she broke down in tears. Dexter took her by the arm and led her off the platform.

For reasons that were unclear to me, Gallo had asked if I'd be willing to say a few words. I told him I was, all the while hoping he might forget. He didn't. He gave O'Leary and me an admiration-filled introduction that made me feel guilty as well as embarrassed. He made it sound as if we were donating our labor to the cause. After we were done speaking, I dragged O'Leary to the donation table and made him match my offering of fifty bucks. At first he said he didn't have that much with him, but he relented as soon as I began searching his pockets.

"I had an interesting chat with Terry Vreeland on Thursday," I told him.

"Yeah, I know. Was she helpful?"

I ignored his question and asked one of my own. "How do you know?"

O'Leary pulled a flask out of his breast pocket. The man knows how to have a picnic. "She called my office and asked for your number—that's how."

So this was the way it was going to be. I figured that once I mentioned Terry, O'Leary would admit that she was Dwight's backdoor girl. Instead, he had decided to play coy with me. Either that or there was another mystery woman in the picture.

I could have asked him outright, but if he was still protecting Terry's wishes, I didn't want to put him on the spot. Sometimes I can be a very thoughtful guy. Besides that, I was planning on asking her myself at the first opportunity.

I refused his offer of the flask. "She was very helpful," I said. "I learned a lot from her. But we're still right where we were to begin with—lots of questions, not enough answers."

He frowned. "What about Shake Johnson?"

I brought him up to date on our visit with Shake and our futile efforts at getting a drink at Pete's. "Right now, Shake's our best possibility," I said. "They didn't spell anything out, but I'd bet my life that Shake wasn't in that bar all evening. But before we can pin anything on him, we have to get some more information."

"How do you plan to do that?"

I shrugged. "Wait things out and see what develops."

"Glad to see you're using nothing but the most modern investigative methods. Meanwhile, my client rots in jail."

"You want us to force the issue?"

"You mean beat it out of him?"

I nodded.

"That's the last thing we need—a coerced confession."

"Exactly. That's why we have to wait." I smiled. "And all the while, I've got the meter running."

"Oh Jesus."

I wasn't sure if O'Leary was reacting to my comment or to Coach Gallo's introduction of a band called Black Power. There were four of them, all high school kids, dressed up in black pants, black turtle neck sweaters and black sneakers. It was probably the first band ever to play in front of the world's first submarine. They looked like they were ready to boogie. So did the crowd. Suddenly, I was feeling very old.

The band opened with a song written especially for the occasion. It was called "Free Dwight Robinson." Their guitars were cranked up to a volume that surely exceeded government safety standards, and they sounded closer to percussion than to stringed instruments. That seemed to be the style these days. It was difficult to make out the lyrics. As far as I could tell, there weren't very many of them.

It turned out I was wrong. As O'Leary and I started moving farther away from the speakers, I noticed Ed Gallo and his wife dancing toward us. The coach's knee didn't appear to be giving him any problems at the moment. It also appeared that he knew all the lyrics, because he was mouthing the words. Either that or he was running short of breath.

They reached us during a long instrumental break, and Gallo paused to introduce his wife. "Are you feeling funky today?" he yelled.

I wasn't exactly sure what he meant, but I told him I was anyway. I needed a couple of aspirin.

He nodded, grinned and continued dancing. Mrs. Gallo dropped out, leaving her husband to do a modified version of the twist. A cluster of kids pointed at him and started to laugh. He began to sing the chorus:

> Look what the white man done,
> We got to free Dwight Robinson.
> They got the brother locked in jail,
> So we got to raise his bail.

The crowd cheered wildly when the song finally ended. I wasn't clocking it, but I figured it must have lasted half an hour. I needed two pulls of O'Leary's flask to get through.

It was hardly a surprise that the coach was the last to stop applauding. After the claps, he let out a couple of wolf whistles that made me wonder if he ever had occasion to use the one he wore around his neck.

"Great band," he said. "They're going to cut a record."

"They're only *talking* about making a record," his wife corrected. I instantly had a sneaking suspicion that one of her primary functions in life was to diminish her husband's enthusiasm. If so, it must have been a full-time job.

"They got a big-time record company interested, and all the radio stations are going to play it," Gallo said, ignoring his wife's comment. I had a feeling he had plenty of practice doing that. "All the proceeds are going to Dwight's bail fund."

"*If* there are any proceeds," his wife added.

The band's next song sounded remarkably similar to the first one. The only difference was that Gallo didn't appear to know the lyrics. He spotted a couple of kids from the baseball team and waved them over to meet us. We chatted with them for a few minutes, but I was more interested in scanning the crowd for Dexter Robinson. I spotted him talking to a pair of girls under a willow tree at the edge of the river. As I excused myself, Gallo invited O'Leary and me to dinner.

"We've got enough, don't we, honey?" he asked his wife.

Mrs. Gallo didn't look so sure. A look of relief spread over her face when we said we had other plans.

O'Leary accompanied me as I approached Dexter. Dwight's brother didn't look especially happy to see us.

"Remember me?" I asked.

"Sure. I know what time it is."

"Good. I wanted to know if you could remember exactly what time it was when you left Pete's bar the night Cynthia was killed."

Dexter thought for a moment, and the two girls started to walk away. "Hey, don't leave," he said. "These cats won't be hanging around long."

One of the girls said they'd talk to him later.

"Damn. Those chicks were hot to trot." He looked as if he were expecting an apology for the interruption. He didn't get one.

"What time did you leave the bar?" I asked.

"Oh, nine-thirty. Right after Tommy and Shake came in."

"Is that why you left?"

He nodded. "This is true. Tommy was drunk as a skunk. I didn't want no trouble, so I split, you know?"

"Where did you go?"

"Back home." He said it as if it were the only possibility.

"What time did you get there?"

"I don't know." Dexter was staring at the ground. "However long it takes to drive home."

"Maybe I should ask your mother."

"No, man, don't do that. Mama goes to sleep real early, you know. She was in bed when I got there."

"What time did Dwight call you?"

"About midnight I guess." Dexter began scanning the crowd. He looked like a kid waiting to be excused from the dinner table. "You got any more questions?"

"Just one. What kind of car do you drive?"

"Me? I got me an Oldsmobile."

"What color is it?"

"It's white. I got a white Oldsmobile."

"Like Dwight's."

"Yeah, this is true. Except he got a Cadillac."

"Thanks for your help."

"Sure. Any time." Dexter looked a bit mystified. Either he couldn't put two and two together or he was telling the truth. Both were distinct possibilities.

I watched him swagger back over toward the stage. O'Leary and I took the long way around to the parking lot, out of the hazardous range of the music.

"What was that all about?" he asked.

"There's something I don't trust about him," I replied.

"I know what you mean. I don't think Dwight's too keen on him, either. Do you think he's the one who killed Cynthia?"

I didn't know what to think. "Probably not. But it's still too early to tell."

I looked at my watch. It was getting late for dinner. O'Leary wanted to stop for a drink, but I turned him down.

"Time is money, Mike. And these days my time is *your* money."

CHAPTER
──18──

It only took me twenty minutes to find my way to Terry Vreeland's house on Beechwood Drive in Packanack Lake. I didn't know anything about the place, but it looked like one of the early prototypes for Mountain Lake. As I drove along the road near a long dam, I could see a nine-hole golf course, tennis courts, baseball fields and, naturally, a lake. Unlike Mountain Lake, this one looked like there had been some natural forces involved in the creation of it.

Packanack looked to be larger than the town Thomas Vreeland had founded. My guess was that there were probably five thousand residents. Judging by the size of the houses, they weren't quite as wealthy as the people of Mr. Vreeland's model community. I figured Packanack was probably a starter club for the social climb up the mountain. It gave the impression of being less snooty. That could have been because it was older, but I think the main difference was that you didn't have to bribe anyone to get in. At least not to visit.

Terry Vreeland was sitting on her front porch waiting for

me when I pulled into the driveway. If I hadn't been sure of the house number, I might not have recognized her. She looked a lot different in a dress than she did in golfing shorts. And a lot better, I might add.

Her brown hair was hanging loose. It fell across the side of her face, so that one of her green eyes played peekaboo through the silky strands. She had put on a little makeup. She didn't need any, but it was a nice touch nonetheless. As I climbed out of the car and watched her coming down the walk toward me, I realized that Terry Vreeland was not just a pretty girl—she was a goddamn knockout.

I told her so, but not exactly in those words. She seemed pleased to hear it. She also appreciated the flowers I had brought along, even though they had wilted somewhat from spending the afternoon in the car.

I was feeling a little wilted myself, so the gin and tonic she mixed for me hit the spot. I was glad to see that she was already working on one. I've got nothing against people who don't drink, but it can be uncomfortable getting hammered with someone who's sober. For some reason, I was in the mood to get hammered.

"I hope you like lasagna," she said. "I only know three recipes."

I told her it was my favorite, which is almost the truth. She said her other specialties were tuna casserole and Polish sausage. I counted my blessings as I drained my drink. She mixed a couple more, then joined me on the couch.

I had felt perfectly comfortable meeting her at the golf course a few days before, but while sitting in her living room I was at something of a loss for words. This is rather unusual for me, since I tend to be a rather suave and confident—some might even say cocky—sort of guy. But I felt more like I was on a date than on a business call. I had a sense that Terry felt the same way. I think that was because we were.

Terry confirmed my suspicions about Packanack Lake being a rung on the local social ladder leading up to Mountain Lake. It was one of those sleepy private communities that barred the sale of houses to blacks and Jews until a few years back. Sections of the town had been developed by her grandfather, and her family had lived there in the forties before moving on to stuffier things. In recent years, the town had been hit with a wave of vandalism, so a group of bored men had formed a vigilante force to patrol the streets. She said the vandals were probably equally bored kids. I figured they regarded the vigilantes as a welcome challenge.

I filled Terry in on the details of the rally for Dwight Robinson. She had been thinking about attending, but she thought doing so would have amounted to a public declaration of war on her father. Instead, she had played thirty-six holes that day, shooting a seventy on the first round and seventy-one on the second.

"Have you recovered from your delightful meeting with my brother?" she asked. She sounded as if she felt somewhat responsible for the altercation.

I told her I had and assured her she wasn't.

"Tommy gets that way when he's drunk," she said.

"It was a little early in the day to be drunk."

"Not for my brother. And not for a lot of people at the country club. I don't drink when I'm there."

"Speaking of people at the country club, I had the pleasure of running into Pete Becker again," I said.

"Lucky you. Where did you see him? Down at the bar?" She got up off the couch and walked to a coffee table in the corner of the room. She picked up a newspaper that was lying on it.

"That's right," I said. "Charming joint. Have you been there?"

She held up a finger. "Once. For five minutes. Tommy hangs out there all the time. I hate the place."

"I'm not especially fond of it myself." I told her about our encounters with Shake, Salvino and Becker. She sat down beside me, still holding the paper in her hand. "Do you know this guy Salvino?"

She shook her head and a few wisps of hair fell across her

face. It looked nice. I hoped she'd have to do it again. Maybe if I asked her a few difficult questions.

"If he's tending bar at Pete's, he's probably a jerk," she said.

"He is."

She handed me the paper. "Look at this. This will give you an idea of what an idiot Pete Becker is."

I smiled. "As if I need convincing."

Terry got up to mix another round of drinks while I looked over the paper. It was a four-page tabloid called *The 19th Hole*, the official newspaper of Mountain Lake. On the upper right corner of the back page, I saw a photo of the beaming golf pro. Pete Becker must have thought he had other talents besides teaching golf and owning a bar. Evidently, nobody had bothered to tell him that writing wasn't one of them.

There was no byline on the column. I didn't know if the omission was an oversight or just an assumption that everyone knew Pete.

AM I RIGHT OR AM I RIGHT?

Never before has there ever been such a big tragedy as the one conflicting upon us today. There is a black cloud hanging over the Country Club and all of our lives and it has the face of Dwight Robinson written all over it. I don't have to tell you that Cynthia Vreeland, the gorgeous young daughter of Mr. Vreeland, was brutally murdered by him in cold blood on Tuesday night May the 9th.

Dwight was always a hot-shot baseball player who turned out to be just another washout and if anybody ever asked me I could have told you years ago what a lazy no-good s.o.b. he was on account of seeing what a lousy caddy he was and raising a ruckus practically every time he walked into my bar like we were supposed to bow down and kiss his feet.

Nothing we do will ever be able to bring Cynthia back from her resting place in heaven but we all have the responsibility to see to it that Robinson pays for it, and I mean he would be getting off easy if he got the electric chair which is exactly what he deserves. I want to offer my sincerest condolences to Mr. Vreeland and his other children Tommy and Terry who have always been my close personal friends and I urge you to all do the same. Without them there wouldn't be any Mountain Lake.

All of which is why I hereby officially propose that we rename the golf course after Cynthia. Am I right or am I right?

"That's the latest issue," Terry said, handing me my drink. "Pete usually writes about the need to clean out sand traps and important issues like that."

"I hope he golfs better than he writes," I answered.

"Dwight was much better. That's one of the reasons Pete couldn't stand him."

"You must be honored to be one of his closest friends."

"What a bunch of bullshit! Pete knows I think he's a jerk."

"But he is friends with your brother."

She nodded. "I told you Tommy isn't a very good judge of character."

Terry got up from the couch. She lost her balance for a moment and had to grab my arm to regain it. "Maybe we should eat," she said. "I think I'm getting drunk." As I stood up, she asked me "Are you hungry?" in a tone that indicated the correct answer was no.

"I could wait for a while."

"Good." She dropped back down on the couch again. "Let's have another drink instead."

That sounded like a fine idea. It was my turn to make them. When I joined her again, she took my arm. "Can I trust you?" she asked.

I told her I was the most trustworthy person she would

ever meet. That may not be true, but I do know how to keep a secret.

"I mean seriously," she said. "I feel like talking."

"What about?"

"Remember I told you how weird my family is? I think there's something you should know. It's about my brother and sister. They had a close relationship."

"How close?"

"Too close."

"Do you mean—"

Terry didn't wait for me to finish the question. "That's right." She closed her eyes and took a deep breath. "I don't know how long it was going on and if somebody had told me about it, I wouldn't have believed it. Except that I saw it with my own eyes. I found them in bed myself."

She opened her eyes again, and I could see that they were slightly damp. Our eyes met and locked. Suddenly, I felt that spark that you get on rare occasions. The one that makes you feel like you're actually seeing inside someone. It's a nice feeling but a little scary.

"When was that?" I asked.

"Five years ago. Tommy was twenty, Cynthia would have been seventeen."

"Did you say anything to them about it?"

She shook her head and the lovely wisps of hair fell across her face again. "Not a word. I guess I should have, but I didn't know what to say. I thought just being discovered like that, I figured that would be enough."

"So you didn't mention it to anyone."

"You mean, like my father?"

I nodded and lit a cigarette. She asked me to light one for her too. "Telling my father wouldn't have done a damn bit of good." She took a long drag on the cigarette and closed her eyes again. A solitary tear rolled down her cheek.

"It was the year after my mother died. My father came home drunk. He was drinking all the time back then but he's cut down quite a bit. But that night, I mean he was blind, staggering drunk."

I knew what was coming, and I didn't want to hear it. The only reason I was listening was because Terry wanted to talk about it. I took her hand, squeezed it and held on to it.

"I was already in bed but I wasn't asleep. He always came in to kiss me goodnight. Sometimes, he'd give me a real slobbering drunken kiss. I couldn't stand that, so I pretended I was asleep. I thought maybe that would make him go away."

She looked at me as if she wanted a reaction. She had stopped crying.

"But it didn't," I said softly.

"No, it didn't." Her voice was calm. But it became louder and shakier as she continued. "First, he started kissing me. Then he began stroking me through the blanket. I still pretended to be asleep. Then he put his hand under the blanket and the next thing I know he's groping me under my nightgown."

Terry shuddered for a moment, and I put my arm around her. "I was only sixteen years old," she said. "I'm his goddamn daughter!"

She covered her face with her hands and sat there silently. I thought about telling her that it happens more often than she probably thinks. I wasn't sure that would be any comfort. Finally, I said, "What did you do?"

She turned to me and smiled. "I started screaming bloody murder. You've never seen a drunk sober up so fast in your entire life. I told him if he ever laid a hand on me again, I'd call the cops and have him arrested."

She handed me her glass. "I need a refill." I thought maybe she needed something else, like coffee, but I went along with her request. When I returned to the couch, she said, "Now you know everything there is to know about me."

Not everything, exactly, and I figured this was as good a time as any to ask the question I had been wondering about for the last three days. Considering the way she had opened up to me, I didn't think she'd feel like I was prying.

"Dwight was having an affair with someone," I said. "Was it you?"

The expression on her face was answer enough, but she let me have it anyway. From where she was sitting, I guess I couldn't blame her.

"Are you kidding? I can't believe it! Dwight Robinson is my brother-in-law!"

I apologized and told her about the mystery woman who had hired Mike O'Leary. She had no idea who it could be. She said she understood why I thought she might have been the one.

"You don't know my standards in men," she added.

I asked just what those might be.

"I make it a rule only to get involved with older guys— guys I know I can beat at golf."

Oh, boy. That was exactly the answer I wanted to hear. It had been a long time since I shot a hole in one. That had been at Ernie Feldman's birthday party, and we were only playing miniature golf. This was the big time, and Ernie's father wasn't on hand to chaperone.

CHAPTER
19

"Tell me about yourself," Terry said.

We were sitting on the couch again after finishing off the lasagna and knocking back a few cups of coffee. For dessert, she had baked brownies. I surprised her and no doubt scored a few points by eating one of the ones with the marijuana in them.

I know I'm a little old for that sort of thing, but Nate uses the stuff and he's pushing fifty. Plus I don't do it very often— only on special occasions. This seemed like one of those.

"What do you want to know?"

"Are you married?"

"Not presently."

She let out one of those throaty laughs and leaned against my arm. "What does that mean? You're just about to get married or you just got divorced?"

I'm usually reserved when it comes to divulging personal information, but there was something about Terry Vreeland that made me feel like talking. Maybe the grass had something to do with it, but it went a lot deeper than that.

The reason I don't talk about that stuff much is probably because I don't have much occasion to do so. The last time I could remember was with the therapist. I came out of that one thinking I had told her too much. I had certainly listened to too much—that's for damn sure.

Whatever the reason, I told Terry just about everything. From growing up in Clifton to the short-lived baseball career, from the accident to my brief stint on the New York police force. Then I told her about Amy, my first wife.

We met in 1953 when I was still a cop. I had dropped out of City College three years before. As with Kathy O'Leary later on, Amy and I were on the four-year plan. We got married in '54, divorced in '58.

It turned out I wasn't the kind of man she was looking for. She found just the right type a few years later. He wanted kids and a house in the suburbs and a lawn to mow on the weekends. So did she. I hadn't realized that when we got married. I wished she had told me. It would have saved me a lot of alimony.

I guess she was hoping I would change. I haven't.

I gave Terry the rundown on my second go-round, the match made in hell with Kathy O'Leary. That account was a little more detailed. For some reason, it was fresher in my mind.

"Do you ever talk to her?" she asked.

"No. But I had a chance to go to her house for dinner tonight."

She looked understandably curious.

"Dwight's lawyer used to be my father-in-law," I explained.

"God," she said, "you've really come full circle. Is he any good?"

"As fathers-in-law go, I guess he was OK."

"You're not very funny," she said, smiling.

"A few people have told me that." Actually, it was more like quite a few. "I've only seen him in action once," I said, answering her question about O'Leary.

"What happened?"

"He stole the goddamn shirt right off my back." *The little prick*, I thought.

"He was the lawyer *against* you?"

"No, that's the curious part. He was on my side. I don't always make the best decisions." I smiled to assure her there were no hard feelings, even as I got the urge to sock the fat little sucker in the puss again.

"I'm glad you decided to turn down her dinner invitation."

"That's one of my good decisions. It's also one of the easiest I've had to make for a long time."

Terry smiled and leaned in closer to me. We looked at each other for a long moment and I felt that spark again as I stared into her eyes. She closed them, a silent signal for a kiss. I complied with her wishes, fulfilling one of mine in the process.

We were nearing the hour of decision. If I had a vote in the matter, it was already fifty-percent decided.

When we came up for air, Terry suggested a nightcap. I didn't raise any objections.

"I had another offer for dinner, too," she said. "My brother. He felt guilty for the scene he made the other day. I guess he thought he could make it up to me by taking me out to dinner."

"It would take an awful lot of dinners to make up for what he did to you," I said. There was a tone of righteousness in my voice that surprised me a little. But I meant it just the same.

"That's exactly how I feel about it. I don't come that cheap."

"Is that the first time he ever hit you?"

"Since we were kids, yes." There was a hesitation in her voice that made me think she was lying. Or at least she was stretching the definition of kids a bit.

"What about Cynthia? Did he ever hit her?"

"I don't know. They had such a weird relationship, I suppose it's anybody's guess. I don't even like to think about it."

I didn't blame her, but it was an important question to me. A little light bulb had gone on in my head when she had told me about Tommy and Cynthia earlier. It hadn't gone off yet.

"You said Tommy drinks a lot."

She nodded. "Too much. I think he's an alcoholic."

"Dexter Robinson said Tommy was already bombed when he came into Pete's the night your sister was killed."

"He's probably right. When Tommy got home that night, he passed out on the living room floor. My father found him when the police called. He had to send Pete Becker over here to pick me up. I let Tommy borrow my car, but he didn't bring it back. That's the night he smashed it up. He ran into a fire hydrant."

Another light bulb went on inside my head. This time it was a big, bright one.

"What kind of car do you have?" I tried to sound as casual as possible.

"It's a nineteen-seventy-one Oldsmobile. Why do you ask?"

I shrugged. "Just curious."

It was a lousy answer. I'm usually pretty quick on my feet, but sometimes my brain doesn't work as fast as my tongue. The combination of booze and pot and the prospect of love tend to slow my mental processes.

Terry didn't look entirely convinced. I couldn't see any point in arousing her suspicions about Tommy. She was already caught in the middle of a family mess, and there was no need to trap her any further. That's why I didn't ask what color her car was.

I leaned in for another kiss, hoping that might take her mind off the subject.

The strategy worked—while we were kissing. But as soon as we stopped, she began spearing me with her green eyes. I'm a master of evasion, but avoiding those eyes was harder than cheating at poker.

"There's something you're not telling me," she said.

It was against my better judgment, but I decided to lay my cards on the table.

"What color is your car?" I asked.

"White. Why?"

I told her about the car that Warren Shepherd had seen pulling away from Dwight's house. I told her about the broken headlight.

"But Tommy was at the bar drinking all night," she said.

"I'm not convinced he was."

She pulled away from me, and I began to wonder if I hadn't blown things in more ways than one. I didn't want Terry thinking that I had only come there to pump her for information. Maybe that's why I had come initially, but my reasons had changed—a lot.

"That doesn't necessarily mean he killed your sister," I reassured her. "It doesn't even mean he went to her house. He could be telling the truth about the car. It could all be—"

"A coincidence?"

I nodded.

"You don't believe much in coincidence, do you?" she asked.

I admitted that I didn't.

"Neither do I." She leaned against me again and took my hand. "I want to do everything I can to help you."

"You've been a big help already."

"I can talk to Tommy if you want."

I shook my head. "Just keep your eyes and ears open." I wagged a finger in front of her nose. "But don't start asking any questions. Let me handle that."

"You sound like you're worried about me." Terry smiled, like she was enjoying the thought of my looking after her best interest. She got up off the couch, steadying herself, then tried to pull me up with her. It worked, but I was helping a bit.

As we stumbled across the living room together, she whispered another enjoyable thought in my ear. Terry had my best interest at heart, too.

CHAPTER
20

It's amazing how good you can feel after a bad night's sleep. Actually, from the standpoint of quality, the sleep I got was great. It was the quantity part that suffered.

I'd be willing to lose a whole lot more, if it meant getting another chance to stay up all night with Terry Vreeland.

It was drizzling when we woke up, so she wasn't in any hurry to get to the golf course. Naturally, this was just fine with me. By nature, I'm not a morning person. On this particular morning, I was practically operating in slow motion. I think the condition had less to do with my metabolism than it did with my pleasant memories of the night before.

Despite her limited culinary repertoire, Terry had mastered the recipe for bacon and eggs. Coffee and cigarettes usually hold me, but I didn't raise any objections.

I had mentioned to Terry that it would be good to have pictures of Shake Johnson and Dexter Robinson. Despite their apparent inability to distinguish one black face from another, I thought it would be a wise idea to show the photos to Anna Paslawski and Warren Shepherd.

Terry dug through a box and unearthed a Mountain Lake Country Club yearbook from three years before that included pictures of all the caddies, as well as a photo of her brother. As I was flipping through it, a shot of a large, muscular guy caught my attention. He had a black face and Afro wig but white arms.

"Who's that?" I asked.

"Oh, that's Pete Becker. On caddy-training day, he always puts black shoe polish on his face. Pretty funny, huh?"

I nodded. "It's a real scream." But I was thinking that my list of possible suspects had just gotten a little longer.

"Was Becker friendly with your sister?" I asked.

"You read his column. Pete was close friends with all of us."

I liked Terry's sarcasm. "I mean, did he ever come on to her?"

"I see what you're getting at." She looked closely at the picture. "The rumor about Pete is that he's a homosexual, but I don't know if it's true. He came on to all the ladies at the club."

"Including you?" I felt a momentary but surprising surge of resentment as I asked the question.

She nodded. "I made sure he got the message right away. I don't know about Cynthia. I think he really had his cap set for my aunt, Melody Winchester."

"Do you think they were having an affair?"

"I don't know. I doubt it. Melody's more of a tease than anything else. She does a lot of flirting, but I think that's basically to remind my uncle that instead of being so concerned about saving the world, he might think about saving their marriage once in a while."

"You think it's in trouble?"

"That's hard to tell. Probably not. Melody's got what she wants—money and prestige. And Bob's got what he wants—a blonde on his arm and his name in the public spotlight. I think they're both pretty happy, in a sick kind of way."

Terry offered to tear the pages out of the book for me. Instead, I took the whole thing. I had a reason, but it had nothing to do with the case. On page 17, there was a picture of Terry Vreeland. I thought it might be nice to look at after I said my bedtime prayers.

By the time I kissed her goodbye and made her promise not to go asking her brother any foolish questions, it was pushing noon. The rain had stopped and she was ready to hit the links. I was off to make my living—asking people foolish questions.

I didn't expect Anna Paslawski to be of much help in identifying the photos. She had only heard and not seen the person she thought was Dwight on the night of the murder. I didn't expect Warren Shepherd to be home on vacation again, unless there was a particularly engaging episode of *The Flintstones* that he didn't want to miss. But there was always the chance I would be surprised.

I was—but for an entirely different reason.

As soon as I turned onto Willow Way, I noticed a definite deterioration in the neighborhood. I'm sure some of the neighbors would have said it started to go bad the moment Dwight Robinson moved in. But the change that caught my attention was a more recent development. Judging by the smell of smoke that was still lingering in the humid air, I figured it might have occurred within the last twenty-four hours.

The cute little Cape Cod starter-home that had once been Ed and Anna Paslawski's dream house didn't look so cute anymore. Very few houses do after they've burned down.

I parked the Corvair on the street and walked up the driveway. The shell of the house was still standing, but it was badly scorched. The windows were nailed shut with wood, a hasty job courtesy of AAA Board-Up. I wondered if Anna Paslawski had placed the order. I wondered if Anna Paslawski was still alive.

I pried one of the boards loose from the window and peered inside. For my trouble, I got a snootful of soot. All I could see was blackness. I went to the front door and examined the cheap padlock on it. The original lock had fallen victim to a fireman's ax. I could have picked the padlock and taken a look inside, but I knew from my glance through the window that I wouldn't find anything of interest. Besides, that's illegal. It's also dangerous.

I strolled around the perimeter of the house, keeping my eyes open for something that didn't look right. There were footprints all over the yard, no doubt made by firemen. Even if some of them weren't, it would be impossible to spot which ones. I didn't find anything until I reached the garage, on the side of the house closest to Dwight's.

I was thinking that I was shit out of luck just as I almost stepped in it. I've been accused of having expertise in the field of bullshit, but that didn't help much. This was clearly a different variety. Nonetheless, I could tell that the dirty deed had been done by a very large dog.

If I were still working as a cop, I would have had to take it in as evidence. There are a lot of advantages to working for yourself.

I headed across the street to Warren Shepherd's house. As I expected, he wasn't home. I decided to try his next-door neighbor.

A young woman came to the door, with two small children hanging on either side of her housedress. They were at the age when it's still difficult to determine their sex without a close inspection.

Her name was Janet Bradley. She said the fire had started about three A.M. Bob—that's her husband—had been the first one to spot it, while getting up to take a leak. Mrs. Norton, Anna Paslawski's next-door neighbor on the far side from Dwight's house, probably would have seen it first, but she was away on vacation.

"And what about Mrs. Paslawski?" I asked, bracing myself for the worst.

"Oh, she's away too. She went on a church tour to the Holy Land."

Indeed. Maybe God does work in wondrous ways, after all.

"Bob talked to the firemen. They said she must have left a cigarette burning. She's very absentminded. I think she's lucky she wasn't killed."

"How could she have left a cigarette burning?" I asked.

"Oh, she only left last night. I saw her loading up the car. Mr. Shepherd from next door was helping her. It was kind of cute."

"What was?"

"Mr. Shepherd and Mrs. Paslawski." A sly smile spread across her face. She began stroking the head of the kid on her left. Janet Bradley was pretty in a plain Jane sort of way.

"She has him over for dinner and things sometimes. I never thought anything of it. You know. I just figured they were both lonely. Until one day, Mr. Shepherd comes over and starts talking to me when I was out in the yard. Well, the next thing you know, as soon as he left, Mrs. Paslawski's over here." She let out a laugh. "Boy, did she ever let me have it. Going on about how I've already got a man, so why am I trying to hook another one. I thought she was joking at first, but then she started quoting scripture. She's really a sweet old lady, but personally, I think she's nuttier than a fruitcake."

I told Janet Bradley she wouldn't get any argument from me on that point. I asked if anyone had gotten hold of Anna Paslawski.

She shook her head. "Nobody knows how to reach her. I thought Mr. Shepherd might, but he just laughed when I suggested it. He said she's not supposed to be back for another ten days. That's why my husband called the board-up company."

"That was thoughtful of you," I said. While I was there, I figured I should take the opportunity to get her thoughts on another subject.

"Does anyone in the neighborhood have a dog?" I asked.

She mulled it over for a moment. "Just the Wolfs. They have a little poodle."

I thought I might be pressing my luck by asking about the night of Cynthia's murder, but she didn't seem to mind. I had a feeling Janet Bradley enjoyed having someone to chat with. At least that's how I'd feel if I had to spend my day talking to small kids.

Unfortunately, she didn't have much to say on the subject. They had gone to bed early that night, and Bob apparently hadn't gotten a nocturnal urge to relieve himself. But Mr. Shepherd had seen the whole thing.

"Do you know Mr. Shepherd well?"

"No. He usually keeps to himself. My husband talks to him once in a while."

"What about Dwight Robinson and his wife? Did you know them?"

That one seemed to make her a bit uncomfortable. "No," she said. "I guess they kind of kept to themselves, too." She patted the kids on their heads. "You understand."

Well, at least I got the point. I thanked her and hopped into the Corvair, then I hightailed it back to the place that there's no other place like—home sweet home.

I popped a beer, flopped down on the couch and listened to my phone messages on the tape gadget that Nate had rigged up for me. There was one from him and one from my ex-father-in-law. O'Leary said his call was urgent. I called Nate.

He whined about Hortense for a while, then got jealous when I told him how smoothly *my* love life had been going. The news came as something of a shock, since I didn't have any love life to speak of the last time we had talked. After promising to join him the next evening to watch *Joe Franklin*, I shocked him again with the news about the fire at Anna Paslawski's house.

"You think Becker must have told Shake your comment about her seeing him the night of the murder. And then he panicked."

That was looking like a distinct possibility. Regardless of what the firemen had said, I didn't think the fire was an accident. I had lied to Becker and Salvino to get a reaction out of them. Evidently, I had triggered more of a reaction than I had expected. I didn't think the world would miss

Anna Paslawski when she departed for other shores. But if she had been in the house when the fire started, you can be sure I would have lost a lot of sleep over it. That's not the sort of thing I like to have on my conscience.

"Yeah," I answered, "but there's another possibility. It's a little farfetched."

"It wouldn't be the first one you've ever presented."

"I wonder if somebody's trying to do an elaborate frame job on Shake."

"With dog shit? That is farfetched."

I told him about the picture of Pete Becker with black shoe polish on his face.

"Well, I guess you might have something there. It would take a guy with shit for brains to think up something like that."

"I'll have to ask Terry if Pete's got a dog."

"Regardless of who's behind the fire, I still think it's a damn tragedy," Nate said. "Now you'll never get the chance to see the old lady's bathroom."

CHAPTER
21

I caught O'Leary just as he was leaving for Happy Hour. As a result, he was only so happy to speak to me. But he still had quite a bit to say.

"I've got lots of good news and a little bit of bad," he said. I braced myself for a long conversation. O'Leary had a habit of telling jokes that started like that, no doubt a result of watching Johnny Carson too often.

This time he wasn't joking.

"You know the lady you've been dying to talk to? I've set up an appointment for you to see her tomorrow morning."

I could tell he was expecting me to thank him profusely. I didn't. But I resisted the temptation of telling him it was about time.

"What's her name?"

"Melody Winchester."

"Melody Winchester?"

"That's right. Surprised?"

Indeed I was. So much for Terry Vreeland's notion that her aunt was only a tease.

"I don't know what surprises me more—that Dwight was

having an affair with her or that you were hired by her. When did you start traveling in such distinguished circles?"

"Fuck you. She remembered me from when I did some work for Winchester—back in the days when he was a decent congressman."

"What century was that?"

"You're an ungrateful bastard, you know that?"

"I do now. What's the bad news?"

"Hold on a second. I've got more good news first. You'll never guess what I discovered when I came into the office this morning."

"A cure for baldness."

"No, asshole. Sometimes I wonder why I bother to put up with you."

"You're going to be wondering a lot harder when you get my bill."

"I found an envelope under my door. It had five thousand dollars in it. The donor wants to remain anonymous. But he read in the paper how much we needed to raise bond for Dwight after the rally. What do you think of that?"

"I think it sounds suspicious. Was there a note with it?"

"Yeah, let me read it to you."

The note indicated that the donation was made by a well-known black athlete.

"Now what do you think?" O'Leary asked.

"I still think it sounds suspicious." I went to the refrigerator and popped open another frosty one. Some people think the telephone is an incredible invention, but I'm more impressed with the miracle of long phone cords.

"Why?"

Other than the fact that it had been left at O'Leary's office instead of with Ed Gallo, I couldn't really come up with a decent reason. But it was another coincidence, and I thought there had been too many of them already.

"I've been scrambling all day to arrange to put up Dwight's car," O'Leary said. "Now you're saying we should let him sit in jail?"

As ridiculous as it sounded, jail almost seemed like the

safest place for him. But I could understand why O'Leary didn't want to be the one explaining that to Dwight Robinson.

"I guess not," I said. "But I think you should keep him away from Wayne Township, just in case."

"I was already thinking of that myself. We could probably put him with Coach Gallo, or I guess he could stay at my place."

I nixed both of those ideas. I wasn't convinced Dwight was in danger, but I didn't think it was safe to assume he wasn't. I suggested my apartment.

"Great," O'Leary said. "We'll send him from the Passaic County Jail to the Manhattan dump."

"You got a better idea?"

Naturally, he didn't.

"When do you think you can get him out?" I asked.

"If things go well, Wednesday afternoon. I'll have to get permission to move him out of state. I could put it off till Thursday, if you need more time to make the place inhabitable."

I told him that wouldn't be necessary. I also directed him to put a lid on his feeble attempts at sarcasm. He said he was only trying to get me back. I told him he was wasting his time. Not to mention mine.

"What about the bad news?" I asked.

"That's a little more complicated. When Melody Winchester retained my services, she said she was only willing to testify at Dwight's trial if it's held *after* election day. She's afraid she might ruin her husband's chances of getting elected if she goes public before then."

"I'd say she's probably right. What's the problem—you got an early trial date?"

"September tenth."

"Can't you get a continuance or something?"

"I just did. Originally, it was scheduled for August. The state's attorney's running for re-election in November, too. I think he'd like to get another conviction under his belt before then. He's one of those young, ambitious types. They make me puke. So now I've got to try to persuade Melody to testify. Unless, of course, you manage to solve the case before then."

I told him there was hope but not enough to start holding his breath.

"Well, maybe you'd be willing to take it up with her. You have such a charming way with the ladies."

"I'll see what I can do. Did you find out anything about the houses on the flood plain?"

"Yeah, I did as a matter of fact. You're going to be very interested to hear about it."

"And when exactly will that be?"

"Right now, if you'll just shut up and listen for a second."

"I'm all ears, counselor."

"It hasn't been determined precisely where the highway is going to be built, but depending on how they map it out, there's probably going to be anywhere from fifty to a hundred homes affected. Sixty of the houses belong to one woman."

He paused to let the suspense build a bit.

"Are you going to tell me her name or do I have to guess?"

"Anna Paslawski."

"Well, I'll be damned." Over the years I've seen enough weird stuff that I rarely have occasion to get surprised. This was one of those rare occasions.

"I thought you'd be interested to hear that." There was a tone approximating smugness in O'Leary's voice. "I think it would be a good idea for you to talk to her about it."

I almost felt guilty one-upping him. "Anna Paslawski's on vacation in the Holy Land. The house she lives in burned down last night."

"Jesus H. Christ!"

I went to the refrigerator and got another beer. We were going to be talking longer than I expected. For starters, I thought O'Leary might know what that middle initial stood for. It was one of the few religious mysteries that interested me.

CHAPTER
22

Melody Winchester lived on Byron Nelson Drive, a couple of blocks over from Thomas Vreeland's estate. The house was set back from the street on a sloping hill that appeared to be the highest point in town. It was a small house compared with Vreeland's, but I figured it could have slept twenty people in a pinch.

As I stood on the front steps waiting for the bell to be answered, I could see the lake and the golf course in the distance to the east. With the morning sun reflecting off the water, it was a pleasant view. But it was nothing compared with the eyeful I got when the huge oak door creaked open.

Given the luxurious aspect of the place, I was a bit surprised that Melody Winchester answered the door herself. That sort of task is usually better left to professionals. She must have felt sheepish about it, because she was quick to explain that it was the maid's day off. I told her I wasn't offended in the least. Dealing with servants has always made me a little uncomfortable.

I had observed that Melody was an attractive woman when I met her at the golf club the previous week, but she looked even better today framed against the doorway in sunshine. In one hand, she was holding a Bloody Mary. On the other, she was wearing a diamond ring the size of a golf ball. I had a feeling it weighed her down a bit, because she was leaning against the door frame for support.

She had ocean-blue eyes that sparkled as she peered out at me against the grain of the sunlight. One look was all it took to realize that Terry Vreeland's aunt was what you call a great piece of work. I tried not to be too obvious about appraising her, but I think maybe that was the intention. Either she had spent a few hours putting herself together or she had already been out to the beauty parlor for the works.

I didn't think the latter possibility was too likely. She was still dressed in her bathrobe.

It was one of those tight-fitting, white gauze affairs that makes a nice contrast on a tanned body. Melody was clearly no stranger to sun worship. And she was still at the age when it hadn't started to exact its inevitable revenge.

The robe ended about eight inches below the point where her thighs began. Whoever bought it for her had failed to take into account that she was a full-figured gal, at least from the waist up. Either that or the store had been out of her regular size. She seemed to be getting the most out of the belt that went with it, although it appeared to limit her freedom of movement a bit. The overall effect was like looking at a pastrami sandwich through a wax-paper wrapper. I happen to be a big pastrami fan.

Melody suggested we go to the living room, then led me through five or ten rooms that could easily have been mistaken for it before we reached our destination. It was a large room with about a hundred square yards of cream-colored wall-to-wall carpeting with a thick, mushy texture. Walking across it was like stepping on a field of marshmallows. I got kind of a pleasant sensation watching Melody negotiate her way through it in a pair of pink high heels.

She motioned for me to take a seat on a black leather sofa that was longer than a subway car. Then she sat down beside me, leaving about the same amount of room you can expect on the subway during rush hour. A pitcher of Bloody Marys was waiting on a glass coffee table in front of us. She leaned over and poured me one without asking if I wanted it.

"I lied about the maid," she said.

"Is that so?" I didn't think to ask why, but she told me anyway.

"Bob fired her. She kept losing his socks when she did the laundry."

"They say it's hard to find good help these days."

"That's not the real reason. I think he's just trying to teach me a lesson. He says I don't appreciate how good I have it. He thinks it would be good exercise for me to clean the house once in a while. If he thinks I'm going to get down on my hands and knees and start being a housekeeper now, I've got news for him."

I tried to stifle the urge to imagine what Melody Winchester might look like bending over to clean the floor in her bathrobe. I was only partially successful.

She let out a harsh laugh and polished off the rest of her drink. "You want another?" she asked.

I showed her my full glass.

"It's his loss," she said. "Now I'm going to have to hire a service to come in and clean the place from top to bottom on Thursday. We're going to have guests coming in and out all weekend on account of the tournament. I told him that, but he just doesn't listen to me. He never listens to me."

I gave her a sympathetic look, all the while thinking that I couldn't blame him. Her parents had no way of knowing at the time, but they had made an ironic selection when they assigned her the name Melody. She was a thrill to behold but a shrill to be heard.

"I take it you and your husband aren't exactly on the best of terms."

"Oh, you are a smart one," she said. "I knew it the first time I laid eyes on you."

She kept laying her eyes on me, and I forced a smile.

"I've been told I'm not as dumb as I look," I said.

She threw back her head and laughed, too long and too hard. At the rate we were moving, I might wind up being there all day. I had a feeling she wouldn't have minded that.

At another time and place, I probably wouldn't have objected myself.

"Does your husband know you're having an affair with Dwight Robinson?"

She seemed startled by the question. I have to admit, it was a little direct. But it seemed to have a sobering effect, which is exactly what I wanted.

"Sure, he knew about him. You want to know how he found out? I told him. I laid it all on the line." She laughed, a short one this time. "Of course, that was after Thomas Vreeland told him about us."

"How did Vreeland find out?"

"Why Cynthia told him, of course!"

"I heard Dwight was under the impression Cynthia didn't know about it."

"Well, Dwight's kind of dumb. But I still like him. He's got some other valuable assets working in his favor." She gave me a knowing smile. I pretended not to see it.

"What did your husband say when you told him?"

She shrugged. "What could he say? My dear husband and I are through. Done. Finished. Over and out. *Kaput.* The only thing he cares about is getting elected to the Senate. We've already agreed to get a divorce. But I promised to wait until after election day. The last thing he needs right now is a domestic scandal. I figured I owed him that much."

Melody leaned her head back and let go with another one of her short laughs. "Besides, he agreed to sweeten the settlement if I would."

This time, I returned her smile. It was clear that Melody Winchester had her share of shortcomings, but beating around the bush wasn't one of them. I kind of liked that.

"Cynthia *was* planning to file for divorce," I said. "Do you think your husband was worried that your name would have surfaced in the divorce petition?"

"Why of course, wouldn't you be?"

I told her I certainly would, giving her just enough time to realize what I was getting at.

"Are you asking if I think *Bob* killed Cynthia?"

I leaned over and poured myself another Bloody Mary.

Except for seeing him on TV a couple of times and reading about him occasionally in the newspaper, I didn't know very much about Congressman Bob Winchester. But I had seen enough to know that I didn't particularly care for him. As politicians go, he probably wasn't any more or less sleazy than the next guy. But to my way of thinking, just the fact that he was a politician made him sleazy enough.

"He wouldn't have had to do it himself," I said. "He could have hired somebody to do it for him."

Melody shook her head. At the same time, she rearranged herself on the couch, affording me a glimpse of smooth, bronze thigh leading right up to the bottom of her panty line. Funny thing, though. I didn't see any panty line. Maybe that's because she wasn't wearing any panties. Maybe the maid had lost them.

I felt a little shiver run up my spine and resolved to keep my attention focused at eye level.

"Bob's a driven man," Melody said. "I know some of the things he's done, and I can tell you he's not the saint that some of the people around here make him out to be. If the people who voted for him knew one-third of what I do about him, they wouldn't vote for him again. But he would never kill anyone. Especially not his own niece."

I wasn't entirely convinced, but I didn't press the point.

"Besides," she added, "I already know who killed Cynthia."

I raised my eyebrows in the form of a question mark. Figuratively speaking, of course.

"Shake Johnson." Her speech slurred a bit when she pronounced the name. I wondered how many drinks she had poured down before I got there.

"What makes you think that?"

"Dwight had a lot of gambling debts. Sometimes I think he was just using me, because he knew I'd give him money when he needed it. Sometimes I wonder if he cares about me at all. As soon as Terry came back from Florida and they started playing golf together, he wasn't so interested in me anymore. I'm not stupid. I can figure out what's going on between them."

I could see tears starting to well up in the corners of her eyes. All of a sudden, I started to feel very sorry for Melody Winchester. I also didn't like the direction she was heading in. I stopped her before she went too far.

"Dwight likes you a lot," I said. "And there's nothing going on between him and Terry—I'm sure of it."

She gave me a hopeful look as I refilled her glass. "You're positive?"

I nodded. "Absolutely."

"You're kind of friendly with Terry, aren't you?" There was a dawn of recognition spreading over her face.

"I only met her last week," I said. "But she seems nice."

I was afraid she might try to pry further. Instead, she pried her calves underneath her thighs and leaned against me. It occurred to me that Terry might have been right about her aunt, after all. Melody came on like a B-movie queen, but I got the impression all she really wanted was a little affection. Unfortunately for her, the way she went about trying to get it was far more likely to elicit lust.

I tried to suppress mine without pulling away from her. It was no easy task, but I'm a professional.

"Yeah, Terry's OK," she said dreamily.

"What about Shake Johnson?" I asked.

"Dwight owed him a thousand dollars. Shake was supposed to go to his house and get it the night Cynthia was killed. When I met him at the motel that night, I gave him the money. He was supposed to meet Shake at ten, but, well . . ." She gave me that knowing smile. "I guess we kind of lost track of time."

"What time did Dwight leave?"

"It was after eleven. No, eleven-thirty. Dwight wanted to watch the sports news. You always have to be quiet when the sports comes on."

"How long would it have taken him to get home?"

"Just a few minutes." She grinned, sheepishly. "We go to the Howard Johnson's on Route 23 up at Ratzer Road."

I told her I knew the place. "Does your husband know you were with Dwight the night Cynthia was killed?"

"I don't think so. He might have figured it out, being I got home so late. But he hasn't said anything." Her voice trailed off a bit. "We really don't speak to each other much. Basically, we just fight a lot."

I started to move away from her a bit, and I could feel an alarm go off inside her.

"You're not going yet, are you?"

I told her I was thinking about it.

She squeezed my arm. "Please stay and have another drink."

I took her up on her offer. I figured she might start crying again if I didn't. Besides, I still had a few more matters to discuss. A third drink wouldn't kill me, even if it was a Bloody Mary. But I wondered again how many Melody had poured down. I had that sinking feeling I might end up carrying her to bed. A situation like that can get pretty messy.

"I've got good news and bad news," I said. I felt like I was imitating Mike O'Leary imitating Johnny Carson. Which means I felt pretty stupid. "The good news is that Dwight's getting out of jail tomorrow."

Good news only to some people apparently. I felt the alarm go off inside Melody Winchester again. It registered on her face as a look of terror. I wondered what she'd look like when I gave her the bad news.

"What's wrong?" I asked.

"I don't think that's a very good idea."

"If you're afraid he's going to talk, I don't think you have to worry about that."

"No, that's not it at all." Her speech was getting really slurred now, and she was starting to feel like a dead weight against me. "I'm worried that he might get hurt."

"By your husband?"

"No. My nephew, Tommy. You saw what a temper he has the other day." She smiled and rubbed my shoulder. "Where did you learn to fight like that?"

I ignored the question, and the massage. "He'll be safe," I assured her. "He's going to stay with me at my apartment. But there's another problem. It's about the trial date. It's going to be earlier than we expected."

"Not before election day."

"I'm afraid so."

"But O'Leary promised . . ."

"There's nothing he could do about it. Unless I can find the killer—"

"I told you: It's Shake Johnson."

"I've got to be able to prove it."

She sighed and leaned forward to reach for her pack of cigarettes on the coffee table. She put the drink on the table and held on to me with one hand for balance. The belt on her robe had come loose, and I got an eyeful of the breast she had to offer.

I lit the cigarette for her and one for me. "Would you be willing to testify?"

She sucked hard on the cigarette. "Fuck it, I don't care." She closed her eyes. I could tell she was fighting off the spins. Before noon. What a goddamn shame. "Sure, I'll testify," she said at last. "I'll do anything you want me to do." She opened her eyes and smiled. "Anything at all."

I slid one arm around her back and the other under her legs. As I lifted her off the couch and stood up, she asked, "Are we going to bed now?"

"Show me the way."

The bedroom was on the second floor, near the top of a grand, spiraling staircase with a white marble railing. If this was a typical drinking day for Melody Winchester, it was a wonder she hadn't fallen down it and broken her beautiful neck.

By the time I put her down on the bed, she had lost both of her shoes, most of her robe and all of her consciousness. When she woke up, she was going to have some kind of headache. What a way to live.

As I pulled out of the driveway, I saw a black Lincoln coming up the street. Congressman Bob Winchester peered out the driver's side window at me when I drove by. I wondered if he had fired his chauffeur. I gave him a friendly nod, but I didn't bother to stop and introduce myself.

CHAPTER
23

"Holy cards," Nate said. "Every goddamn inch of the wall was plastered with holy cards. Now I've heard of some weird concepts in wallpapering, but you've never seen anything so bizarre in your whole life as a room the size of a doghouse with five thousand little pictures of Jesus Christ staring at you."

Nate is not usually so lively in the A.M., but this morning he had a new and captive audience—Terry Vreeland.

We were on our way out to Jersey. Yes, again. After I left Melody Winchester's the day before—and after knocking back a few real drinks at a saloon in Mountain View called Gabriel's—I decided to drop by Terry's house for a visit. One thing led to another, and the next thing I knew, she was accompanying me back to New York to watch the *Joe Franklin Show* at Nate's apartment. I took that as a sign that she was either crazy about me or just plain crazy.

The program had been edited, just as Nate predicted. But they had left in his plug for the Sarah Winchester Vreeland Memorial Golf tournament, which earned him a few points with Terry.

"But where in the world did you get the idea that Frank Sinatra and Dean Martin are going to be there?" she asked.

Nate got an expression on his face that looked like an equal mix of bafflement and disappointment. If he were forty years younger, you might have thought he had just learned there wasn't any Santa Claus.

"You mean to tell me they're not?" he asked.

"I think you were misinformed," Terry said. "It's Frank Sinatra, *Junior* and *Dino* Martin."

"You've got to be kidding. Couldn't you get anybody bigger than that?"

Terry shrugged. "Well, I heard Morey Amsterdam is coming—you know, the short guy from the *Dick Van Dyke Show*."

"Oh, he's real big," Nate answered. "What's the matter? Couldn't you get Dick Van Dyke?"

She shook her head. "No, but *Jerry* Van Dyke may be coming."

"Oh, yeah, he's big, too. And funny. He's even funnier than Don Knotts. Of course, that's just my personal opinion. What about females?"

Terry grinned and shot me a helpless look. "You're talking to the wrong person. I don't pay much attention to this stuff. But I heard somebody mention something about Joey Heatherton and Peggy Lipton."

"Who's Peggy Lipton?" I asked.

"*The Mod Squad*," Nate answered. That didn't clarify things any for me, but I figured she must have been with a rock band.

"Let's see." Terry was touching the pretty little pinky of one hand with the slender index finger of her other, getting ready to count off. She ran out of celebrities before she ran out of fingers. "Trini Lopez, Orson Bean, Alan Hale, Kitty Carlisle . . ." She pronounced each name almost as a question. I couldn't tell whether she was unsure they were coming or uncertain that they existed at all.

"Oh," she said, "I thought of somebody. Is there a hockey player named Gump something?"

"Worsley," I said. He was a goalie who used to play for the Rangers. He was good—after they traded him to Montreal. I recalled a game I had seen at Madison Square Garden when he had been hit by a frozen egg thrown by some balcony savage and had to be carried off the ice. The Rangers lost the game.

"I don't know if you'd count this guy as a celebrity," Terry said. "Have you ever heard of Roy Cohn?"

"Oh, Jesus," Nate said. "What's he going to be doing there—investigating communist infiltration among the caddies?"

Terry laughed. "Roy Cohn is my father's lawyer," she said.

Nate let out a soft whistle, then finished off his beer. I hadn't been counting, but I think he had consumed the equivalent of a keg. "Yeah, that's quite a lineup you've got there."

"Now I understand why you were invited," I told him.

"Just be sure to remember who's the celebrity and who's along to carry the bag," he answered.

We left him sitting on the sofa in his living room, gleefully groaning out the names of numerous second-rate show business personalities. The man is a living encyclopedia of useless information. When we picked him up the next morning, he started in right where he left off. By the time we passed through the so-called Meadowlands, a swampy burial ground for mobsters that a gaggle of Jersey politicians was plotting to turn into a sports complex, he had moved on to the subject of Anna Paslawski's bathroom.

Ever the gentleman, Nate had insisted on letting Terry have the front seat. I didn't know how he had managed to get himself into the backseat, but I was sure getting him out wouldn't be as easy. His voice was booming in my ear.

"So there I am trying to get up the nerve to take a leak with Jesus staring at me from all sides," he said. "When I go to lift the seat cover, what do I see but a huge black-and-white photo of her husband—right on the goddamn commode."

"How did you know it was her husband?" Terry asked.

"Because she had his name printed right underneath it—

in red crayon. And it says, 'Rest in peace.' How's the poor guy supposed to rest in peace when . . ." Nate's voice trailed off. I think he caught himself just before he was about to say something that he thought might have offended Terry. He's a thoughtful kind of guy.

"But the best part is that it must have been the last photo ever taken of old Ed. He was already laid out in the coffin."

"That's bizarre," Terry said.

"I'm glad you agree," Nate replied. "I was afraid maybe it was just me."

We dropped Terry off at her house before going to Paterson to pick up Dwight Robinson. Terry wanted to see Dwight, but she was concerned there might be TV cameras on hand to cover his release. She didn't want to get caught in a family controversy.

It was a legitimate concern. The story of Dwight's mystery donor had made the front page of the New York *Daily News* that morning. The night before, Thomas Vreeland and Bob Winchester had made the rounds on TV, both condemning the decision to let Dwight out on bail. When Nate and I arrived at the county courthouse, a crowd of reporters was gathered on Hamilton Street waiting for a juicy quote.

They didn't get one.

I'm sure Mike O'Leary wouldn't have minded a few minutes in the glare of the media spotlight, but his better judgment told him to keep Dwight out of it. O'Leary has good judgment. He just doesn't use it very often.

We hustled Dwight out a side door and into O'Leary's car before the press corps could get to us. After a short visit with his mother up in Singac, Dwight, Nate and I were on our way back to New York.

O'Leary hadn't been too keen on swapping his Buick for my Corvair overnight, but he was roundly out-voted. His client wasn't too keen on going anywhere with us, but he didn't even get a vote. Once we got him liquored up and stuffed full of non-prison chow at Downey's steak house, he stopped complaining. It probably didn't hurt that we entertained him with stories about our encounters with Shake

Johnson and Pete Becker. As the evening wore on, you might even say Dwight got friendly.

"O'Leary says you used to play ball, Renzler."

I told him it was true.

"You any good?"

"Some people thought so." I told him about my conversation with Coach Gallo and his recollection of pitching against me.

Dwight shook his head and laughed. It was a nice, easy, deceptive laugh. When he wasn't brooding, he sounded like a guy who didn't have a care in the world.

"Coach understands the theory of the game, but I don't think he was too good at the execution part," he said. "Me— I was the best. They've had a lot of good Robinsons playing ball in the big leagues—Jackie Robinson, Frank Robinson, Brooks Robinson, Floyd Robinson—but they said I was better than any of them."

I nodded politely, figuring it wouldn't do any good to remind Dwight that he had never made the major leagues.

"You know what they used to call me?" he asked. "They used to call me the black Mickey Mantle."

"They used to call Renzler the next Jerry Coleman," Nate said.

"Who's that?"

"Before your time," I explained.

"Why'd you quit?"

I told him the story. It seemed like I had been telling it an awful lot lately.

"Damn!" he said, when I finished. "You and me got a lot in common. And I thought *I* got fucked."

"Yeah, we do and you did," I told him. "But we've been hearing some people think it didn't have to be that way. Some people seem to think you got busted on account of your brother."

Robinson had been slouching in his chair, but he sat up straight at the mention of Dexter. The smile that had been forming steadily at the corners of his mouth disappeared quicker than a Sandy Koufax fastball.

"What's between me and my brother stays between me and my brother," he said. "You understand where I'm coming from?"

"Your brother's a goddamn cretin," Nate answered. "You understand where *I'm* coming from?"

I don't think Dwight was familiar with the term, but he understood its meaning from the tone and context. He was back inside the brooding shell again, staring at Nate as if he were thinking about taking a swing at him. Something made him decide not to. It might have been the realization that Nate had knocked the lights out of Pete Becker and Shake Johnson's dog. Or maybe it had something to do with knowing that Nate was right about Dexter.

Dwight leaned back in his chair and tapped himself on the chest a couple of times with a long finger. The guy did look like a natural athlete. Even his fingers were in shape.

"All the same, that's my problem," he said. "I'm the one that's got to deal with it. I got a problem with my brother, I take care of it my own way."

"Fair enough," I said. I had been thinking about raising the question of whether Dexter might have had something to do with Cynthia's murder. Now it seemed like a good idea not to press him on it. At least not yet. "We just don't like to see you taking the rap for something that he did."

"What? You think I do? Don't get the idea I like it any more than you do. Because I don't. I just got my own ways of dealing with some things." He didn't bother to elaborate on what that might be.

I raised a cautioning finger. "I just hope your ways don't get you in any more trouble. Because right now, that's the last thing you need."

"Yeah, I hear you."

CHAPTER
——24——

We kissed Nate good-bye outside a deli on Columbus Avenue near Seventy-second Street. Then we went inside and bought Dwight a fifth of Boone's Farm Apple Wine. I had stocked the refrigerator with beer and the liquor cabinet with booze in anticipation of his visit, but somehow I had overlooked the Boone's Farm.

"This stuff goes down real smooth, man," he said, clutching the bottle and grinning.

I told him I'd take his word for it.

Dwight stalked through the apartment silently, checking the place out like a cat marking off new turf. The only difference was he went to the bathroom to relieve himself.

"Does it meet your approval?" I asked him.

He shrugged. "I stayed in worse dumps before." The smirk was in evidence again. "It's better than the place I stayed last night."

"That nice?" We did have a lot in common. This kid was a smartass, too. "Well, make yourself at home," I said. "Think of yourself as a jewel on the cushion of hospitality."

He nodded. "Sounds all right. But where do I sleep?"

"I'll take the couch and you can have the bedroom. I put clean sheets on the bed for you this morning."

"Man, you're like a regular housewife almost."

"Almost. Just don't expect breakfast in bed, sweetheart."

"Shit. From a wife? Man, you're lucky just to get a piece of ass once a month."

"Well, don't expect that from me, either."

Dwight gave me a skeptical look, then cracked the smile barrier. He refused my offer of a glass, preferring to drink his wine right from the bottle. I got myself a beer, and sat down across from him at the kitchen table.

"You mind if I ask you a few questions?"

"Go ahead. I got all day."

That was the same thing he had said to me the first time I had asked him that question. This time, I expected to get a lot more out of him. I had told him about talking with Terry Vreeland and Melody Winchester. There was no good reason for him not to trust me now.

"Was Cynthia seeing someone else?"

Dwight shrugged and took a pull off his bottle. "I don't know. I suppose it's possible. Things were pretty weird around our house. I sure wasn't getting any." He smirked. "Not from her, at least."

"Terry told me that Cynthia and Tommy used to play around together."

I caught him in mid-swallow, and Dwight sent a shower of apple wine across the table. Being out of paper towels, I wiped up the mess with a handful of toilet paper.

"She told you about *that*?" At first I thought he was angry, then I realized he might have been relieved.

I nodded. "She told me a lot of stuff."

"Man, that's a *strange* family. White folks think *we* got problems. Terry, too. She could be on the tour right now, if she'd just go out and do it instead of sitting around thinking about all the reasons it might not work out."

I had a feeling Dwight was right, but I didn't want to get into a discussion about Terry. "What about Tommy and Cynthia? How did you find out about them?"

"Terry told me. She said she was worried about me, but I think maybe she just didn't like Cynthia. They had kind of a rivalry going on."

"Did you ever think they might still be involved—after you and she got married?"

"I don't spend too much time thinking about things I don't like to think about. Tommy, you see, he and me used to be friends, but it changed almost as soon as he found out me and Cynthia were thinking about getting married. I think maybe that was the reason. I just wish she'd have told me about it sooner. Then I wouldn't be in this fucking mess."

"What were they like together—Tommy and Cynthia?"

"Weird. Man, that's the only way to describe it—weird. They used to fight all the time, you know, but it wasn't like just arguing."

"You mean like nagging."

"Yeah, man, that's it. Nagging. Now that I look back on it, I think maybe they were still doing it. You know, when I was playing ball, Cynthia never wanted to come with me. I don't know what she was doing." The smirk came back on his face. "But I didn't care. I was having a good time of my own."

Dwight rocked back on his chair and listened while I explained to him what was on my mind. I wondered if Cynthia Vreeland might have taken up with a new lover and what her brother might have done if she had. I wondered if Tommy might have gotten mad enough to kill her.

"Damn. I don't know. I don't think Tommy would've *tried* to kill her, but that boy's got a bad temper on him. Real bad. He jumped all over me one night for no reason."

"Yeah, I heard he paid for it, too." I told him about my encounter with Tommy and the conversation I had with Pop when I was leaving the country club.

"That's right, man, he paid for it. But when the police get there, they're saying *I* started it. Any time you get a white guy and a black guy, they're always going to take the word of the white guy. That's how it works. White justice. All the time. Just like the time with that asshole living across the street from us."

"Who's that? Not Warren Shepherd?"

"I don't know what his name is. Yeah, Shepherd—maybe that's it. Yeah, that's it. Just another crazy cracker asshole to me."

"What happened?"

"I got arrested—that's what happened."

"Why?" I resisted the urge to tell Dwight that people don't get arrested for no reason. He wouldn't have believed me. Then again, I might have been wrong.

"I told him I was going to kill him—that's why."

"And why did you do that?"

"A lot of reasons. He used to come over and talk to Cynthia sometimes. And then sometimes I used to see him watching us out of his picture window. With binoculars."

"Did you call the police?"

Dwight gave me a look that told me what a dumb question I had asked. I put up my arms in defense. "I know, I know," I said. "White justice."

"Yeah, believe it. I told that motherfucker if I ever seen him spying on us again, he'd be eating binoculars for the rest of his life, which wouldn't be all that long considering the circumstances."

"Did you hit him?"

"Shit, no. I just grabbed him by the collar, you know, and shook him around a bit. He wasn't hurt. I just scared his ass a little."

I tried to picture Dwight shaking Warren Shepherd. It was a good bet that Shepherd was more than a little scared. "So then he called the cops," I said.

"No, man, Cynthia did that! She was afraid I would've killed the dude. I wouldn't have done that. I could've killed her, though, for calling them." I caught Dwight's eyes, and he realized what he had said. "I don't mean that. But I sure was pissed at her, you better believe it. She's the one that brought it on in the first place."

"What do you mean?"

"She was always walking around the house with nothing on, or just her underwear. I told her she shouldn't go walking around with her tits showing, but she didn't listen to me. She wouldn't even pull the shades down. I figure that dude must've been froze to the window every night beating his meat."

"Did you ever hit Cynthia?"

"Shit. Who told you that—Terry?"

I shook my head. "I got it third-hand. That's what Tommy Vreeland told the police."

"That motherfucker." He took a swig from the wine bottle and licked his lips. Then he held up a finger. "One time. Only one time and that was it. And all I did was slap her. You should've seen what she did to me. She was in a *rage*. She used to get like that—all of a sudden. I don't even remember what I did, but all of sudden she's screaming and yelling and she comes at me swinging a vase. She hit me right across here."

He leaned over the table and pointed his finger at a spot on his temple. There might have been a small scar, but I couldn't see it. I nodded anyway, pretending that I did. I was willing to take his word for it. But I still had a nagging doubt that Dwight wasn't telling me everything. I didn't think he had killed his wife, but I had the distinct impression he wasn't the slightest bit unhappy she was dead.

"What about Pete Becker?" I asked. "Did he ever show any interest in Cynthia?"

"Man, you kidding? Becker's a queer. Everybody knows that."

I was going to ask him just how everybody knew, but the ringing of the telephone put an end to our conversation. Melody Winchester sounded a bit more coherent than the last time I had spoken with her. She apologized for passing out on me, and I assured her that I didn't mind. We chatted for a moment, but it was clear she wasn't calling to speak to me. She wanted to talk to my roommate.

I held the phone to my ear while waiting for Dwight to pick up the extension in the bedroom. I thought I heard a click on the line right after he came on, but it could have been my imagination.

"Is there a third party on the line?" I asked.

I didn't hear anything, except for Dwight's booming voice.

"Yeah, dude, and you're it. How about letting me have a private chat with the lady?"

"Go right ahead, sir," I answered. "Just let me know when you want me to come in and fluff up your pillow."

CHAPTER
25

On Thursday morning, I made Dwight promise not to leave the apartment for more than three hours. I would have made it less, but there was a Pam Grier movie playing on Forty-second Street that he was just dying to see. I couldn't see any harm in that, and I figured it might keep him from going stir-crazy. It might also make him easier to put up with when I got back home.

While making the car switch at O'Leary's office in Paterson, I asked him to run a check on Warren Shepherd. I could have done it myself, but that sort of thing can get time-consuming. Since O'Leary had done such a good job investigating Thomas Vreeland's land holdings, I figured I'd reward him with another assignment.

It was nearing the end of lunch hour by the time Nate and I reached the Felsway Corporation on Riverview Drive in Wayne. It was a hideous brown-and-white building, set back from the road in a sprawling cluster of undistinguished flat-roofed warehouses that developers like to call an industrial "park." I guess it was only fitting that Felsway headquarters looked like a giant shoe box. The company operated Shoe-

Town, a chain of discount stores littering every highway in New Jersey, part of the ongoing campaign to keep the Garden State ugly.

I knew a little something about the outfit, because I had once spent a very long evening with a friend of my brother-in-law who worked there. He was the kind of dull guy who can talk for hours about his job, always referring to his company as "we" and "us." Of course, he had some lofty title like vice-president in charge of sneakers. Something told me Warren Shepherd wasn't inclined to speak of his employer in such close, personal terms.

I usually don't go to see people while they're working, because they tend to get uncomfortable. In Shepherd's case, I was more than willing to make an exception. Making him uncomfortable was exactly what I wanted to do.

We found him sitting on a stack of cardboard slabs near the back of the warehouse, eating a baloney sandwich on white bread and drinking a carton of chocolate milk. I wouldn't say he looked especially happy to see us.

I told him we only wanted to ask a couple of questions, but that didn't improve his demeanor. He told us we had no business being there. If we didn't leave right away, he'd call his boss.

"Fine," I answered. "We'd be glad to ask your boss how he feels about having an employee who likes to go around peering into his neighbors' windows. I hear forklift operators aren't too hard to replace."

Shepherd thought it over while finishing off his carton of milk. It left a brown mustache over his curled upper lip. He wiped the mustache away on the sleeve of his work shirt and said, "Where'd you get that bullshit?"

"We heard all about how you used to stand at your picture window with your binoculars, peeping on Cynthia Vreeland," I said.

"Bullshit. That asshole told you that. He doesn't know what the fuck he's talkin' about."

"I suppose he must have imagined it. I suppose you don't even own a pair of binoculars."

He got up from his lunch table. "Sure I do. But I got better things to do than spy on some jig. I like to watch birds. It's my hobby."

If Warren Shepherd was a bird watcher, I was a goddamn nuclear physicist. I opened the Mountain Lake yearbook to the page with the caddy pictures. I pointed to the picture of Shake Johnson. "Have you ever seen this guy before?"

Shepherd pretended to glance at the picture casually, but he was taking a good, long look. After a moment, he shrugged. "I don't know. This picture is awful small. Should I have?"

"He probably had a dog with him. A big, black one."

"Oh, yeah, sure. I used to see him going over to their house once in a while. That's the guy from the golf course. Matter of fact, he came around to Mrs. Paslawski's house just the other day. Scared her half to death."

"How do you know that? Did you see him?"

"No. She told me about it."

"Did she say what he wanted?"

"You kiddin'? She didn't even open the door and talk to him. I don't blame her."

"We hear you and Mrs. Paslawski are kind of friendly," Nate said.

Shepherd seemed startled. "She's a lonely old lady. I go over there once in a while, have a bowl of soup, help her with the chores around the yard." He glowered at Nate. "There ain't a law against that, is there?"

I pointed at Shake Johnson's picture again. "You didn't see him the night of the murder, did you?"

He shook his head. "I already told you everything I saw that night." He looked at his watch. "Now, if you don't mind, I got to get back to work."

"What about this guy?" I pointed to the picture of Dexter Robinson.

Shepherd studied it casually for a few seconds. "That's him," he said.

"Who? Dwight Robinson?"

"Yeah, that's him."

"Are you positive?"

"Hey, what is this?"

"Just answer the question," Nate said.

Shepherd gave him a long, cold stare. "Yeah, I'm positive."

"This is Dwight Robinson," I said, moving my finger to another photo. "That one was his brother."

"Aw, fuck. So you tricked me. Big deal. How're you supposed to tell these boogies apart?"

"That's your problem," I said. "You're the witness."

"Hey, I already talked to the police. I don't have to talk to you guys." He began to walk away.

We joined him, one of us on either side. I think he was feeling a little flustered.

"You said you saw Dwight Robinson driving away from his house in a white Oldsmobile the night of the murder. Is that right?"

He ignored the question and kept on walking.

"Is that right?"

Shepherd stopped in his tracks. This time, he raised his voice. "Yeah, that's right."

"Wrong," I said. "Robinson drives a Cadillac, not an Oldsmobile."

"Aw, what's the fuckin' difference? It was a nigger in a pimpmobile."

I answered his glare with a big smile. "Thanks, that's exactly what we wanted to hear."

Shepherd shook his head in disgust and turned quickly away.

"What a shame," Nate said. "I think we ruined his lunch hour."

We watched Warren Shepherd moping his way toward a cluster of guys who were starting to work. Before he reached them, a beefy red-haired guy with a mug like one of those holiday cheese balls appeared from behind a stack of boxes. I figured him for the foreman, as soon as I glimpsed the necktie with Rheingold beer logos.

"Hey, Shepherd," he said. "Lunchtime's over. Get back to

work. Just because you gave two week's notice don't mean you can take early retirement."

Shepherd's boss rotated his head slowly and circum-navigated his way into our orbit. He began giving us the once-over. Now that I got the benefit of a full-figure profile, I realized he looked like a cheese ball short stack.

"Your friends can meet you at the gin mill later on," he said.

Nate assured him that we most certainly were not friends. When we hit the parking lot, he said, "Curious that old Warren should be quitting his job."

Yes it was. And it was clear that he hadn't wanted us to know. Otherwise he would have fetched the cheese ball as soon as we started pressing him.

"Well, at least I've finally figured out what Warren's story is," he said.

"Yes?"

"I think Warren Shepherd's just a triple-E man living in a double-E world."

CHAPTER
26

It appeared that nothing had changed at the Wayne police station since the last time we were there. Hal Pucinsky had just finished sinking an eight-foot putt into one of those aluminum golf cups when we stepped into his office. I guess he didn't care about making an impression on us. Either that, or he was suffering from a bad case of tournament fever.

The chunky chief motioned for us to take the chairs across from his desk, but he continued with his putting.

"I've been getting some complaints on you guys," he said, without looking up. "Bothering Mr. Vreeland at his house, then starting a fight with his son at the golf course, then picking another fight at Pete's. I thought I told you guys to stay out of trouble."

"We haven't started any of it," I answered. "We left Vreeland's house as soon as he told us to. I only slugged the kid *after* he smacked his sister. And there wasn't any trouble at the bar until Pete Becker pulled a gun on us."

Pucinsky sank a short putt, then walked to his desk and lit a cigarette. "I've got to give up these goddamn cancer

171

sticks," he muttered. Then he looked down his beak at me. "That's not the way I heard it. It's funny how different people give you different stories."

"We've been running into a lot of that ourselves lately," Nate said.

"So what's the occasion for your visit?" the chief asked.

"You come up with any murder suspects?"

"Yeah, too many," I said.

Pucinsky didn't ask who they were, and I didn't bother to tell him. If I mentioned all the names on our list, he would have laughed us right out of his office. I asked him some of my own questions instead.

"You told us Shake Johnson was drinking at Pete's the night of the murder. Who supplied his alibi?"

Pucinsky crushed out his cigarette and went back to work with his putter.

"I already told you—Tommy Vreeland. They were drinking together."

"Tommy was drunk that night. So drunk that he banged up his sister Terry's car. You want to know what kind it is?"

He didn't look up. "I've seen it. It's a white Olds."

"We just had a chat with Warren Shepherd," I said. "He can't tell the difference between an Oldsmobile and a Cadillac. We also showed him a couple of pictures. It turns out he can't tell Dwight Robinson from his brother, Dexter."

Pucinsky looked up and yawned. At least we had eye contact again. "He gave us a positive ID when we took his statement. He gave a positive ID to the D.A. when they took a deposition. Far as I'm concerned, that's all we need."

"Believe me," I said. "The guy's not going to hold up in court."

"That's the prosecutor's problem—not mine."

And this guy said *I* had a bad attitude. "Doesn't that make you wonder even a little?"

"About what?"

"Whether or not Tommy Vreeland and Shake Johnson were at the bar all night."

He let out an impatient sigh. "Pete Becker and Ray Salvino said they were."

"We talked to them," Nate said. "We got the impression they weren't so sure about that."

"Is that so?" Pucinsky moved to the desk and sat down. It seemed like we almost had his interest. "Did they tell you that?" he asked.

I shook my head. "Not in so many words. We read their reaction to something I said."

"And what would that be?"

I felt sheepish saying it, but that didn't stop me. After all, Pucinsky was the top cop in town, and he didn't have anything better to do than stroke his putter all day.

"I told them Anna Paslawski saw Shake go into Dwight and Cynthia's place the night she was killed."

Pucinsky started giving me the eyeball treatment. I thought his brow had gotten thicker since the last time we saw him. "And just why the fuck did you do that?"

"To make them think a little. And it might have worked. Two days later, Anna Paslawski's house burned down. I don't think it was a coincidence. Do you?"

"It was an accidental fire," he said. "She probably left a cigarette burning."

"Another thing we found out: Thomas Vreeland has been buying up houses along the flood plain. His brother-in-law, the congressman, is feeding him info on where the new interstate highway is going through. The owner of the houses is listed as Anna Paslawski. That's a curious coincidence, don't you think?"

Pucinsky scratched a pimple on his chin. It looked like his thoughtful pose. Like me, he hadn't shaved that morning. I hoped it was the only thing we had in common.

"Yeah, I guess it is kind of curious," he said at last. "So what are you implying—that Mr. Vreeland and Mr. Winchester hired somebody to torch the house? What would they have to gain from that?"

"I don't know. I'm not saying they had anything to do with it. My point is that there seem to be quite a few cozy little relationships in this town that elude the attention of the local authorities." I didn't bother to add that eluding the local authorities was probably easier than taking a leak.

"I checked around the outside of the house," I said. "I found a clue that your guys must have overlooked."

"We didn't investigate it," he corrected. "That's the fire department's responsibility."

I resisted the urge to ask him if golfing was part of his job description.

"So what was this clue you found?"

I knew what his response would be. He started to chuckle as soon as I told him. The chuckle increased in intensity until it reached a crescendo of gasping laughter. Between breaths, he managed to blurt out, "Dog shit, huh? You didn't ask it any questions, did you? I mean—to see if you could read its reaction?"

The police chief's joke triggered a wave of self-congratulatory laughter. He began coughing, and his chubby face got more bloated as the blood rushed into it. If Hal Pacinsky howled himself into a heart attack, I wouldn't be in any hurry to call the paramedics.

"You guys are a piece of work," he managed, still heaving.

Nate stood up. "I think we're wasting our time," he said to me.

"And mine," Pucinsky added, wiping tears from his eyes. He started to laugh again, then caught himself. It can get lonely laughing alone. "Listen," he said in a suddenly serious voice, "if it was anybody else but Dwight Robinson, I might be inclined to believe you. But you guys just don't seem to get it: You just can't trust that kid."

"I got it now," Nate replied. "But guys like Thomas Vreeland and Bob Winchester—they're as honest as the day is long."

"That's right," I told him. "And if you're a small-town cop, what they lack in honesty they make up for in bestowing privileges. Free greens fees can go a long way."

Pucinsky stood up and pointed at the door. For some reason, he wasn't laughing anymore. He wasn't even smiling. "Get the hell out of here," he said. "I've given you two jerks enough of my valuable time for one day."

As we turned to leave, I heard a crunch of metal to my right. I looked in time to see one of Nate's size-13 boots stepping off a stroke of bad luck on the police chief's putting tray.

Nate bent over slowly and picked it up. "Sorry about that." He dropped it on the desk and smiled. "It was an accident. You know—kind of like Anna Paslawski's fire."

Pucinsky glowered and we got out of there before he decided to arrest us for illegal trespass.

CHAPTER
27

On our way out of town, we took a swing down through Mountain View. Since we seemed to be doing such a bang-up job of making people uncomfortable, I thought it might be a good idea to stop by Pete's and have one for the road.

Maybe they saw us coming. When we pulled into the gravel parking lot, the tavern was shut up tighter than a mobster testifying before a grand jury. It seemed a little surprising that a bar would be closed around the start of Happy Hour. But Pete's was the sort of place that's filled with surprises.

Unfortunately, that wasn't the only one we encountered.

Nate volunteered to join my new roommate and me for dinner again. He's always willing to eat, especially if the meal is free. But when we got back to my apartment, a note on the kitchen table made me lose my appetite.

It was written in a shaky scrawl, along the lines of what you'd expect from a fourth-grader. Evidently, Dwight Robinson had never been subjected to the torture of the Palmer Method.

The note said: "Went out for air, catch you later. D." It had been written at noon.

"Six hours worth of air seems like an awful lot to me," Nate said.

My sentiments exactly.

I called downstairs to Pressie, our combination doorman and security guard. The security part is a joke. Pressie has to be at least eighty years old, and he has considerable difficulty just opening the door. Like me, he's blind in one eye. This isn't a severe occupational handicap, because he spends most of the day with his eyes closed, listening to Coleman Hawkins on a portable tape recorder that I think predates the airplane.

It was unlikely that Pressie would have noticed Dwight Robinson. But since Dwight liked to chat with Pop at the golf course, I figured there was a chance he might have initiated a conversation with Pressie.

Apparently, he hadn't. Or if he had, Pressie didn't remember. Most of Pressie's recollections start and end before the war.

I got on the horn to Mike O'Leary. Instead of my ex-father-in-law, I got another surprise—my ex-wife.

"What a pleasant surprise!" Kathy said.

For her, maybe. "What are you doing there?" was all I could manage in response.

"I always come over on Thursday nights to do Dad's laundry," she explained. "Mitch has bowling on Thursdays."

How interesting. I offered the bare minimum of pleasantries, then told her I had to talk to Mike right away.

"He's not home," she said. "Something urgent came up. But he said he has to talk to you. It's real important."

Regrettably, she didn't have the foggiest notion of what it was. Mike didn't entrust her with information. Housekeeping was where he drew the line.

"Why don't you come out here for dinner? I'm making a meat loaf."

I resisted the urge to tell her that I would sooner eat her father's dirty underwear. Instead, I said I was on a special diet.

Maybe some other time. Perhaps in some other life.

Nate went out for corned beef sandwiches and beer while I waited for O'Leary to call back. By the time he did, we had finished off a six-pack.

"I've got bad news," he said. "Dexter Robinson's in the hospital. He's got a concussion and a pair of cracked ribs. He says Shake Johnson and Tommy Vreeland beat him up."

"When did it happen?"

"Late this afternoon."

"Where?"

"They jumped him in the parking lot at the Willowbrook Mall."

"Were there any witnesses?"

"Just Dexter."

"Did you talk to the police?"

"About an hour ago. They still hadn't picked up Vreeland or Shake."

That sounded about right. If Pucinsky was any example, the Wayne police probably patrolled the streets in golf carts.

"I've got worse news," I said. "Dwight's disappeared."

O'Leary let out a gasp that was followed by the sound of the phone dropping to the floor. Then came a lengthy silence that made me suspect he might have suffered a heart attack. That would not have been an unreasonable price to pay for being spared Kathy's meat loaf.

No such luck. I heard a few distant but choice cuss words, then the sound of the phone being picked up again, then the sonic boom of O'Leary's voice.

"Sorry," he said, "I had to get a fucking drink."

I knew just the feeling.

"Are you sure he's disappeared?"

"No, Mike. There's a chance he might have vanished."

"Cut the wise guy shit. You were supposed to be watching him. What happened?"

"What did you expect me to do—chain him to the goddamn bed? Remember, I'm the one who was content to let him sit in jail."

"All right, all right. You just don't know how fucked up this is. I'm supposed to have him with me in court tomorrow. I got another hearing on a continuance. If he's not there, I'll have to tell the judge he's skipped bail."

"Don't worry," I said. "He'll turn up."

"What makes you think so?"

"I don't. I'm just trying to be positive. I get that way when I'm not acting like a wise guy."

"I like you better when you're being an asshole. Do you think this has something to do with our anonymous bail donor?"

"I'm figuring it has everything to do with it. Unless your client's stupider than we think."

"But how could they have figured out where he was staying?"

It was a good question. I answered it with one of my own.

"Just who could 'they' have been?"

"There's always the chance he did skip out," O'Leary said.

Yeah, wouldn't that be a bitch.

"Now what the fuck are we supposed to do?" he asked.

"Have another drink," I advised. "I'm going to make some calls. You call me if you hear from him."

"Natch."

It took a few minutes for Ed Gallo to come to the phone after his wife answered it. He assured me that he hadn't been napping, but his yawns were a dead giveaway. I didn't really expect to locate Dwight Robinson at Gallo's house, but longshots do come in on rare occasion.

This wasn't one of them.

I tried to be casual about checking for Dwight, but there was no fooling the coach. He didn't take the news very well.

"You don't think he would've run away, do you?"

I told him I didn't know what to think.

"Jesus, that would be terrible," he said.

Indeed it would. If Dwight had skipped bail, his old coach would be wiping egg off his face for the rest of his life.

"I'm afraid the alternative would be even worse," I said.

"Yeah, much worse." There was a long silence at his end of the line. "I don't think he would have taken off," he said at last.

For Gallo's sake, I hoped he was right. For Dwight's, I hoped he was wrong.

"Is there anything I can do to help?" There was a tone of desperation in his voice that was just begging for an assignment.

I couldn't think of a damn thing. But just as I was about to hang up, an idea dawned on me.

"Do you play golf?" I asked.

"About once a year."

"Have you ever caddied?"

"Not for twenty years or so. Why?"

"How would you like to come out of retirement this weekend?"

I gave the coach some background on the tournament. If something was finally going to break on this goddamn case, it was going to happen at Mountain Lake over the weekend. With the exception of Dwight and his brother, most of the principals involved were going to be there. If something didn't happen, I just might decide to force the issue. How I was going to do that, I didn't exactly know. But it would be a good idea to have a little help on hand, in case things got a little out of hand.

"I'd do anything in the world to help," he said.

Terry Vreeland was in the same frame of mind. She was glad to take Gallo on as her caddy. She was also a little frantic.

"I've been trying to reach you," she said. "My father called a little while ago. The police were over at the house questioning Tommy. Somebody beat up Dexter Robinson, and he's saying that Tommy did it."

"I know," I said. "Tommy and Shake."

"Do you think it's true?"

"I can't think of any reason why Dexter would lie," I said. But there was one at the back of my mind. I just didn't bother mentioning it to Terry. It would only complicate things.

"My father's going crazy," she said. "He called his lawyer, and he's talking about filing a suit against the police if they arrest Tommy."

I tried to picture Roy Cohn, Joe McCarthy's commie-hunting assistant, going up against Hal Pucinsky in court. The whole situation was getting too bizarre for words.

"Did Tommy have an alibi?" I asked.

"I don't know. I think he might have been drinking at Pete's."

That would have been about right. I didn't tell Terry that Pete's was closed.

"I have this terrible feeling," she said. "I have this feeling that something horrible is going to happen."

"I'm afraid it might have happened already." I told her about Dwight. I could hear her starting to cry.

"Everything's so screwed up," she sobbed.

I didn't dispute that. But I did stay on the phone a while longer in an effort to cheer her up. Nate was standing by to cheer me with a steady supply of beers.

I wasn't sure there was any point in calling Dahlia Robinson. I figured if she had seen her son, she would have mentioned it to O'Leary at the hospital. I was wrong.

Dwight had stopped by his mother's house early in the afternoon. He had brought her a dozen roses. He said he had taken the bus to the Willowbrook Mall. When he left, he said he was going to visit Dexter. The next thing Mrs. Robinson knew, the police were on the phone, saying Dexter was in the hospital.

It wasn't the right time to do it, but I asked Dahlia Robinson about Dexter's whereabouts the night of Cynthia's murder anyway. She said he came home around nine, just as he had said. He didn't go out again until Dwight called around midnight.

I agreed with Mrs. Robinson that she had wonderful sons. It just about broke my goddamn heart to tell her one of them was now missing.

Hers, too. I drained a beer and smoked a cigarette while listening to her weep. Sometimes this job doesn't seem to pay enough.

"Why does God let things like this happen?" she blurted out.

I resisted the temptation to tell her that the man upstairs might have less interest in her affairs than she was inclined to believe. I simply said I didn't know.

CHAPTER
28

I tend to be kind of an irritable guy. I think that's because quite a few things tend to irritate me.

Like waiting. Probably nothing irritates me more than having to sit around and wait. Except maybe having to *stand* around and wait.

This can be quite the occupational shortcoming. Patience is a valuable asset in my line of work. Some people might even say it's a prerequisite. You have to do an awful lot of watching and waiting. Maybe that's why I'm getting so goddamn sick of the business.

When I was younger I used to be very patient, but not anymore. I know this is a reverse of the normal pattern, but being normal is not something I've ever aspired to. I figure you're born with a fixed allotment of patience, and mine just happens to be running out. That's one of the major reasons I'd like to go into early retirement. Unfortunately, my reservoir of liquid assets seems to dry up at about the same rate that my supply of patience dwindles.

It's a dilemma, and it makes me irritable. But luckily, I'm

also an adaptable guy. Over the years, I've found two surefire home remedies for relieving the symptoms of impatience—getting drunk and going to sleep. While waiting for some word about Dwight Robinson, I decided to employ both methods of treatment.

I had just stolen the puck off Bobby Orr's stick and was about to score the winning goal in the seventh game of the Stanley Cup finals when the ringing of the phone delivered a crushing check to my head. My biological clock told me there were two minutes left in the third period. The Utica Club beer clock on my night table told me otherwise. It was two A.M.

As I reached to pick up the phone, I thought maybe the prayers I had forgotten to say had been answered. Or maybe Dahlia Robinson had managed to recruit Saint Anthony's assistance in locating her lost son.

Not in my wildest dreams.

Her voice was only a whisper, but the tone of hysteria in it was loud enough to shake Madison Square Garden from New York to kingdom come. Even in beer-soaked somnolence, I could tell that Melody Winchester was one very scared lady.

"Did I wake you?"

"No."

"I'm sorry. But it's important."

"That's OK. What is it?"

"It's about Dwight. I'm worried about him. Bob had a meeting here tonight with Pete Becker. I heard them talking about Dwight. I think they're planning on doing something to him. And it's all my fault."

"Did you tell him where Dwight was staying?"

"No, of course not. But we had a huge fight last night. I told him everything else. About being with Dwight the night of the murder. I told him I was going to testify at the trial. I have to see you. I can't talk now."

"We have to get you out of that house," I said. "I'll be there in an hour."

"No, don't. I'll be OK. They don't know I heard them."

I started to tell her that didn't make any difference, but she interrupted me.

"I've got to go. I think he just woke up. Don't worry about me. I'll be OK. Come in the morning—after nine-thirty. He'll be gone by then."

"Are you sure—"

She hung up.

I sat there in the dark, staring at the green light of my cigarette and thinking things through. If Bob Winchester had decided to get rid of Dwight Robinson, he would have to get rid of his wife, too. My instincts told me I should go to their house right away. I usually trust my instincts. But there were some logistical problems to consider—like getting into Mountain Lake in the middle of the night.

After thinking it over for a few cigarettes, I managed to convince myself that Melody Winchester probably wasn't in any immediate danger. Her husband was, after all, a politician. They never do anything quickly. Even if he had already made up his mind to shut up his wife, he'd be sure to do it cleanly, with a lot of advance planning. I thought it was highly unlikely he'd do something that stupid right before the start of a celebrity golf tournament at which he'd be occupying center stage.

But I've been wrong before. Especially when I don't trust my instincts.

I called Nate and told him to be ready for an early start. Then I had a shot of bourbon and went to bed. It took me a long while to get back to sleep. I never made it back to center ice.

I was just getting ready to leave my apartment when I got a call from the expectant ex-father-in-law.

"Bad news," he said.

"I figured that. It's only no news that's ever any good." But it could have been a lot worse. At least Dwight Robinson was still alive.

"He called me a few minutes ago—that no-good prick. He's decided to split. He started mouthing off that goddamn line about white justice again. Can you believe that ass-hole—after all I've done for him?"

"No, I don't believe it." I didn't bother to remind O'Leary that he wasn't the only one sticking his neck out on Dwight's behalf. I did tell him about Dwight's visit to his mother's house the day before and my late-night phone conversation with Melody Winchester.

"Jesus Christ! They're going to kill the poor kid."

It's amazing how far a little information will go toward changing a man's opinion of someone. "You mean the no-good prick," I reminded him.

"Come on," he answered. "I was just blowing off steam. What should we do?"

"I'm going to see Melody Winchester and find out if she knows any more details. After that, I don't know."

"What about me? My ass is in a goddamn sling. I've got to go to court this afternoon."

"I'd hold off on that."

"What do you mean? Lie? I can't do that."

"It wouldn't be the first time."

"What am I supposed to say—your honor, I'd like to get a continuance on my motion for a continuance?"

"You're the lawyer. You'll think of something. But whatever you do, don't tell anyone Dwight's missing. Bob Winchester may be a jerk, but he's not stupid. My guess is he's going to wait until the news gets out that Dwight skipped bail, then arrange for him to have an accident. Chances are it's going to occur some place far from here. Our only hope is that they don't kill him before they take him away."

"Oh, Christ. I wish I'd never gotten into this mess."

"Just think of all the money you're going to make, Mike."

"Fuck the money. My nerves are so shot, I got the chills all over. I feel like I'm going to puke."

It would be a cold day in hell before the thought of money didn't warm Mike O'Leary's heart. "Maybe it's not just your nerves," I said.

"What do you mean?"

"Are you sure it doesn't have something to do with last night's dinner?"

"Hell, no. Kathy made meat loaf."

"I rest my case."

CHAPTER
29

"God, what a festive atmosphere," Nate said, as we turned off Route 23 onto Boonton Avenue in Mountain View. "It's amazing what you can accomplish when you turn a bunch of kids loose with a set of Magic Markers and some old sheets."

His reference was to a series of enormous banners announcing the Tenth Annual Sarah Winchester Vreeland Memorial Golf Tournament. They were hanging over the street, attached with wire to telephone poles, street lights and any other available vertical supports. The overall effect was to transform the normally drab little town into a drab little town with large ugly banners hanging over its main street.

"I think that last one must have been donated by an old folks home," he said, as we turned up the hill toward Mountain Lake. "There's clear evidence of long-term incontinence."

"It rained last night," I reminded him. Ordinarily, I would have laughed, but I was feeling somewhat apprehensive as we pulled up to Checkpoint Charlie. I was having second

186

thoughts about having waited until the morning to go see Melody Winchester.

Instead of our acne-faced, pot head buddy, the entrance to the promised land was being guarded by an expressionless, middle-aged man in a faded, navy-blue uniform.

"They must have pulled it out of mothballs," I said.

"Yeah, and him with it," Nate added.

I began to feel more apprehensive when the new guard told us there was no answer at Melody Winchester's house.

"Well, she's expecting us," I assured him.

He looked me over with a hollow gaze. His expression, or the lack thereof, hadn't changed since we pulled up. I had a feeling this guy was going to require more than a ten-dollar bill.

The bastard refused my offer of a twenty. "That's a bribe," he said. "That's illegal."

"Hey, I'm a celebrity in the tournament." Nate pulled his crumpled registration packet from the pocket of his rumpled sports jacket.

The man looked at his watch and shook his head. "Registration don't start till four. You have to get special permission to come in any earlier."

"I'll bet you wouldn't turn away Jerry Van Dyke," Nate said indignantly.

Poker face stood pat.

"Who do we have to talk to about getting permission?" I asked.

He thought it over for a minute. "Well, you could be one of Mr. Vreeland's special guests or Congressman Winchester's, but they're having the VIP party at Mr. Vreeland's house this year, so I don't suppose he'll be having any special guests. So you got to be on Mr. Vreeland's list on account of that's where Mr. Winchester is, too. Course I suppose you could speak to Mrs. Heatherton."

"Monica Heatherton?"

"That's right. She's the chairman this year."

I thought about the former Miss New Jersey contestant I had met the week before. It seemed like it had been months ago. Then I thought about the phone ringing off the hook at Melody Winchester's house.

"I've got a better idea," I said.

"So do I." Nate hopped out of the car and began walking around the front end toward the gate.

"Hold it right there, mister."

I looked up to see the guard pointing a revolver at my best friend. His hand was shaking. I was tempted to reach through the window and grab the gun, but it would have been a difficult maneuver. The uniform was a clear tip-off that this guy took his job rather seriously. I had a feeling he wouldn't hesitate to shoot.

"It's nothin' personal against you, mister," he said. "But you can't be too careful with all these hijackers around these days."

Nate threw up his arms and searched the sky. "Welcome to Mountain Lake," he shouted. "What the fuck is going on around this place? Do you think we're going to hijack the goddamn golf course?"

The guard didn't answer the question. If his expression was any indicator, the gun was probably loaded with blanks. That didn't seem like a wise assumption to make.

Nate got back into the car. "What's your idea?" he said.

I told the idiot to hand me the telephone. He kept the gun trained on me while I called the golf course. I reached Pop at the clubhouse and asked him to go find Terry. I told him it was urgent.

She came to the phone five minutes later. Five minutes after that, she had persuaded vacuum head to grant us security clearance.

As we began to pull away, he started to chuckle. "The gun wasn't even loaded," he said.

Nate buried his face in his hands and shook his head. If we didn't have more pressing business to attend to, he might have gotten out of the car and tried to pummel some sense into the man. "Jesus Christ," he muttered, "there's nothing like humor in uniform."

Nate was still grumbling by the time we had followed

Terry to Melody Winchester's house and began heading up the winding walk.

"That's Preston Carswell," Terry said. "He's Pete Becker's half-brother."

"Half-*wit* brother's more like it," Nate said.

"He used to be the full-time guard, but now he only works on tournament weekend. He had a nervous breakdown."

"That can happen when you work a stressful job," I said.

"I don't understand why you're coming to see Melody," Terry said, as we got to the front porch.

"It's a long story." I gave her an abbreviated version while we waited for someone to answer the door.

Nobody did.

I tried the knob. It was unlocked.

I looked at Terry, who was still reeling over the revelation that Dwight Robinson was having an affair with her aunt. "Do you want to wait here?" I asked.

She bit her lip and shook her head. I think she was too anxious to speak.

Our search of the first floor didn't turn up any sign of Melody Winchester.

"Maybe she forgot you were coming and went out." There was a sense of hopefulness in Terry's voice.

I didn't want to ruin it, but there was no such tone in mine. "Yeah, maybe."

"It smells kind of funny in here," Nate said, as we mounted the staircase.

"Yeah, it does," Terry agreed. "I think it might be shoe polish."

I didn't smell a damn thing, but I was willing to take her word for it. When it comes to the senses, smell has never been one of my strong suits. But I did notice an odor when we neared the bathroom. This one would have been difficult to miss. But it was hard to identify. At first I thought it was the smell of something burning. But there was another odor mixed in with it. Stale water, maybe.

That turned out to be a good guess.

As I pushed the bathroom door open cautiously and peered into the room, I could see Melody Winchester staring back at me. Her blue eyes were lacking some of their usual sparkle. That can happen when your head is under water. Terry let out a scream and put her head against my chest. I pulled her closer and surveyed the room while she sobbed into my shirt.

It didn't take a genius to reconstruct what had happened. Terry's aunt had decided to take a bath. Before getting into the tub, she had mixed herself a pitcher of Bloody Marys. She had put the pitcher on the windowsill above and a little over from the end of the tub. Right next to the clock radio. When she reached up to get herself a refill, she had knocked the pitcher to the floor. That's why the tile was now covered with glass shards, vodka and Mr. T's. In the process, she had pulled the radio into the tub with her.

It was one of those bizarre home accidents that are more common than most people realize. A personal tragedy that could have been prevented if not for a momentary, careless lapse. At least that's the scenario Melody's killer wanted the police to believe. From what we had seen of the cops so far, it was reasonable to expect they would.

It was a good plan, as murder plans go. But the killer hadn't counted on a key variable: He had no way of knowing that we'd be the ones to find the body.

I looked at Nate. "You want to call?"

He nodded. "The police chief and I have an excellent working relationship."

I pulled the shower curtain closed, then helped Terry down the stairs. She said she needed some fresh air. That sounded like a very good idea. I left her on the front porch, then went back inside to see if I could find anything of interest. I did.

You had to have a good eye to notice it and luckily the one I've got is perfect. There wasn't enough polish for a shoe shine, but black's not my color anyway.

A couple of minutes later, Nate and I joined Terry outside. "Pucinsky's on his way," he said.

"A lot of good that will do," she answered. "Hal Pucinsky might as well be on my uncle's payroll."

"It wouldn't surprise me if he already is," I said. But this time, I had a feeling the police chief might not be so inclined to look the other way.

He looked me straight in the eye as he padded up the walk to the house, followed by three cops in uniform and two paramedics. "Did you touch anything inside?" he demanded.

"Only the shower curtain."

We led the chief and his entourage up to the bathroom. Terry stayed outside. Pucinsky took a quick look around, shook his head disgustedly, then told one of the cops to go down to the golf course and find Bob Winchester.

"I think he's over at Thomas Vreeland's house," Nate said. "He got special permission to go there from the guard at the gate."

Pucinsky gave Nate a baffled look. "Try Mr. Vreeland's place first," he told the cop. Then, to me, he said, "You want to tell me what you were doing here?"

I thought about suggesting we move out of the range of the other cops, then decided it wouldn't be such a bad idea if a few witnesses were on hand to hear the story. Pucinsky must have been reading my thoughts.

"Let's move outside," he said.

I started from the beginning, telling him about Dwight Robinson's affair with Melody Winchester.

He didn't believe it. I hadn't expected that he would.

"Mrs. Winchester called me last night and told me to come here to see her. She was upset. She said her husband had a meeting with Pete Becker. They talked about Dwight Robinson. She was afraid they were going to do something to him. She should have been afraid for her own life, as well."

"Are you implying that Mr. Winchester hired Pete Becker to kill his wife?"

"I most certainly am."

Pucinsky snorted and lit a cigarette. "You guys are fucking crazy." Then, to Terry, he said, "Pardon my French, Miss Vreeland."

"Fuck you, Hal," she retorted.

"I know you're upset about your sister and your aunt, but

I don't know how these guys got you to start believing all their fairy tales. If you'd like my advice, I think you should stay away from him."

"When I want your dumb advice, I'll ask for it, Hal."

"If I were you, I wouldn't hold your breath," Nate advised.

Pucinsky glared at Nate, then turned his eyeballs on me. "Did you see anything up there that makes you think this wasn't an accident? We all knew Melody had a drinking problem."

"Take another look," I said. "You tell me how she could have pulled the radio into the water without knocking her cocktail glass off the rim of the tub. And then you'd have to have a good nose to notice it, but there's also the smell of shoe polish."

Pucinsky shook his head and cracked a smile. "I may have a big one, but that doesn't mean I got a good one."

If I had thought it was the time for size-is-not-important jokes, I might have pointed out that the chief's schnozz was ugly, too. Instead, I said, "If you look closely, you'll see a couple of polish smudges on the bannister. Becker must have slipped on his way out and bumped against it."

"Becker, shoe polish. What the hell are you talking about, Renzler?"

"He liked to put it on his face on caddy-training day," I said. "If anybody saw him come here, he might have been mistaken for a black guy."

Pucinsky scratched at his beak and ran his tongue around the inside of his mouth. "You guys better get going," he said at last. "It wouldn't be such a good idea for you to start making accusations the minute Mr. Winchester gets here. Terry, you stay with me. We're going to say you're the one that found the body."

"And what's that supposed to accomplish?" I asked.

Pucinsky let out a long, loud sigh. "Let me handle this my way. I can assure you that I intend to conduct a thorough investigation."

"I guess there's a first time for everything," Nate said.

CHAPTER
30

Our first stop after leaving Mountain Lake was Pete's bar. Finding Melody Winchester's body had killed our appetites, but it had produced a king-sized thirst for a good, stiff drink.

Of course, we had more reason than that for going to Pete's.

The place was empty when we entered, except for the bartender, who had his head buried in the racing page of the *Daily News*.

"Hello, Ray," I said, as we made our way to the bar.

"I'm not Ray," Salvino replied.

"Oh, Christ, here we go again," Nate said.

But this time, it was our mistake. On second glance, I realized that the man behind the bar had been cursed with Ray Salvino's bad looks, but he still had an original head of hair. It just looked like an ill-fitting rug naturally.

"I'm Ray's brother, Tony," he explained. "Are you friends of his?"

"You could beat him in a look-alike contest," I said.

"Yeah, but who'd have the bad taste to hold one?" Nate added.

Unless Tony was dumber than his brother, I think that answered his question about whether we were friends. He eyed us warily as we ordered shots and beers.

"Where is old Ray today?" I asked, as he set the drinks down on the Formica-topped shelf in front of us.

"He's up at the golf course helping Pete set up for the tournament. I'm filling in for him."

"Well aren't you a nice brother," Nate said.

I watched the anxiety on Tony's face spread into a look of fear, as his eyes followed Nate to the door. Nate locked it, then pulled the shade down over the front window.

"You wouldn't mind taking us on a little tour of the place, would you, Tony?" I asked.

Of course he wouldn't. Not while he was staring down the barrel of my gun.

Tony led us through the backroom to the basement, but we couldn't find any sign of Dwight Robinson. Likewise at the dreary little apartment upstairs that Ray Salvino called home. When we got back down to the bar, Nate told Tony to bring him the phone book. He tore out the page with Pete Becker's address.

"Thanks for letting us bring a little sunshine into your day," I said.

Pete Becker owned a large, pink split-level house in a development off Alps Road called Tall Oaks. It was an imaginative name, considering the absence of trees. Becker's place wasn't impressive compared with the Winchester and Vreeland estates, but it was big enough to make a person wonder where Pete got his money. He certainly didn't get enough business at his bar, and golf pros at dumps like Mountain Lake generally get paid for what they are— glorified caddies and clubhouse bouncers.

I figured there was a good possibility Becker was getting a cut of Ray Salvino's gambling profits. Or Shake Johnson's drug profits. Or maybe he earned extra cash doing favors for Thomas Vreeland and Bob Winchester.

"He's got that column in the newspaper," Nate said. "Maybe he's one of those guys who makes money writing short paragraphs."

"They'd have to be very short," I replied.

On initial inspection, the house looked to be sealed up tighter than most of the girls I used to date in high school. As with a few of them, I managed to find a way in. There was a key right where most people leave one—under the welcome mat on the back porch.

As we stepped inside, I found out the answer to one of the questions I'd been meaning to ask somebody: Pete Becker didn't have a dog. Or if he did, he must have taken it to his office. Once again, we didn't find Dwight Robinson or anything to indicate that he had been a recent house guest. Which is not to say that there wasn't anybody home.

Nate was the one who had the pleasure of making the discovery. The next time we search a house, he probably let me take the bedroom. I was downstairs when I heard him yell. When I got to the bedroom, he was standing at the corner of the bed and gaping. Pete Becker's house guest was lying on top of the sheets. They were badly in need of changing.

"Most guys keep these things *under* the bed," Nate said, quickly adding, "Not that I speak from personal experience."

"Of course not," I assured him. "I've only seen ads for them in the back of dirty magazines. This is the first time I've seen one in the flesh."

"Yeah, so to speak. I saw a lump under the covers. That's why I pulled the blanket back. I thought it might be another body."

"I suppose you could say that it is."

"I suppose." He rolled his eyes. "Gorgeous, isn't she?"

"A real knockout."

"There's a lot to be said for having a girl like this. She wouldn't put up any resistance. I'd say she's the perfect date for a blowhard like Pete Becker."

I agreed. "So much for Dwight Robinson's characterization of Becker as a queer."

"Oh, yeah," Nate answered. "This looks perfectly normal to me. Would you at least be willing to accept *odd*?"

"That's not exactly what I meant. Plus I was using Dwight's choice of words."

He nodded. "I understand what you meant. I think that may be the reason he has *this*." Nate pulled at the pillow under the inflatable doll's head with the tips of his thumb and index finger. As he flipped the pillow over, he jumped back a step, as if he were expecting to find a coiled snake underneath.

It wasn't nearly as long as any snake I've seen, but it was definitely wider than some. On the right guy, it would probably be more menacing than a lot of snakes.

"I've never seen a black one before," I said.

"You just don't read the right kind of dirty magazines. If you want to see another take a peek in the closet. He's got a whole boxful of dildos in there. He's also got three Afro wigs and another girl, if you're interested. I guess he keeps her around in case this one has a headache."

I told him I'd take his word for it. "Leave the bedspread down," I said. "I want this guy to know that somebody was here."

"Good idea. Maybe he'll get suspicious that she's having an affair with one of the neighbors."

Despite the interesting possibilities that our visit to Becker's had opened up, there was only one more possibility that I could think of where somebody might be hiding Dwight Robinson. As we pulled away in the Corvair, still wagging our heads in disbelief, I remembered that the dog would be home at Shake Johnson's shack.

We stopped by a Food-Town and bought half a pound of ground beef. Nate always packs a supply of downers and amphetamines when he's traveling long distances, in case he feels the need to go to sleep or wake up. We spiced up the meat with enough reds to make an elephant snore like a sailor.

When we got to Shake Johnson's place, the dirty-faced kids were still playing baseball. This time they were using a shovel and an old penny loafer. If that had been the recreation to look forward to when I was in school, I would have spent a lot of time staying after to help the teacher.

As we expected, Shake was not at home. We figured he'd

be off helping Ray Salvino help Pete Becker get ready for the tournament. I distracted Badass at the front door, while Nate went around back, broke a window and delivered a late lunch or early dinner, depending on how you wanted to look at it. I'm sure it was just a between-meal snack to Badass. By the time we finished knocking back a beer, the dog had decided to catch thirty winks.

It took all of about thirty seconds to search his master's house.

"What a shame," Nate said. "A complete waste of good drugs."

"You could have raided Shake's supply again."

"I thought of that. It was empty. I think we tapped him out last time."

We were pretty much tapped out of ideas about where to look for Dwight. I wasn't about to call O'Leary just yet, but I had begun to wonder whether Mr. Robinson had taken off on his own after all. Stranger things have happened—quite a few of them on that day already.

We still had a couple of hours until the opening-night banquet, and we still had a few things to do. Like check in at a motel, eat lunch and rent Nate some golf clubs. I thought it made sense to stay close to Mountain Lake for the next day or so.

We took care of the first chore under the orange roof where Dwight Robinson and Melody Winchester used to romp, then knocked back lunch at a place called the Triangle Hofbrau on Route 23 that wasn't half bad. We got the clubs at a cinder block joint in Pompton Plains run by a fat guy claiming to be able to rent "absolutely, positively everything." Except perhaps his elderly mother, who was breaking her back trying to load a lawn mower into a station wagon when we arrived. We didn't inquire if she was available, but she would have made a hell of a caddy.

We got back to our temporary residence in time to see the evening news. There was no mention of Dwight's disappearance, which meant that Mike O'Leary had managed to think up a yarn to tell the judge. But there was a lengthy report on the death of Melody Winchester.

Her husband was unavailable for comment, but an aide said he would be holding a press conference the next morning. He also read a statement that said Winchester was "absolutely, positively distraught by this tragic accident."

"Bullshit," Nate grumbled. He has a habit of talking back to the TV during newscasts—and during sporting events, sitcoms and talk shows, for that matter. That psychology student I had dated for thirty seconds told me it was "the first sign of something."

"First sign of what?" I asked her.

"I don't know," she said. "*Some*thing."

I reminded Nate about her suspicions. He ignored me, just as he had ignored her, and continued his conversation.

"I'll bet Winchester's over at the Vreeland house right now, sipping cocktails with that scumbag Roy Cohn."

Maybe so. But when we got to the cocktail party, Bob Winchester was nowhere to be seen. Terry Vreeland was stationed at the clubhouse registration table. She told us she was filling in for Monica Heatherton, who was so absolutely crushed over the death of her friend that she had gotten positively shit-faced.

Terry asked another woman to cover for her for a moment, so she could have a word with me. Naturally, she was still upset herself.

"I think you might be wrong about Melody," she said. "Bob seemed genuinely shocked when he arrived back at the house. He broke down and started crying. It was really creepy."

I wasn't so easily convinced, but I didn't see any gain in pressing her. Nate wouldn't have shown such restraint, but he had gone to the bar to redeem his free-drink coupon.

"I talked to my father a little while ago," Terry said. "Bob's holding a press conference here tomorrow morning. Dad says he's planning to announce that he's dropping out of the Senate race. That's surprising, don't you think?"

"Yeah, very." Almost unbelievable, in fact.

Nate ambled back with three drinks and a fistful of tickets for refills. "I found our table," he said. "It's in the far corner.

If this room were a golf course, we'd be at the bottom of a frog pond. I think somebody in high places doesn't like us."

Terry smiled. She looked beautiful. I was tempted to lean in and give her a kiss, but that wouldn't be right in a public place. Especially not in this public place. Across the room, I could see her father and brother chatting it up with Trini Lopez.

"You were just late to register," Terry assured Nate. "If you'd like, I'll come over and sit with you."

"Oh, that's OK, we'll manage," he answered. "You go ahead and press the flesh with the important people."

Terry returned to her post, and we wandered through the crowd. I'm sure the atmosphere was subdued on account of Melody Winchester's death, but with a hundred people all talking about it at once over booze, it was hard to tell. If your idea of a good time is mingling with show business personalities, the place was heaven on earth. To me, it seemed closer to a night in hell.

"There's Julie from *The Mod Squad*," said Nate, who watches more TV in a week than most nursing home residents do in a year. He pointed to a fresh-faced girl with straight blonde hair who was standing between a tall, thin black guy and a short, stocky white guy. "And she's got Pete and Linc with her."

I made a calculated assumption about which one was which on the basis of their names, but I didn't bother to ask which one played drums and which one played guitar. "It wouldn't be *The Mod Squad* if Linc was missing, would it?"

Nate suggested we chat with them, but I was more interested in a scene to our left, where Pete Becker was having his photo taken with a miniature blonde in an even more miniature sequined dress.

"Joey Heatherton!" Nate blurted out, as if he were a contestant bidding for a washer and dryer on a quiz show.

"I wonder how she'd feel about sitting on Becker's lap if she knew about the dame lying back home in his bed."

"From what I know about Joey's love life, even Pete might be a step up," he replied, scanning the crowd for more stars.

I did the same, only I wasn't searching for Hollywood's finest. I wanted to locate Shake Johnson and Ray Salvino. As long as we were able to keep an eye on Becker, Tommy Vreeland and them, I figured we had half a chance of finding Dwight. Assuming, of course, that one or more of them had kidnapped him and hadn't disposed of him yet.

While Nate ventured off to swap one-liners with Jerry Van Dyke and Morey Amsterdam, I ambled over to a table along the wall where I had spotted my old pal George Grimaldi, the former assistant Wayne police chief, sitting alongside Hal Pucinsky. I figured it wouldn't hurt to plant the reminder in Pucinsky's head that George thought I was good people. And I thought I might learn something more about Melody Winchester's "accident."

No such luck. The two cops were engaged in riveting conversation about the comparative merits of nine irons and pitching wedges with another fellow, whom I didn't notice until it was too late to turn back. I knew from personal experience that the guy was fully capable of speaking on the subject all night long.

I put on my happy face and shook hands with my goddamn brother-in-law, Dick Derkovich.

"Well, well, small world," Dick said.

"Golfing's always been kind of a clubby sport," I replied.

I remained standing, despite their invitation to make it a foursome, but sank deeper and deeper into a sand trap of chitchat nonetheless. I got a lucky bounce when a fat lady at the next table told me we were all supposed to take our seats.

Nate was waiting for me back at our table with a fresh drink. "I was beginning to get worried about you," he said. "I was afraid someone had decided to take you hostage."

"You could say that."

"I think Frank Sinatra, Jr., is going to sing the national anthem—his way."

It wasn't quite that bad. Thomas Vreeland was about to say a few words.

CHAPTER

31

At the front of the room, Thomas Vreeland stood before a podium in the center of two long tables on a makeshift stage. I guess you'd call it a dais. There were two empty chairs on either side of him, one of which was his. Terry and Tommy were seated to his right. Sitting to their right and to the left of the other unoccupied chairs was a row of celebrities that Nate identified for me one by one.

"We're talking superstars, no doubt about it," he whispered. "Trini Lopez, Orson Bean, Kitty Carlisle, Frank Sinatra, Jr., Joey Heatherton, Dean Martin, Jr., Roy Cohn, *The Mod Squad*, Jerry Van Dyke, Morey Amsterdam. When's the last time you saw that much talent gathered in the same place at the same time?"

I thought about it for a moment. "Not since last year's Jerry Lewis telethon, I guess."

"Exactly. By the way, you may find this hard to believe, but Jerry Van Dyke and Morey Amsterdam are even funnier in person than they are on TV."

The drone of people talking gradually died down until the

only sound that could be heard in the room was the clinking of ice cubes in cocktail glasses. Vreeland's speech was brief, I'll give him that.

"My lifelong friends, Congressman Bob Winchester and his wonderful wife, Melody, cannot be with us tonight," he said in a somber voice already verging on tears. "Most of you have no doubt heard by now that Melody had a tragic accident this morning. Like my wife, Bob's sister, who this wonderful tournament is named after, Melody has gone to meet her maker."

A few murmurs went up in the room from people who apparently were not fortunate enough to be on the primary stems of the gossip grapevine.

"Naturally, Bob is terribly distraught by this tragic news and because he couldn't be with you all here tonight, as he has been for the last nine years. He asked me to welcome you here tonight on his behalf and assured me he will be with us tomorrow morning. He also asked that you all remember Melody in your prayers. I implore each of you to remember Bob as well."

Vreeland paused for so long that I thought the speech might be over. No such luck.

"I speak from personal experience when I tell you that I know exactly what Bob is going through tonight," he continued. "I'll never forget the pain I felt upon learning that my wife, Sarah, had died. And I'm sorry to say that Melody's death is not the only tragedy that has befallen our Mountain Lake family this year. By now, I'm sure all of you have heard about the personal tragedy that was suffered by my family and myself. My beautiful daughter Cynthia was brutally murdered by her husband less than three weeks ago."

Vreeland's voice began to tremble. I winced when I looked at Terry, who was shaking her head and covering her face with her hands.

"I can assure you that we're looking to see that justice is done, but that will never bring my daughter back to life. As we get ready to start this year's tournament, we can only hope that the good lord has found a place for all three of them in heaven. I'd like to think that right now, at this very moment, Sarah, Melody and Cynthia are together, looking down on us, wishing they were here with us, as we all wish they could be, too."

Vreeland struggled to choke back his sobs, but he lost the battle and had to step away from the microphone. "I'm sorry," he blurted.

He wasn't the only one. As I glanced around the room, I saw a lot of suddenly sober people squirming in their seats.

At that moment, Terry Vreeland got up from her chair and walked to her father. She put her arm around his shoulder and led him to his seat. Her brother, meanwhile, stood up and began frowning at a guy in a black robe who was standing in the wings. The minister got the hint only after Tommy abandoned subtlety and began waving frantically.

The whole scene probably took less than thirty seconds, but it felt like an eternity in the midst of the pall that had been cast over the room. Even the guest comics looked like they would have been hard pressed to think of something lighthearted to say.

The minister walked quickly to the microphone and said, "Let us pray." He didn't have to ask anyone to bow their heads.

After a fast "Our Father," Tommy took charge again. "I want to welcome all our guests," he said. "Thank you for coming. In spite of everything, we're going to try to make the tenth annual tournament the best one we ever had."

"Good luck," Nate muttered.

Amen.

The silence was quickly broken when the old waiter, Pops, led a parade of kids in white jackets carrying plates of food into the room. If Thomas Vreeland hadn't made everybody lose their appetites, one look at the dinner offering should have. It was a new breed of chicken that appeared to have been mated with old truck tires, instant mashed potatoes the texture of river mud, and carrots that even Bugs Bunny would have taken a pass on. And, of course, there was peach cobbler for dessert.

"Just pretend you're on an airplane," Nate said.

"On an airplane, they give you a vomit bag," I reminded him. I was getting motion sickness just from watching him pack it in.

When he finished his dinner, he started in on mine, claiming he needed the practice in case his celebrity status ever landed him an extended stint on the rubber chicken circuit. While he was busy doing that, I went to the bar for refills and did a quick circuit of the room.

Terry was still trapped on the dais, caught between a rock and a hard place—personified by Kitty Carlisle and Orson Bean. She managed to mime an apology in my direction with a shrug of quiet desperation. In the front corner of the room, near an exit door, I noticed Pete Becker, Tommy Vreeland, Ray Salvino and Shake Johnson engaged in conversation.

I pulled Nate away from his second dessert and suggested that we join them. He was all for the idea.

Needless to say, they weren't.

"What the fuck are you doing here?" Tommy Vreeland demanded.

Nate pulled his ID tag from his jacket pocket. He had refused to pin it on. "I'm a celebrity, junior."

"Yeah," Becker said, "he's a professional asshole."

Shake began laughing and Tommy Vreeland cracked a smile.

"Blow it out your barracks bag, Becker," Nate said. He turned to me and added, "I bet they've never heard that one before."

Probably not. It was my first time, too.

Becker looked at us uneasily. I wondered if he had been back to his house since we were there.

"Why don't you get the fuck out of here before one of you gets hurt," he said.

"You've got an awfully short memory, Pete," I replied.

While the golf pro was mulling over the previous day's encounter, Shake took over for him. "There's two of them and four of us, kicking their asses would be no *fuss*."

"This guy's quite the literary light," Nate said to me.

"When he goes in the slammer, he's liable to become a regular Jean Genet."

Ten points for their team, ten points for ours. I felt like we had wandered onto the wrong side of the dance floor at a rival high school. Apparently, that's what it seemed like to some of the people at nearby tables. A small crowd of onlookers was beginning to gather behind us.

I spoke to Nate, raising my volume a notch to make sure the boys would hear me. "I had a chat with Warren Shepherd the day before yesterday. He's the guy who lives across the street from Dwight Robinson. I showed him a picture of Shake Johnson. He thinks Shake might have been the guy he saw driving away from their house the night Cynthia was killed."

I glanced at Shake, but he was looking at the floor.

"I wouldn't say that too loud," Nate cautioned. "Somebody might get nervous and burn down the guy's house."

Tommy Vreeland lowered the level of dialogue but raised the level of volume. "Why don't you just get the fuck out of here, douche bag."

Behind us, I could sense the crowd getting bigger. We backed up a bit to give ourselves more operating room in case the dispute escalated to fisticuffs.

"Young man's kind of a nerve case," Nate said. "Shepherd didn't mention anything about another guy being in the car, did he? Like maybe a white kid—"

"What the hell's going on here?" Tommy's dad to the rescue. And right in the nick of time.

Well, almost.

The founding father of Mountain Lake pushed his way to the front of the crowd just as his son lost control. Tommy responded to Nate's latest verbal assault by hurling his cocktail glass at him. But his elbow hit Ray Salvino's shoulder at the moment of release, resulting in a rather ineffectual effort.

The glass floated lazily over our heads and off to our left, where it struck an innocent bystander. Not just any bystander, and not exactly an innocent one, now that I think of it. I turned in time to see the heavy bottom of the tumbler hit flush against the cheekbone of my beloved brother-in-law, Dick Derkovich.

With his father now standing between us, Tommy was spared the prospect of physical retaliation from Nate. He took advantage of the reprieve by saying something stupid. He shouted it, to be precise.

The idea behind confronting guys like Tommy Vreeland with juvenile banter is to get them so rattled that they say something they'll regret. I had no doubt that if we could get all the principals assembled in one place, we'd have the whole matter sorted out in no time—from the murder of Cynthia Vreeland to the fire at Anna Paslawski's house. Of course, it's a lot easier to orchestrate an event like that when you're a cop.

"If you're so fucking sure Dwight Robinson didn't kill my sister, then how come he jumped bail?" Tommy shouted.

"Who says he jumped bail?" I shot back.

I didn't get any answer, but I did see Shake Johnson give young Vreeland a cuff on the arm. It was at that moment that Hal Pucinsky paraded into the big picture.

"Arrest these two at once," Thomas Vreeland ordered.

Pucinsky put up his arms. "I'm not going to arrest anybody."

"What do you mean? Yesterday you accuse my son of a crime and now you let these two jerks come in here and cause trouble." He wheeled to face us. "How *did* you get in here?"

Nate grinned and held up his ID tag. "You invited me. Maybe you didn't realize how many big names you'd be able to draw."

"Well consider yourself uninvited. If you show up here tomorrow morning, I'll have you carted out."

"Oh no you won't." As Terry Vreeland stepped into the fray, it occurred to me that the voice of reason often seems to originate in the mouths of females. Her voice was the nicest sound I had heard all day.

Terry glared at her father and brother, spearing them with

those beautiful green daggers. It was just a typical blow-up for your not-so-typical nuclear family. I felt sorry that she was being forced to draw the line, but I appreciated where she had decided to draw it.

"If he can't play, I don't play," she said.

Her father let out a gasp of astonishment. In all fairness to him, I'd say he was having one hell of a bad day.

"I don't know what happened," Terry said. "But the way Tommy's been acting lately, I'm sure they're not the ones who started the trouble."

Pucinsky took two steps toward me and tugged at my sleeve. "I think it's about time you went home," he said. "I'll walk you out. I want to have a word with you guys."

Fine with me.

"Thanks, Terry," I said, as we turned away.

She forced a smile, but I don't think she was too happy with me, either. I couldn't blame her.

The members of *The Mod Squad* stared at us as we filed through the crowd. "Close call, Linc," Nate said. "For a minute there, I thought we were going to need a little backup."

Linc responded with a thumbs-up signal, and Nate finished off the exchange with a peace sign. Sometimes, he can be an awful embarrassment.

I took a short detour to the table where my brother-in-law was holding an ice pack against his face.

"Why is it that every time you and me are in the same room together somebody seems to get hurt?" he asked.

I put my hand on his shoulder. "Just one of the mysteries of life, Dick." I didn't bother to add that as long as I wasn't the one to get hurt, I didn't have any interest in pondering it.

George Grimaldi accompanied us outside with Pucinsky. "You haven't changed a bit, Renzler," he said. "Always in the middle of whatever trouble's going on."

"Trouble's my middle name, George."

"Cut the crap," Pucinsky said. "You guys are a goddamn pain in the ass is what you are. But I'm beginning to think you're not totally full of shit. What's all this crap about Dwight Robinson skipping bail?"

I thanked him for the compliment, then laid it out, omitting any mention of our efforts to find Dwight that day.

"So how the hell does Tommy Vreeland know about it?"

"That's what we'd like to know."

Pucinsky exhaled some smoke, then stomped out his cigarette. "You think somebody snatched him. I think he probably took off like a bat out of hell."

"Do you want to make a bet?" Nate suggested.

"Shut up. I don't gamble."

"Just to be on the safe side, you could put a watch on Pete Becker's house and bar and Shake Johnson's house," I said.

"I'll do better than that. I'll put out an APB."

"All Points Bulletin," I explained to Nate.

"I know," he said. "Broderick Crawford on *Highway Patrol* was like a god to me."

"What happened with Dexter Robinson yesterday?" I asked Pucinsky.

"Somebody beat the living crap out of him—that's what happened."

"I heard he said it was Tommy and Shake."

"He's a goddamn liar. Both of them had alibis."

"Don't tell me they were drinking at Pete's."

"I won't. They were sitting right here in the clubhouse, getting stoned off their ass."

"Who said so—Pete Becker?"

"No. The head waiter. A guy named Pop. Surprised?"

I had to admit I was. "Are you making any headway with Melody Winchester?"

"Now, that's none of your damn business, is it?"

CHAPTER
32

Getting Pucinsky to agree to put a watch on Pete's bar, Becker's house and Shake's shack saved us from having to stay up all night and try to be in three places at once. So I guess we should have felt well-rested when we got up on the morning of the big tournament.

We didn't. Or at least I didn't. Somehow I had managed to forget that, among his many charms, my partner is probably the world's loudest snorer. Next time, I'll be sure to get two rooms on separate floors instead of letting myself get talked into Howard Johnson's concept of an executive suite. At the time it sounded like a good idea, if only because it cost Mike O'Leary more money.

I rang O'Leary on the horn while gulping down room-service coffee. He started in on me right away.

"Where the hell have you been? I've been trying to call you."

I told him it was too damn early to be nagging like an old queen. Besides, I didn't have time for it. Then I treated him to a one-minute report on the previous day's events.

"Hey, hold on a sec," he said, as I started to hang up. "Don't you want to hear what I told the judge yesterday?" There was a smug tone in his voice indicating that he was just dying to give an account of his legal creativity.

"Another time, Mike." You never want to give a guy like O'Leary too much encouragement. "I'm more interested in hearing what Bob Winchester tells the press. He's giving a statement in half an hour."

"Yeah, I heard on the news last night that he's planning on pulling out of the Senate race. I'd like to see that myself. Plus I got some information for you."

"Why don't you meet us at Mountain Lake?"

"How the hell do I get in? They've got that place guarded like a fortress."

"Get your ass down there quickly and say your name's Dick Derkovich."

"Who's that?"

"Just another goddamn in-law. By the way, if the guard pulls a gun on you, don't panic. It's not loaded."

"Huh?"

As we got into the Corvair, Nate pointed at a gold Rambler American parked next to it. "Isn't that Anna Paslawski's car?"

"It would be a miracle if it is. She's supposed to be off in the Holy Land."

He shook his head. "It's a miraculous resemblance. Looks like it's even got the same rust stains."

"I think they're all designed that way."

"What about a JESUS LOVES YOU bumper sticker? Is that standard equipment?"

No, it probably wasn't. I figured Anna Paslawski had either returned early and relocated to the motel or loaned her car to a friend. Whatever her Rambler was doing there, we didn't have time to hang around and wonder. We had some rambling of our own to do.

I had to test the limits of the Corvair, and the patience of early morning drivers on Route 23, to get to Mountain Lake in time for Bob Winchester's announcement. This time, Pete Becker's half-brother didn't give us any problems getting through the gate. We didn't give him half a chance. We pulled up on the rear bumper of a Lincoln Continental and shot right through behind it, like a trotting horse racing with cover.

By the time we parked the car and I lugged Nate's clubs across the lot, a hundred or more people had already gathered on the lawn outside the clubhouse. Among them were three TV news crews, a dozen photographers and a gaggle of newspaper reporters, identifiable by steno pads and ill-fitting suits. And, of course, there was a galaxy of stars, none of whom were twinkling as much as the night before, when the atmosphere and their veins had been full of booze.

From our position on the edge of the crowd, I could make out the silver rim of Congressman Bob Winchester's stately blow-dried haircut glistening in the morning sun. It was a beautiful day for golf, assuming you like to play golf. I knew from experience that there was no such thing as a beautiful day for caddying.

We pushed our way forward to see Thomas Vreeland and a young Ivy League type in a three-piece suit standing next to Winchester. On the practice putting green about twenty-five yards to our left, Pete Becker, Tommy Vreeland and Shake Johnson were giving last-minute instructions to a cluster of caddies.

The suit stepped up to a waiting microphone and announced that Winchester would be reading a brief statement. "But I want to remind you," he cautioned reporters, "that this is not a press conference. In the interest of getting the tournament started on time, Congressman Winchester will not be answering any questions."

"I think he means in the interest of not giving any answers, the tournament will start on time," Nate muttered.

It was clear that he and I were in a minority of detractors. As Winchester strode forward to speak, he was greeted with a thunderous round of applause. When the clapping finally faded out, he repeated the reminder that his aide had just made. Then he said:

"All my life, all I've ever wanted to do is run for public

office and have the opportunity to serve the people of this wonderful community. When I was a young boy in high school, my dream was to someday become a member of the United States House of Representatives. After achieving that dream and living it for the last twelve years, I realized that I could be of even greater service if I were elected to the United States Senate. For the last year, that has been my only goal.

"By now, all of you are aware of the terrible personal tragedy I suffered yesterday. My niece, Terry Vreeland, went to my house to visit her Aunt Melody. I cringe when I think of how traumatic it must have been for her to find Melody, alone, in the bathtub, dead."

Winchester paused for a moment and panned the crowd with a somber face. "This guy is slick," Nate said. "Real slick."

"When Thomas Vreeland and I started this tournament in honor of my sister Sarah—his wife—ten years ago, we did so in the hope that we would benefit two important causes— flood relief for the unfortunate citizens of this area living in the flood zone, and alcoholism.

"Some of you may know that Melody, like Sarah, had a serious drinking problem. Being acutely aware of the horrible ramifications and consequences of this condition, I urged—begged and pleaded with—Melody to seek help. Unfortunately she refused, and now the biggest regret of my life is that I didn't insist upon it, even if it was against her will. By not doing so, I feel that I failed in my obligation as a husband."

Winchester did his eye-contact number again while taking a sip from a glass of water that Vreeland handed to him.

"The last twenty hours have been the most difficult of my entire life. And I've spent them trying to make the most difficult decision of my entire life. When you're a public servant, you have an obligation not only to yourself and your loved ones but to the constituents who have chosen you to provide leadership and work to improve the quality of their lives. This is a responsibility I have never taken lightly.

"I never thought that anything could happen that would

upset me so much that it would shake my long-standing devotion to the people who have supported me over the years. But yesterday, it did. Yesterday, I learned that there is something more important than being a member of Congress. I'm only sorry for Melody's sake that I learned that lesson too late.

"Last night, I spent a sleepless night deciding it would be in my best interest to withdraw from the race for U.S. Senate. It was only after I came to this decision that I was able to finally get a couple of restless hours of badly needed sleep."

A murmur of protest went up through the crowd. Winchester quelled it by raising his hands. Slick or not, it was still impossible for me to believe that anyone could take seriously—no less find inspiration in—a guy wearing madras shorts, a lime-colored knit shirt and white golf shoes. But then, Richard Nixon did get elected president.

"This morning, I realized that what is in my own best interest is not necessarily in the best interest of my loyal constituents. Melody, rest her soul, is already dead, and I am partly to blame for that. I don't want to make another mistake. It is for this reason that I have decided to *stay* in the race for Senate and dedicate my campaign to her loving memory. Melody wouldn't have wanted it any other way."

Winchester's "thank you" was lost in the roar of audience approval. You would have thought Winchester had just announced a plan to give each of them a million bucks instead of twenty-five cents worth of bullshit.

Nate shook his head sadly. "Mencken once said nobody ever went broke underestimating the taste of the American public. Here's his proof."

"As if we needed any more."

While Bob Winchester made his way through the crowd, glad-handing every paw he could find, his brother-in-law stepped up to the microphone.

"I have an important announcement to make." Thomas Vreeland stood in the morning sunlight, beaming. In a few moments, a hush fell over the assembly. "Let the tournament begin."

CHAPTER
33

Despite the reservoir of musical talent on hand, the task of soaking the national anthem for all it was worth was left to Melody Winchester's friend Monica Heatherton, who appeared to have recovered from her bender of the previous day. Terry Vreeland told us it was an annual tradition, reprising Monica's performance in the talent segment of the Miss New Jersey pageant years ago.

"*Many* years ago, I would imagine," Nate said.

"Not as long as you might think," Terry answered. Her voice lacked some of its usual cheer. Between her aunt's death and our antisocial behavior of the night before, I wasn't surprised. I was just glad to find out we were still on speaking terms.

Over her father's objections Terry had arranged to switch to our foursome, which was scheduled to tee-off last. In addition to Terry and Nate, it consisted of two roly-poly retirees named Fred and Barney, who we quickly learned had gotten stinking rich together in the trash-hauling business. We refrained from asking if their last names were Flintstone and Rubble, but I don't think they would have been offended if we had. Fred was hard-of-hearing, and Barney was a non-stop talker.

"You may not believe this, but there's great money in garbage," he told us. Either he was in the habit of repeating things for Fred's benefit or we looked dubious, because he said it three times.

"I'll look into it as soon as I get home," Nate assured him.

For caddying partners, Gallo and I drew a tall, quiet black kid named Julius and the acne-scarred day sentinel who had socked me for a sawbuck on our first visit to Mountain Lake. He said his name was Jonathan Chadwick Mills III, but all his friends called him Blotter. He told us we should feel comfortable doing the same. Nate told him that wasn't too likely.

Frank Sinatra, Jr., playing in the first group with Joey Heatherton, Bob Winchester, and Dino Martin, started the tournament rolling by dribbling a shot no more than fifty yards off the first tee.

"The guy golfs lousier than he sings," Nate said. "Even I can do better than that."

But an hour later, after retiring to the clubhouse for a morning eye-opener and waiting out the thundering hordes of eager hackers, my friend learned that the game isn't as easy as it looks.

"Goddamn, it's a tiny little sucker, isn't it?" he said, as he leaned over the ball with seven pairs of eyes watching him. Terry had started things off with a perfect drive down the center of the fairway, and Barney and Fred had followed with marginal shots.

Nate took three unsuccessful roundhouse swipes at the ball, the first received by grins, the second by chuckles and the third by all-out laughter. On his fourth attempt, he actually made contact with the ball. In terms of sheer distance, it might well have been the longest shot on record. Accuracy, of course, was another matter altogether.

"Now all you gotta do is straighten it out," Julius said, after watching the ball sail over the twenty-foot cyclone fence along the left side of the first fairway, across Byron

Nelson Drive and onto a perfectly manicured lawn that was in the process of being mowed, narrowly missing the man who was in the process of mowing it.

Nate shrugged. "That's what I've got a caddy for." He turned to me. "Go fetch."

"Go to hell."

"I think I'm already there."

"At least you hit it far," Barney said.

"Huh?" Fred asked, thinking that his friend was speaking to him.

"I said at least he hit it far."

Nate looked at Terry expectantly. Somehow, I didn't think anything she said was going to make a significant improvement in the quality of his game.

She smiled. "Try to let the club do the work for you."

"I've got a better idea," Nate said, turning to Gallo. "I'll let you do the work for me. Do you mind?"

Gallo shrugged and took the driver out of Nate's hand. As he stepped to the tee, Barney said, "Better not. I think you can get disqualified for that."

"Huh?" Fred asked.

"I said I think you can get disqualified for that."

"Put a lid on it, Barney," Nate advised. I had a feeling it was going to be a long day.

The coach had not exactly mastered the art of the graceful hip swivel, but he managed to put the ball in play. "You sure you don't want to give it another try?" he asked Nate, when we got to the ball.

"That's all right. I'll have a lot more fun laughing at you."

But there weren't many laughs to be had. Even when you're doing it for Terry Vreeland, caddying isn't a lot of fun. The charm of Fred and Barney wore off fast, and they moved as swiftly as a pair of box turtles. By the time we got to the eighth tee, we could see Bob Winchester's leadoff foursome creeping up on us in the distance. I had spoken briefly with Hal Pucinsky before the tournament started, and he told me the night watch had not turned up any sign of Dwight

Robinson. Mike O'Leary had not shown up, as promised, so I didn't get the information he wanted to pass along.

While we waited impatiently for Fred to finish four-putting the eighth hole, I had pretty much concluded that participating in the tournament was a major waste of time. And with Dwight now missing for almost forty-eight hours, time was the one thing we couldn't afford to waste.

My view of the situation turned out be a little premature. That can happen when you're running out of patience, especially if you happen to be a naturally impatient guy.

The ninth hole was a par-five with a dogleg to the left that started about a hundred yards from the tee. Normally, two caddies would go ahead as scouts to spot the balls, and two would remain behind with the golfers. As we got to the tee, Blotter pulled me aside and asked if I'd mind accompanying Julius and him down the fairway. When we reached the beginning of the dogleg, he grinned and pulled a hand-rolled cigarette out of his shirt pocket.

"We want to smoke some reefer," he said, nodding toward the old caddy shack, about twenty-five yards from the left side of the fairway. "I told Julius you were cool."

"Yeah," Julius said, "it's kind of like a tradition. You'll cover for us, right?"

I told him I had nothing but the utmost respect for people's traditions. I turned to watch the tee shots, while they trotted to the abandoned building that Cynthia Vreeland used to call the Stable.

Terry's drive hooked perfectly at the start of the dogleg and landed smack in the center of the fairway. Aside from the two screwdrivers I had washed down in the clubhouse bar, watching her play was the only pleasure of the day. Dwight Robinson was right about Terry's holding herself back. If the girl didn't try out for the goddamn LPGA tour soon, I was going to threaten to break her clubs.

Gallo stepped up to the tee to hit next, but I didn't bother to watch his shot. I got distracted by the shouts of my caddying partners. I couldn't make out what they were yelling, but I thought I heard Julius say something about Dwight Robinson.

They were waving their arms wildly at me when I turned to look. As I started running toward them, I saw a first-class horse's ass coming out of the stable. Ray Salvino began shouting at the caddies, but he switched his strategy from fight to flight the instant he saw me coming.

Salvino took off on an angle that led through a grove of trees and back toward the ninth tee. I adjusted my angle and veered left, but he had too big a lead for me to cut him off.

No problem. If Salvino thought he was out of the woods, he was in for a big surprise. Ed Gallo was waiting for him on the other side of the trees. I stopped and reversed direction, heading back toward the start of the dogleg, in case Salvino got any ideas about doubling back down the fairway.

He didn't. He didn't have time to think about anything.

I didn't get back to the fairway in time to see it, but Nate later told me that the coach flattened Salvino with a body block that would have dented a dump truck. The force of the collision had dislodged the rug on Salvino's head, adding insult to injury.

From my vantage on the fairway, it didn't look like they needed any assistance, so I ran back to the shack where the two caddies were peering into a ground-level window.

"It's Dwight Robinson!" Julius said, pointing. "He ain't movin'. I think he's dead."

I didn't bother to look in the window. I kicked in the door and hurried down the steps that led to the basement.

Julius was right about Dwight not moving. But as soon as I saw the tape over his mouth, I knew he was wrong about Dwight being dead.

His ankles were tied with rope, and his hands were taped behind his back. There were bruises on his face, and one eye was swollen closed. He was shivering from lying on the damp cement floor.

I pulled the gag off his mouth first, then tilted his head up and offered him a hit off the flask of Bombay Gin I was carrying in my hip pocket.

"Damn! What is that rot-gut?"

For the first time since I had met him, Dwight Robinson had a bona fide shit-eating grin on his face. Given the way it had been rearranged, that was no small accomplishment.

"If I had known you were going to be here, I would've brought along a bottle of Boone's Farm Apple Wine."

"Yeah, that would've been *real* nice."

CHAPTER
34

"It was this asshole and that motherfucker Shake Johnson," Dwight said, pointing a menacing finger at Ray Salvino. It would have been very menacing if he hadn't been leaning on Terry Vreeland for support and clutching at his left side. Dwight had told me he was fine, but I figured he was good for at least one cracked rib.

All things considered, Ray Salvino should have felt lucky that Dwight was injured. But I'm sure he didn't. The bartender was lying perfectly still on the edge of the ninth fairway. Ed Gallo was using his chest for a lounge chair.

I had sent Julius and Blotter off to fetch Hal Pucinsky, who, according to Terry's examination of the lineup sheet, was probably shooting on the twelfth or thirteenth hole. At least that's what it would have been on a real golf course. In the meantime, we had created a major traffic jam on the links. After a few minutes of shouting from the tee, Bob Winchester sauntered down the fairway to investigate the cause for the delay.

"What's going on here?" he demanded, as he approached

our group. "Mr. Sinatra has to appear in the Poconos tonight."

"That sounds like another good reason to avoid the Poconos," I said.

A look of shock spread over Winchester's face when he got close enough to notice Dwight Robinson. He came to a dead stop. I wondered what was going through his mind while I followed his gaze from Terry to Salvino.

"Nice speech this morning, Congressman," Nate said. "Very sincere. I like that."

Winchester looked nervously at his niece. "What's going on, Terry?"

She avoided his stare by looking at the ground. I took the liberty of answering for her. "Why don't you tell us."

"I don't have the slightest idea what you're talking about. But I don't like your tone. Why don't you move off the fairway and let us play through."

"Fine with me," I said.

As Winchester turned on his heels, Nate said, "Better enjoy it, Bob. This could be the last chance you get to play for a long time."

Winchester looked back without stopping, then shook his head in disgust.

"How the hell can he be thinking about golf at a time like this?" Terry said.

"He's not," I answered. "He's trying to figure out his next move. He's wondering if Salvino's going to spill his guts."

Gallo got up, then yanked Salvino roughly to his feet. "Isn't that right, Ray?" I said.

Salvino replied with a sullen stare. Fred handed him his hairpiece, and the bartender put it back on his head.

"Here comes the chief," Barney said.

"Huh?" Fred asked.

"The chief's coming."

I turned to see Hal Pucinsky slowly approaching, with Julius and Blotter on either side of him. "Goddamnit, Renzler, I was putting for a birdie and what happens—"

The sight of Dwight Robinson stopped him in mid-sentence. I thought the caddies would have filled him in, but perhaps the police chief hadn't given them a chance. Or maybe they were too high to make any sense. Julius had told me it was "killer weed."

"Jesus Christ, what happened to you?" Pucinsky demanded.

Dwight answered with a disinterested shrug. I think he just didn't like cops. It was no wonder they didn't like him.

"He was kidnapped by Mr. Salvino here and Shake Johnson," I said. "They were holding him over in the caddy shack."

"Well I'll be damned. You guys were right after all." To no one in particular, Pucinsky said, "Where the hell's Shake?"

"He's caddying for my father," Terry said. "They're probably on sixteen or seventeen."

Pucinsky lit a cigarette. "We'll wait for him back at the clubhouse. Let's get this kid to a goddamn hospital. Can you walk OK or should we get you a cart?"

"I'm fine." The grimace on Dwight's face undermined his credibility a bit. "No way I'm going to any hospital."

"The hell you're not," Gallo said. "And I'm going along for the ride—just to make sure you get there."

"Me, too," Terry said.

Dwight failed in his effort to suppress a smile. "Shit. Where the hell am I supposed to sit?"

"Don't worry, young man," Barney assured him. "Ambulances are very roomy. We used to use an old one to haul trash. You wouldn't believe how much garbage you can cram into the back of one of those things. Right, Fred?"

Fred offered his usual reply. I suggested to his partner that they continue with their game. He was about to reject my motion until Pucinsky seconded it in a tone that was closer to an order than a suggestion. The chief and I were finally starting to see eye to eye.

A look of disappointment spread over Barney's face. He probably hadn't experienced this much excitement since the invention of the trash compactor. Needless to say, the caddies also looked a bit dispirited.

As we cut across the fairway toward the clubhouse, Nate noticed a familiar form searching for a ball in the rough on the second hole. "If this is a celebrity tournament, what's a lowlife like Warren Shepherd doing here?"

His question was directed at Terry. She must have been getting tired of having to account for tournament regulations, but she answered with her customary patience. "Any jerk who's willing to pay fifty bucks is eligible to play."

"That seems like a pretty stiff nut for a guy like Shepherd to cough up," Nate said to me.

Yes it did, especially considering that our pal Warren was about to quit his job. I figured he'd be saving every nickel he could get his hands on. But when we got back to the patio off the clubhouse, where Mike O'Leary was slouched behind a tumbler of scotch and chatting away with Pop, we learned something that started the old light bulbs blinking inside my head again.

"I got that information you were looking for," he said, after Dwight had been loaded into an ambulance and Terry and Gallo had left for the hospital. "Warren Shepherd lived in Nutley until about five years ago. He used to be an electrician. For some reason, he got kicked out of the union. I wasn't able to find out why. But I did find out something else."

He paused to let the drama build. Whenever O'Leary had an audience of more than one person, he liked to pretend he was Perry Mason in a courtroom. We had already suffered through the melodrama of how he outwitted Pete Becker's half-brother by flashing a toy FBI badge.

"I should hope so," I said. "You've been checking on the guy for a couple of days now."

O'Leary scowled. "I found out, you ungrateful son of a bitch, that Warren Shepherd was arrested six years ago for exposing himself to a teenage girl who lived next door to him."

"Was he convicted?" Pucinsky asked.

"No, he got off. It was her word against his, and I guess the girl was sixteen going on thirty-five. Shepherd's wife died the year before, so the judge went easy on him. But I talked to a lawyer I know who lives there, and he told me a lady friend of his came home from work one day and found a guy standing buck naked in her kitchen. She thought it was Shepherd, but she couldn't pick him out of the lineup." He laughed. "I guess she got a good look at everything except his face."

"Well, I guess that tells us everything we need to know," Pucinsky said. "I always suspected there was something that wasn't quite right about that guy."

Nate and I exchanged incredulous looks. He was about to give the beefy cop a quick refresher course in memory dynamics, but I silenced him with a cautioning shake of the head. Pucinsky may have been a jerk, but he was our jerk now. Besides, I've dealt with enough headstrong guys over the years to know that they never learn from their mistakes—they just rush headlong into new ones. His assumption that Warren Shepherd was a murderer was fresh evidence of that.

"Shepherd didn't kill Cynthia," I said.

"What do you mean?" Pucinsky barked.

"I think Shepherd knows who killed her. He's being paid off to say it was Dwight."

"That would explain how he can afford to quit his job," Nate said.

"Well, if he didn't kill her, then who the hell did?"

"I don't know for sure. But if you can arrange to get them all together, I think we'll be able to figure it out."

CHAPTER
35

Separating the truths from the half-truths, the little white lies from the big boldfaced ones, and the guilty from the not so guilty was harder than sorting out penalties after a bench-clearing brawl in a hockey game. Some of the people in the room had committed major infractions, others relatively minor ones. A couple of them were liable for nothing more than unsportsmanlike conduct. After a lifetime of complaining about botched calls, I was feeling suddenly sympathetic toward linesmen and referees.

Pucinsky had shepherded all the players into the clubhouse bar, including a baffled Warren Shepherd, who I think may have been expecting a trophy for his performance out on the links. Given their underlying suspicions and fears, I was surprised that most of them filed in willingly, raising only minor objections.

The major exception was Thomas Vreeland, who was guilty of delay of game for protesting when Pucinsky told one of his men to slap the cuffs on Shake Johnson and sit him down in the corner-table penalty box beside Ray Salvino.

"This is a complete outrage," he complained. "You're

going to ruin the entire tournament. Just who do you think you are?"

"I'm the police chief here in town, Mr. Vreeland," Pucinsky answered calmly. "Believe it or not, there are more important things in life than golf."

Nate and I exchanged bemused glances at the chubby cop's blasphemous remark. I wasn't entirely convinced that he believed it. He was probably feeling a little sour grapes because he hadn't been able to finish out his round.

Vreeland cut right to the heart of the matter. "If you feel that way, I could easily have your golfing privileges suspended."

Pucinsky scowled. "Fine, Mr. Vreeland. From now on, I'll do my shooting over at the county course."

Nate added a supporting sentiment. "I hear they've even got eighteen holes over there, Chief."

Vreeland gave Nate a dismissive frown. "Well, we demand to have our attorney present," he said, presumably speaking for the entire group. He pointed toward a short man beside him who had the face of a ferret and the body of a throw pillow.

Pucinsky shrugged. For all he knew, Roy Cohn was just another two-bit lawyer from Paramus. "You can bring your hairdresser for all I care. Let's just go inside and talk. Of course, if you prefer, we can all take a ride down to the station."

"I can assure you that won't be necessary."

There were plenty of seats in the room, but nobody seemed to feel like sitting down. There was also a buffet table set up, but I didn't think anybody would be hanging on the feed bag quite yet. I went behind the bar and began mixing drinks, while Pucinsky started to deliver an introduction to the proceedings.

Tommy Vreeland interrupted it. "Are you going to pay for those?" he demanded.

I pulled out a twenty and put it down on the bar. "Yeah," I said, "First round's on me."

"Now be quiet and listen up," Pucinsky said. "I know you're all kind of tense, but this won't take long. A couple weeks ago, Mr. Vreeland's daughter was murdered. Renzler and his partner and O'Leary here have been saying all along that Dwight Robinson didn't do it. I know most of you don't believe it, and neither did I. It wasn't until yesterday, when Melody Winchester was murdered, that I started to think—"

"Murdered! What do you mean—murdered?"

Pucinsky nodded. "That's right, Mr. Winchester—your wife was murdered."

"Is that what *he* told you?" Winchester pointed at me.

Pucinsky waved his arm like he was swatting away mosquitoes. I figured he had a lot of practice. After all, the mosquito is the state bird of Jersey.

"Let me finish, Mr. Winchester, then you can have your say." Pucinsky lit a cigarette. "Where was I? Oh, yeah. It wasn't until yesterday that I began to wonder myself. Today, when I found out Shake and Salvino here kidnapped Dwight Robinson and were holding him in the old caddy shack—"

"Who told you that?" Thomas Vreeland asked. "Shake was caddying for me all day."

Pucinsky knitted his eyebrow. "Dwight Robinson told me, Mr. Vreeland. Robinson was beaten up pretty badly. I don't think anyone in his right mind believes that this guy"—he pointed at Salvino—"could have done that to Robinson alone."

Pucinsky looked at Salvino, then at Shake. "Does one of you want to tell me who hired you?"

Apparently, they didn't.

The police chief turned to me. "You're on. Try not to be too long-winded."

I took my bottle of beer and came out from behind the bar. Without looking up, I said, "One of the reasons nobody believed Dwight Robinson when he said he didn't kill Cynthia was because he didn't give an alibi. But that doesn't mean he didn't have one. He was merely keeping his mouth shut to protect someone. The person Dwight was protecting hired Mike O'Leary to defend him." I stopped in the corner next to Nate and looked up. "Melody Winchester and Dwight were having an affair. She was with him the night—"

"This is slander." Thomas Vreeland's attorney stepped into

the middle of the room. Evidently, he was on retainer to Bob Winchester, too. He pointed a finger at me. "We'll sue your ass, buddy."

"You're a good one to talk about slander," O'Leary shot back. "Of course, I guess you're an expert on the subject."

Cohn turned his accusing finger on O'Leary and sneered. "Listen, small fry, I eat nobodies like you for breakfast."

O'Leary took two steps forward to answer the challenge. I wondered how many scotches he had downed while waiting for us. "I hear that's not all you do with them."

The two attorneys got poised to square off, finger to finger, mouth to mouth. They looked like a pair of midget wrestlers.

"I'm filing suit on Monday against you, Jack," Cohn snarled. "When I get through—"

"Shut up, goddamnit!" Pucinsky raised his arms. "I didn't interrupt the best round of golf I ever played in my whole life to watch a pair of goddamn lawyers have a goddamn pissing match. I don't want to hear another peep out of either one of you."

Yes, your honor. They dropped their fingers back to their sides, still glowering.

"Don't worry," Cohn whispered to Winchester. "This guy can't prove a thing."

The congressman nodded. He had an expression of impatient amusement on his face. "I know. I'm just taking it all in. We'll get him back in court."

"Are you through, Mr. Winchester?" I asked.

He responded with a smug, contemptuous stare. That would change, at least the smugness would, in a few moments.

"Melody told me you knew about her and Dwight, but she wasn't sure if you knew she was with him the night of Cynthia's murder. I think you probably did, or at least you thought she might have been, because you put five thousand dollars in an envelope and had one of your flunkies deliver it to Mike O'Leary's office. Who did that? Was it you, Pete?"

"Nonsense," Winchester said. "I didn't do anything of the kind."

Cohn put his hand on Winchester's shoulder and whispered something in his ear. I figured he was telling him to keep his mouth shut. It was good advice.

"That's supposition on my part," I admitted. "There's somebody else here who could have done that. Like you, Tommy. You were so mad at Dwight Robinson for killing your sister that you wanted to kill him. Maybe you talked to your buddies about it, maybe you decided to do it alone."

"You better be careful before making charges against my son."

I smiled at Thomas Vreeland. "That's nothing compared with some of the charges I *could* make against him. *And* you, for that matter. But this is only a minor point. To figure out who donated the money, all we have to do is subpoena a few bank records. That should take about twenty minutes. Of course, Tommy could be in a whole lot of trouble if he doesn't own up. He could be implicated in Dwight's kidnapping, too."

"Bullshit. I didn't have anything to do with that." I had figured that Tommy Vreeland would be the easiest one to intimidate. He was basically just a bully. He wasn't accustomed to having someone put the heat on him.

"OK, I admit it, I put up the money. But I didn't have anything to do with beating him up. I couldn't even find out where the son of a bitch was staying."

"That didn't stop you from beating up his brother," O'Leary said.

"Bullshit. I didn't do that either. I was right here, in this very room."

I turned to O'Leary. "He's right. He didn't do anything to Dexter, and neither did Shake."

"What do you mean?"

"Dwight did that," I said. "He was sick and tired of Dexter screwing up. He gave him a lousy alibi for the night of the murder, and then last year he got him busted and thrown out of baseball. Dwight likes to take care of his problems his own way, especially family problems."

"I asked you not to be too long-winded," Pucinsky reminded me.

"That's right, come on," Thomas Vreeland said, looking at his watch. "The buffet's supposed to start in half an hour."

The spirit of impatience seemed to be contagious. Even Warren Shepherd was feeling brave. "Yeah, where's all this going? Why do I have to stay here?"

"I'll get to you in a minute," I said. Then I turned my attention back to Winchester. "So you didn't put up the money. But on Wednesday night, you and Melody had an argument, and she told you everything. She went back on the deal you two made about not filing for divorce until after the election. She decided she didn't need to wait for the payoff you were going to give her. She told you she was planning to testify for Dwight. That's when you called in Becker."

Winchester rolled his eyes, but the golf pro was beginning to look a bit anxious.

"You look like you could use a drink, Pete," I said. "Who's buying the next round?"

Nate grinned and walked to the bar. Within a minute, all the guys except Shake and Salvino were stationed there for refills. It was just like a party, except that only a few of us were enjoying it.

"Melody overheard her husband and Pete talking about Dwight," I said to the room. "She was afraid the next senator from New Jersey was planning to have him killed. She was right. It's too bad she didn't realize he was planning to get rid of her, too."

"That's a goddamn lie," Winchester said.

The congressman's lawyer pulled on his sleeve. Winchester nodded.

"Becker subcontracted the job on Dwight. But he wanted to take care of Melody himself." I turned to face Becker, who was leaning against the middle of the bar. "Am I right or am I right?"

The golf pro glowered at me. Beneath his anger, I could see real fear beginning to spread over his face. It wasn't warm enough in the room for a guy to be perspiring that much. I'm a world-class sweater, and I was as dry as a good martini.

"You tried to make it look like an accident, but you didn't do a very good job," I said. "You left shoe polish smudges on the bannister, for one thing. You put that on your face so that anyone who saw you go into the house would think you were black."

"You're crazy," Becker sputtered. "You can't prove a fucking thing, asshole."

He was right. I couldn't. But I was hoping Pucinsky could.

"One of the neighbors saw a black guy entering the house," the police chief said. "She said he was about your size, Pete."

Becker laughed, but I don't think he convinced anyone that he was amused.

"Did the coroner find any evidence of sexual assault?" I asked.

"Yeah, in a manner of speaking. There was no sign of semen. But the walls of Mrs. Winchester's . . . you know . . . her vagina had been scratched and stretched. He said someone must have penetrated her with a fairly large object."

"Like a dildo, maybe," Nate said.

"Yeah, exactly. That's what he said."

I looked at Becker, then at Winchester, who was glaring at Becker. The congressman let out a scream. It wasn't likely he was going to heed his attorney's advice now. Even guys as slick as Bob Winchester lose their cool eventually.

He charged at the golf pro, shouting, "You raped her! You goddamn animal, you raped her!"

I didn't see any reason to add that she was dead at the time of the assault.

Becker put up his arms to defend himself, but Winchester began pummeling him with both hands. He was no match for the younger and larger golf pro, who pushed back with both forearms. He sent Winchester sprawling sideways into Thomas Vreeland, who grabbed at a table beside him for support. But Winchester's stumbling momentum knocked him backward, and the founding fathers of Mountain Lake landed side by side, like two peas in the proverbial pod, in the largest mound of three-bean salad that anybody's ever had the bad taste to make. A foot or so to the left, and they would have been just another pair of cocktail franks swimming in the baked beans.

Pucinsky opened the door behind him and beckoned the two cops he had stationed outside. He ordered them to handcuff Becker, who was busy fending off another assault, this one courtesy of Tommy Vreeland.

As the two cops tried to pull Tommy away from him, Becker spotted his chance to make a break for it. There was another door to the room, at the end of the bar, on the opposite wall from where Thomas Vreeland and Bob Winchester were still busy marinating. Becker slugged at one of the cops with his left arm, then turned to his right and slid along the edge of the bar. Six steps and he would be making his exit.

Fat chance. Mike O'Leary put out his foot as Becker went past, tripping him up and sending him crashing against the wall beside the door. He regained his balance, but only momentarily. Nate pushed O'Leary out of the way, then leveled the golf pro with a shoulder block that caught him right in the midsection. Becker let out a gasp that sounded like air gushing out of a leaking tire, but he wasn't done yet. He was a big guy, and he was fighting for his life.

Becker hit back at Nate with his forearm, but he didn't have the leverage to make it count for much. Nate backed off a step before letting him have it with a right hand that would have stunned King Kong. Becker's head snapped as it hit the wall, and he managed one more futile, powerless swing with his left hand. Nate took it on the right side of his face, then followed with a left of his own that landed squarely on Becker's jaw. I heard a sickening crunch of bone, then watched the burly golf pro slump to the floor.

Nate turned and winced in pain. "Shit," he said, grasping his left wrist. "I think I broke my goddamn hand." He grimaced for a few seconds, then forced a grin through clenched teeth.

"Just think," he said, "I may never be able to play golf again."

CHAPTER
36

"**S**o who killed my daughter?"
Thomas Vreeland asked. As far as I could recall, it was the
first time he had spoken to me in a civil voice. But there was
still a tone of impatience lingering beneath his newfound
respect.

I resisted the temptation of asking him if he was in a hurry
to go play another eighteen. If he had cooperated with me to
begin with, I might have been able to answer his question
sooner. It would have saved some people, including me, a
whole lot of trouble.

It probably would have saved Melody Winchester's life.

But as I looked around the room, starting at the corner
table holding cell where Shake, Salvino and Becker sat
downtrodden and handcuffed, I figured Thomas Vreeland
had done his share of suffering. After all, his daughter had
been killed. And now, his best friend and political fix-it man
had been charged with murdering his own wife, Vreeland's
sister-in-law.

Vreeland had watched in horror as Winchester, handcuffed, was led from the room, trailed by his celebrity

lawyer, who had demanded immediate medical attention for his client.

"I think twenty-five Valium ought to do the trick," said Nate, who had swallowed a couple himself to cope with his busted hand. Pucinsky suggested that he go to the hospital too, but Nate refused. He said he wanted to stick around until the show was over.

As I returned Thomas Vreeland's stare, it was clear that things were never going to be quite the same again around the perfect little controlled community that he had built for himself.

Plus, of course, I wasn't through with him yet. Even after I got done giving Vreeland the satisfaction of finally knowing who was responsible for his daughter's death, he was going to be sorry he had ever met me.

I was almost positive who killed Cynthia. It would have been faster to start there and work backwards, but I wanted to get some satisfaction out of it, too. Making people I don't like squirm a bit is one of the ways I go about getting it. I began at the beginning.

"Your daughter had quite a few visitors the night she was murdered," I said to Vreeland. "Let's start with your son."

I turned my gaze on Tommy, who was standing beside his father at the bar, and savored the scene, as the old block and the young chip eyed each other warily.

"No, Dad," Tommy protested. "He's talking crazy shit. I never would have killed Cynthia. You know that." He wheeled to face me, a pair of icy blue slits peering out from beyond blowsy cheeks. His expression must have made a nice contrast to my cheery countenance.

"I didn't say you killed her. I merely said you were one of her visitors. You borrowed Terry's car that night. You were drunk. It's possible you might have killed her. It wouldn't have been the first time you lost your temper and hit one of your sisters, would it?"

"I didn't do it!" He was yelling now.

I answered in a calm, quiet voice. "But you went there, didn't you?"

"Yeah, OK, I went there. But I didn't even go into the house."

"Because you were shit-faced. You were so bombed, you let Shake drive. He had an appointment with Dwight that night, to collect on some gambling debts."

"What?" Pucinsky had been strangely quiet.

"Oh yeah," I said offhandedly. "Shake deals dope, handles action, does all sorts of favors for Ray and Pete. Don't you, Shake?"

The man whom the country club honkies had nicknamed Shakespeare was looking a little sickly o'er the pale cast of thought.

"What's the matter?" Nate asked him. "Lost your poetic license?"

"You drove the car and went into the house alone, because Tommy passed out," I said. "You were probably glad to find out Dwight wasn't home, because you figured you might be able to get a piece."

"That's outrageous! You're a liar!" The denial came from Thomas Vreeland. He might have been speaking on Shake's behalf, but I imagine he was trying to protect his daughter's reputation in memoriam. Too little, too late.

I ignored Vreeland. "You better start talking, Shake. If you don't, somebody's going to think you killed her. After all, you did try to frame Dwight for it by bashing in the headlight on Terry's car, knowing full well you smashed his headlight the week before."

"Man, this is all *jive* man." Shake rose to his feet. "I just drove outta there *fast*. I wasn't thinking of nothin' but gettin' *my* ass outa there. She was dead, man, when I found her."

"What about the trophy?" Pucinsky asked. I think the chief thought he had found his killer.

"I don't know shit about no trophy. I went in the house and saw her there. You know, laid out right on the floor. The place smelled kind of funny, like . . . I don't know."

"Like shoe polish?" O'Leary asked.

"Yeah, man, that's what it was." Shake turned slowly to face Becker. "Shoe polish."

"You goddamn prick, you killed her, too!" Thomas Vreeland was across the room and pounding on the golf pro before Becker could spit out a denial. The neighborhood bully was really taking his lumps.

"He didn't do it," I shouted, while Pucinsky's finest were pulling Vreeland away.

I turned to Pucinsky. This was the part I had to double-check. "The coroner didn't find any signs of sexual assault on Cynthia, right?"

He nodded. "That's one of the reasons we figured it was Dwight Robinson." He smiled, as if to explain. "You know how it is with married couples."

I nodded and looked at O'Leary. Boy, did I ever.

"Becker went over to Cynthia's and played whatever little games the two of them played together. I assume it involved him dressing up like a caddy."

Thomas Vreeland shook his head in disgust. The year-round tan had drained out of his face, replaced by a ghastly shade of gray that matched his hair.

"Was she alive when you left the house?" I asked Becker.

As I watched him nod, even with my lousy peripheral vision, I was able to notice Warren Shepherd inching his way along the bar toward the far door. If he was smart, he would have learned from Pete Becker's recent experience. With Shepherd, of course, that was a very big if.

Naturally, I wasn't the only one who saw him.

Shepherd didn't even get as far as Becker had. Pucinsky ordered him to stop about ten feet from the door. That's when the surly little sucker decided to pull the weapon out of his Shoe-Town windbreaker.

It was one of those cheap, white-handled steak knives, the kind you get at gas station giveaways. About the only thing you can cut with them is a TV dinner. I figured Warren Shepherd for the sort of guy who had collected the entire set—two dollars of low octane at a time.

One of Pucinsky's finest pulled out his gun. With the kind of marksmanship you can expect from suburban cops, I felt a clear and present danger. Anybody in the room was fair game.

"Put away the knife, Warren," I said.

"Get away from me," he snarled, waving the knife in the air. In fact, I had already taken two steps back to escape the probable line of fire.

"You two assholes thought I did it right from the start," he said. "You've been jerking my chain, thinking you could get me to confess. Pair of goddamn nigger lovers." Shepherd's expression changed to something approximating a smile. "Well you're wrong. I didn't do it. And you're not going to pin it on me."

"I know you didn't do it. But you were there in the house when it happened, weren't you? She got back from church early that night and walked in on you."

Shepherd looked so shocked, I thought his eyes might come right out of their baggy sockets. He put the knife down on the bar.

"Yeah, that's right." There was a tone of amazement and relief in his voice.

"You must have been in a fairly compromising position to make the old lady that mad, Warren," I said. "Did she catch you with your pants down?"

Shepherd answered with the sheepish stare of a kid who's been caught with one hand in the cookie jar and the other on his prong.

"Well?" I asked.

He looked at the floor. "Yeah, that's right."

"Now you've lost me totally," Pucinsky said. "What's going on, what are you talking about?"

"Shepherd didn't kill Cynthia," I said. "His girlfriend did."

"Who's his girlfriend?" Pucinsky asked.

I ignored his question. The floor was mine, so I figured I'd dazzle them with my deductive skills for a few moments.

"This wasn't a premeditated murder. Somebody just hauled off and slugged Cynthia. If any of the men in this room had gotten angry enough to hit her, they probably would have used their hands. They're all bigger than she was." I nodded toward Shepherd. "Even this little sack of shit. Only somebody smaller than Cynthia would have grabbed for the trophy. That's why the blow that killed her landed on the *side* of her head."

"So who the fuck's his girlfriend?" Pucinsky repeated. I guess he wasn't dazzled.

Nate grinned. "My favorite suspect—Anna Paslawski."

"The next-door neighbor? Why the hell did she kill her?"

"A couple of reasons. First of all, you've got to imagine how desperate somebody would have to be to link up with Shepherd. Warren used to peep on Cynthia, and Anna Paslawski is a very jealous old lady. Probably because of her own twisted religious slant, she believes that all women are evil temptresses of men. She once accused the lady across the street of trying to seduce Shepherd when *he* came over to hit on *her*."

I paused and gazed at the far end of the bar, where Thomas Vreeland had rejoined his son and regained his color. But not for long.

"I'm sure Mr. Vreeland could explain the other reason," I said.

"What? I haven't the slightest idea what you're talking about."

I looked at Mike O'Leary. "You're the one who made the discovery. You want to explain it?"

"I'd be glad to. It's been tough keeping my yapper shut all this while."

O'Leary sauntered forward to the center of the room, working the theatrics he'd like to practice on a jury sometime. Mike's one of those lawyers who's never actually been in a courtroom.

"I submit, Mr. Vreeland, that you have been systematically buying up houses on the flood plain. More precisely, you've been buying houses on the proposed sight of Route 287, very likely acting on illegal information supplied by your brother-in-law, the dishonorable Bob Winchester.

"I further submit that, in an effort to hide these land holdings, you have been paying off Anna Paslawski to put the properties in her name. However, Mrs. Paslawski apparently wanted more out of the arrangement—or perhaps you decided to reduce her cut. As a result, you and, very possibly, your daughter were at the top of the old lady's shit list."

Vreeland was no doubt incensed at the implication that he had been an indirect cause in his daughter's murder. But it was a little farfetched to suggest that Anna Paslawski was thinking about him when she went into a jealous rage, and I'm sure he was more concerned with the discovery of his real estate dealings. Without his lawyer there to froth for him, he went on the attack himself.

Vreeland forced a sarcastic laugh. "Very interesting. But I don't think this is exactly a matter for Chief Pucinsky's jurisdiction."

Pucinsky nodded. "You're right about that, Mr. Vreeland. But I'm afraid I'll have to turn the information over to the Feds."

"There's one more thing you should know," I told the cop. "Shepherd decided to blackmail Mrs. Paslawski. He burned down her house for her to collect the insurance money."

"That's a bunch of crap!" Shepherd suddenly didn't look so relieved anymore.

"You're an electrician," I said. "I'm sure you could figure out how to screw up the wiring." I turned to one of the cops. "If you check his pockets, I bet you'll find the key to her house."

This time Shepherd didn't even try to go for the knife. He just hollered. "You can't prove a fuckin' thing."

"With Anna Paslawski's cooperation, it shouldn't be too hard," I answered. Then, to Pucinsky, I said, "She was in on the fire to get the money to pay him off. I guess she figured she could move into one of the other houses she owned. She came up with the hoax of going to the Holy Land as an excuse."

"What? You mean she didn't go away?" The day had been full of surprises for Hal Pucinsky.

"She's staying at the Howard Johnson's," Nate told him. "You know the one on Route 23 at Ratzer Road? My guess is, she's using an alias. She's a crafty old lady, likes those detective magazines. She's probably reading one right now."

Pucinsky nodded, dumbfounded.

"While you're up there," Nate added, "be sure to try the fried clams."

CHAPTER
37

Picking up Anna Paslawski should have been strictly routine, but Hal Pucinsky insisted that I accompany him, anyway. The next thing you know, he'd want to make me an honorary deputy.

I was kind of curious to get another look at the old gal, but Nate required some medical attention. Pucinsky was willing to wait while we picked up a couple of six packs and dropped him off at Chilton Memorial Hospital in Pequannock, where Terry Vreeland, Ed Gallo and Dwight Robinson were already having a little party.

Anna Paslawski's Rambler American was still parked in the same space in the lot when Pucinsky, two of his boys and I arrived at the Howard Johnson's. The desk clerk was only too pleased to let the chief of police have a glance at the register.

Nate was correct about the need to look for an alias. The crafty old dame had changed her name—from Anna Paslawski to Edna Paslawski.

"I don't get it," Pucinsky said.

"You just don't know Anna," I explained. "She's got a thing for her dead husband. His name was Ed."

"I still don't get it."

Her room was on the second floor, three doors down and across the hall from the suite where Nate and I were camping out. As we stood outside the door, I could hear Joe Franklin's voice booming behind it. Evidently, Anna Paslawski could withstand *Down Memory Lane* at the same volume Warren Shepherd took his *Flintstones*.

Anna didn't answer Pucinsky's polite knock. She probably couldn't hear it. He began pounding on the second go-round, and I heard the volume on the TV fade out.

"Yes, who is it?" There was a spooky quality to Anna Paslawski's voice that I hadn't noticed the first time we met. Of course, I hadn't known then what I knew about her now.

"Police," Pucinsky barked. "Open up."

That seemed a little gruff to me, considering the person he was dealing with. I figured she might be having a few second thoughts about letting us in. Quite a few, if the amount of time it took her to unbolt the chain lock was any indication.

Finally the door swung open, and Anna Paslawski peered out at us over the rims of her bifocals. She was clad in the same tattered blue bathrobe and pink pajamas that she had worn during our last meeting. She had forsaken the shower cap, so I could see that her hair really did match the robe.

"Oh, hello, it's you again," she said to me, smiling. "And where's that other nice young man today?"

I didn't think it would get us anywhere if I pointed out that Nate was presently sitting right behind her, next to Joe Franklin on the TV set. Memory Lane was a dead-end street for Anna Paslawski today.

"He couldn't make it," I said. "But he asked me to give you his regards."

She nodded, then looked at Pucinsky. "I guess you came to tell me 'The game's up, sister.'" I was impressed that she could still manage to maintain her TV cop manner.

Pucinsky responded with a passable Jack Webb. "Yes, ma'am, I'm afraid I have to."

"Are you going to slap the cuffs on me?"

"No, ma'am, I don't think that'll be necessary."

It would be overstating it to say she looked disappointed. I guess chagrined is more like it.

"Well come inside and make yourself at home." She gestured with her arm. "You don't mind if I step into the lavatory and slip into something more comfortable before we go."

"Of course not." Pucinsky shifted on his feet and glanced around the room. "Why don't you two wait out in the hall," he said to his men.

As Anna Paslawski walked toward the closet, I noticed that she was clutching something in her left hand. It suddenly occurred to me that she might be planning to slip into something really comfortable—like permanent unconsciousness.

False alarm.

"What's in your hand, Anna?" I asked.

I could see tears beginning to form behind her glasses, as she unclenched her fist to reveal a religious medal.

"Saint Christopher is my protector, sonny. I don't care what you say. They can't take him away from me."

I apologized sheepishly. I hadn't exactly been keeping tabs on the movement to defrock old Chris. I figured he had his work cut out for him today.

We pretended not to watch as Anna selected her police-station outfit. It was on a hanger in a dry-cleaning bag, but it was well past the point when conventional methods of cleaning cease to have any effect.

At one time the suit had been white. Now it was the color of margarine. The lingering grease stains were a tip-off that someone had gotten a lot of use out of it.

Anna Paslawski turned and held the costume up for us to see. On the right pocket, there was an orange patch with the Flying-A service station logo. On the left pocket, in script, was the name "Ed." Underneath the name was the word "Manager."

"Well, what do you think?" she asked.

"Very nice," I lied.

"It was Ed's, you know. He wore it every day. I used to stay up all night washing it."

I resisted the urge to ask why he didn't have any extras. Pucinsky and I stared silently at each other as she walked past us to the bathroom.

"This feels more like a goddamn mugging than an arrest," he muttered.

I nodded and lit a cigarette and sat down on the edge of the bed. It was unmade, and there was a copy of *True Detective* magazine and a paperback Bible on it. The sheets had the odor of old people's houses. I guess at some point they carry it with them wherever they go.

Anna Paslawski stopped at the door to the bathroom and wheeled to face us. "I know it was wrong to do," she said. "But that filthy little whore had it coming to her for a long time. And you want to know the thing that bothered me most? I gave her my magazines *all* the time. But do you think she ever gave any to me? Not on your life. Oh, she said she would. But she didn't."

"It's in your own best interest not to say anything until you see your lawyer," Pucinsky said. "If you don't have a lawyer, the judge will appoint one for you."

"God is my judge," she said. "He's the only judge."

Amen.

We chain smoked in silence until Pucinsky noticed the TV. "Hey, isn't that your buddy?" he asked.

"Yeah, it's a repeat," I said.

"Then he really is a celebrity!"

"Oh, yeah. One of the biggest."

Pucinsky was about to turn up the volume when we heard the first shriek. It didn't even sound like Anna Paslawski. But it surely was the voice of a mad woman.

"You'll never take me alive!" she shouted. Then she let out a scream that was probably the most mortifying sound I've ever heard.

I felt a sudden stab of nausea as I pushed off the bed and stumbled across the room. This time, I knew, it wasn't a false alarm.

The sign on the bathroom door said "Ed's Room." I didn't know if she had ordered a new one or taken the original with her when she had made her exodus before the great fire. I got my answer when Pucinsky shot the lock and kicked open the door.

The old lady had carted away the contents of "Ed's Room" and used them to redecorate every inch of space in her HoJo crapper. Now I'd be able to tell Nate that I knew what it felt like to have five thousand little pictures of Jesus staring at me. Except I don't think they were staring at me. For some reason, their gaze seemed to be focused on Anna Paslawski.

She was sitting right where Ed would have been if he were still with us—on the throne. She was tilted to the right, and her left hand was clasped under the rim of the seat. I would have bet the farm that Saint Christopher was still hanging on in there for dear life. The front of the yellowed uniform was drenched with blood, causing the orange Flying-A logo to take on the appearance of a scarlet letter. How's that for symbolism?

The white plastic handle of a gas station giveaway steak knife was sticking out of her heart. So much for my notion that the goddamn things weren't sharp enough to cut into a pot pie. The blade was about halfway in. It had entered flat, so that Ed's name was perfectly underlined.

Anna Paslawski's face was still contorted in an expression of agonizing pain. She wasn't feeling pain anymore, but she wasn't resting in peace yet, either.

The note on the counter near the sink said, "I'm finely coming to meet you, Darling."

"This is un-fuckin'-believable," Pucinsky said.

The chief and I had found another point that we could agree on. He looked like he was about to retch. I knew exactly how he felt.

"You can use the can in my room," I said. "It's about time for me to check out of this place, anyway."

CHAPTER
38

T erry Vreeland turned on her side and leaned in toward me, her gorgeous green eyes playing peekaboo behind strands of silky brown hair that had come loose from her ponytail.

We were back in the park without a name, near the submarine without an explanation, behind John F. Kennedy High School, on the banks of the scenic Passaic River, in beautiful Paterson, New Jersey. It was a great day for a picnic—sunny, warm, a cool breeze blowing in over the hill from Haledon. It was Memorial Day, and we were playing dead on a blanket—Nate, Terry and I.

The picnic was Ed Gallo's idea. He wanted to do a replay of the fund-raising bash, complete with an encore performance by Black Power, whose record had become an instant best-seller, at least in North Jersey. It seemed like a month had passed since the first party, but a quick glance at the calendar slot on my Timex revealed it had only been eight days.

The central event of the day had been Dwight Robinson's press conference, at which his attorney and the Wayne chief-of-police formally announced that all charges against Dwight had been dropped. With his mother and brother standing by his side, the man Thomas Vreeland had nicknamed the black Mickey Mantle announced his intention of becoming the black Arnold Palmer. Dwight Robinson had decided to try out for the professional golfers tour.

"You want to go for a little stroll?" Terry asked me.

"Yeah, that sounds like a good idea—stretch the old legs," Nate said, letting out a giant yawn as he rolled over to face us.

Terry responded with her customary smile. You had to be watching closely to catch the momentary furrowing of her brow. I was. Apparently, my partner was, too.

"Oh, I get it." Nate lowered his voice to a whisper. "You two love birds want to be alone."

"Three's a crowd," I said.

"And too many cooks spoil the broth," he answered, leaning on his good arm to get to his feet. "You guys stay here and steam up the blanket. I'm going to wander over to party central and see if I can find me a woman to dance with." As he ambled off, he stopped and turned, raising a cautioning finger. "But be careful not to get any impure thoughts."

"I have an announcement of my own to make today," Terry said, tilting her head slightly to avoid full contact with my hypnotic love stare. "I hope you don't take it the wrong way."

I told her I hoped I didn't, either.

"I've talked to Larry a couple of times on the phone this week—that's my old boyfriend."

I nodded. "The one in Florida who doesn't know how lucky he is."

"Yeah, that's right." She was smiling, but her eyes were beginning to dampen, like dew on the early morning grass. "I've decided to go back there. I'm going to make the big jump to the tour."

"I think that's a good idea."

"You do? I thought . . . well, I was afraid I might hurt your feelings."

"You did. But I'll get over it." I tried to make it sound easier than it was, for my sake as much as hers.

"I don't want to go away from here with you being mad at me."

I took her head in my hands and forced a smile. I got that feeling you get when you see inside someone. Only this time, it wasn't scary. "I'm not mad," I said. "I just have two questions for you."

"What are they?" A pair of tears rolled down each cheek.

I wiped off the left side with my finger. "Is he older than you are?" Then the right. "Can you beat him at golf?"

She laughed and kissed me and the tears started flowing freely. A light drizzle, not a downpour. "I've got to go," she said, pulling away and scrambling to start gathering up her things. "I'm acting stupid. I kind of lose control of myself when I drink."

We wouldn't want that to happen now, would we?

I walked her to her car. We did the parting embrace and I held the door for her while she got in. She put the window down and studied my face one last time. The crying was over now.

"I'll think of you a lot," she said softly. I could barely hear her voice above the distant roar of Black Power. Then, as she began to pull away, she said, "It was really wonderful."

My sentiments exactly. But somehow I didn't think Terry and I had much of a future, even if she had stayed around. I just couldn't see myself fitting into the Vreeland family. That would have been murder-in-law.

Nate and I arrived back at our blanket at about the same time. "You're looking a little down in the mouth," he said. "What happened? A kiss-off instead of a kiss?"

"A little of each."

"That's too bad. I liked her a lot."

So did I. Still do.

As I told him about Terry's plans over the last of our beer, Mike O'Leary stopped by to see us. "Well, you guys did one hell of a job. You both deserve a pat on the back." He chuckled. "I'd say you deserve a goddamn massage."

"We're expecting more than that, O'Leary." Nate got up and stood chest to nose with him. "You said today was the day."

"Oh, yeah, that. Well, there's been some problems, as you can imagine. I mean, with Melody Winchester dead, you know, we technically don't have a client."

"Our fee, Mike." I said.

"No problem. Eventually—"

"*Now*." Nate reached out and grabbed the lawyer by his collar, lifting him about an inch off the ground. O'Leary was a small guy, but Nate only had the use of one hand.

"OK, OK, put me down," he whined. "Let's see." He reached into his inside breast pocket and pulled out a money clip. He counted out five hundred-dollar bills and put them in my outstretched hand. "That will have to do for now. As an advance, until Melody Winchester's estate is settled. But then there's another matter."

"What's that?" Nate asked.

O'Leary snatched the bills out of my hand. "Renzler never finished paying Kathy all her alimony. I think we ought to do some negotiating."

I glared at the little fireplug of a guy and thought back to the time the mutt on Seventh Avenue had mistaken him for one. The perpetual grin gradually disappeared and gave way to a look of fear. The only other time I had seen that expression on his face was the moment before I had decked him at Downey's bar four short years ago.

I clenched my hand into a fist and thought about whether or not I should do it again.

"Just like old times, isn't it, Mike?"